TRUE HARMONY

AMY KNUPP

CHAPTER ONE

*E*liza Bancroft knew something was up the minute she walked into her duplex on a Tuesday afternoon in August. It was written all over her roommate's face.

"What's wrong?" Eliza asked, eyes narrowed, pulse ramping up as she set her shoulder bag and her fiddle on the bench by the back door.

"Who says something's wrong?" Grace threw back, trying for a nonchalant tone.

Eliza could see right through it. "You. Your eyes. You're watching me like you expect me to flip my shit."

Grace pushed the half-full dishwasher trays in and closed the door of the appliance, then, after too much of a pause, she swiveled to face Eliza. "You're going to flip your shit."

"Is Calvin—"

"He's fine. Still napping with Blitz. Preschool wore him out but good." Grace took two long-legged strides to the kitchen table, picked up a magazine, flipped through the pages as though on a mission. "Here." She set the magazine on the table and tapped it. "Familiar?"

Eliza moved closer, eyes on the full-color, full-page photo, and half a heartbeat later, she sucked in her breath. "Oh, my God." She pressed a fist to her chest to try to stop herself from stroking out.

"His name is Mason North," Grace told her in a quiet, matter-of-fact voice. "Your baby daddy is the CEO of North Brothers Sports."

With her breath stopped cold in her lungs, Eliza snatched up the magazine and avidly dug in to the article. "Most eligible bachelor of *Nashville*?" she let out, her voice climbing higher. "I thought he was from out of town."

"Sit down, sugar." Grace pulled out one of the kitchen chairs, but Eliza barely registered it until her roommate eased her down with a gentle hand on her shoulder. "You're pale. I'll get you some tea."

Eliza continued reading as she sat, inhaling the words with her eyes, soaking up every morsel of info on the man she'd spent a grand total of six, maybe seven hours with. Unfortunately, it seemed the *Nashville Heat* hadn't actually interviewed Mason North for the piece, had simply put together whatever info was public—his job running North Brothers Sports, his family's nonprofit foundation, his immediate family, including a younger brother, Drake, who had made the publication's Most Eligible Bachelor list a few years back.

Add to that information what Eliza knew—he loved the St. Louis Cardinals and expensive whiskey, was irresistible in a suit, and appreciated the hell out of the tattoo of stars and music notes and ribbons that curved over her hip at her bikini line—and she still knew more, at least twice as much, about the musicians she'd played with in the studio today.

"He's been here all along." She grasped the tall, cold glass of tea Grace set in front of her, mainly for something to hold on to, as she let that nugget sink in. "I feel so dumb."

Grace plopped down in the chair next to hers and took her hand. "We've been over this a thousand times, Eliza. You're not dumb. You got caught up in a little magic with a scrumptious man and let yourself go for it. Part of the reason it was so magical is that you *didn't* ask for each other's life story or pertinent information. If you hadn't ended up pregnant, you wouldn't have thought anything of it."

Oh, she would've thought about it. She *had* thought about it, about *him*, the man who had rocked her world for a few hours before she'd crept out of his hotel room. Mason-with-no-last-name had been a once-in-a-lifetime event. A few spectacular hours she could hold in her memory forever—the kind that had likely ruined all other men for her for the rest of her life.

Luckily for her, she hadn't had room in her life for men in the four and a half years since. All of her energy and time went to her son and her career. Everything she did was to try to give her boy the best life possible.

"What am I supposed do with this information?" Eliza said, still staring at the magazine photo, which had him in a tux at some formal evening event, looking admittedly gorgeous.

She couldn't help comparing this man's classy, sedate life to hers, filled with little-boy noise, music, chaos, an energetic dog, and eternal scrambling. Scrambling was her middle name— scrambling to pay the bills, scrambling to pick up more work, scrambling to make sure her boy had consistent care when she did work.

"Well, it seems to me you have two options," Grace said, leaning forward to try to force eye contact with her piercing blue eyes, her long blond waves falling over her shoulders. "You can track him down and tell him he's a father, or you can *not* and keep on keeping on the way you have been."

"Both make me want to throw up."

"Understandable." Grace glanced at the clock on the microwave.

"You have to work," Eliza said, suddenly remembering the reason she'd had to hurry home after the afternoon recording session.

"Not for a few minutes yet." Grace hopped up, went over to the fridge, took out a string cheese. "Can I get you a cupcake?"

Eliza shook her head in a rare rejection of her favorite vice, store-bought, processed, heaven-sent chocolate cupcakes with cream filling.

"Here's the thing," Grace said. "You don't have to figure it out today. You've got time to think it over."

Eliza tried to breathe, nodding, knowing her roommate had a

point despite the choking panic that had gripped Eliza from the moment she'd seen Mason's face in the photo.

Mason North. Calvin's father.

Tears burned in her eyes out of nowhere, because how many nights had she lain awake wishing for the one thing her boy couldn't have? A two-parent family. A daddy who loved him, who could teach him how to hit the Little Tikes T-Ball in their tiny backyard, who could go to Family Day at preschool.

Eliza threw her head back, closed her eyes, and blew out all the air from her lungs. "Maybe I could've tried harder to find him."

"What?" Grace's alto voice went soprano with the one-word question. She rushed back to her seat, grabbed Eliza's wrist. "Eliza, you did everything you could to find your mystery man back then. The hotel wouldn't release his info, the business conference he was attending was a dead-end, the internet searching with no last name was a bust. There was nothing else we could've done."

"I still wonder if I could've hired an investigator."

"Sure," Grace said, "if we skipped paying rent for a few months, went without food. Come on, Eliza. If we could have, we would have. It wasn't a possibility back then."

It still wasn't. Even though Eliza had gotten her foot in the door as a session musician and made her money that way rather than hustling for live gigs now, which was a definite step up financially, there was never an extra dime at the end of the month.

"I could've tried the hotel front desk again. The guy I talked to was a jerk."

Grace stuck the last of the cheese in her mouth and shook her head vigorously. "Wouldn't have worked and you know it. A hotel can't and won't release a customer's info."

"I know," Eliza said, the despair of four years ago coming back to her in droves.

"You need to forgive yourself for not getting his last name or contact info. You didn't know you'd need it. It was one night of being carefree, and if anybody deserves that, it's you, sugar."

"It was part of the fantasy," Eliza admitted, thinking back to that night.

Both she and Grace had been working the music scene hard even back then, bartending on Broadway, making industry connections by the dozens, getting called to fill in for more and more gigs. Her one rule was never to date or sleep with someone in the industry. It was too small, and you never knew where you'd next run into your ex-lover.

Grace had had a second bartending job at a downtown hotel, and that evening, she'd texted Eliza that a music VIP was sitting alone at the hotel bar and to get her butt over there ASAP. By the time Eliza made it, the VIP was gone, so she'd settled into a barstool for a drink and the Cardinals spring training game and to keep her roomie company for her slow weeknight shift.

Mason had appeared next to her at some point, and they'd bonded over the St. Louis Cardinals. It didn't sound romantic, but they'd watched the game together, flirting like crazy until the last out. Between his killer blue eyes, his reluctant but sexy laugh, and the complete escape from her normal world of music and working it twenty-four seven, she'd been all in for a rare night of no-strings sex. Even now, *especially* now, it sounded tough to swallow and a little ridiculous, but somehow, in those few hours at the bar, they'd truly connected on some level, a level far outside of their everyday lives.

"If I ever needed proof that fantasies aren't real and magic doesn't exist..." Eliza shook her head, let out a humorless, self-deprecating laugh. "Thank you, universe. Message received."

"Stop," Grace ordered her. "Maybe magic doesn't last, but you, sugar, are one of the lucky ones who experienced it for a blink of time."

"I don't feel lucky. How in the ever-loving hell can I tell this man I don't know that he has—"

"Mama!" Calvin appeared at the doorway between the kitchen and the living room, looking rumpled, wearing his Young, Wild, and Three T-shirt that Lettie, their dear next-door neighbor, had given him for his birthday last year. Next to him, Blitz, the irresistible black-and-white mutt they'd rescued just over a year ago, wagged his tail and looked between Grace and Eliza, as if gauging who would be more likely to give him a treat.

"Hey, baby." Eliza scooted the chair back and held out her arms for a hug, and her still-waking-up boy raced over to her and jumped at her with full force, just like he did everything. Blitz galloped over to Grace, who'd gone to the treat jar and held out a canine snack.

Eliza held Calvin to her, inhaled the scent of his baby shampoo that still twisted her heart every day, and thanked God for the millionth time for letting her be this boy's mom. "How's my favorite boy in the whole wide world?"

"Hungry!" He spotted the empty cheese wrapper Grace had left on the table. "String cheese!"

"String cheese what, little man?" Grace said. "And where's my hug?"

"String cheese please," Calvin said as Eliza lowered him to the floor, and then he hugged Grace with just as much enthusiasm.

"How was preschool?" Eliza asked as Grace went after a string cheese and Blitz finished crunching his treat and settled on the floor at her feet, giving her his best puppy-dog eyes in hopes that maybe she, too, would succumb to his charms. She patted him on the head and steeled herself against the sad-dog look.

"Fun! Jacob was the Star of the Week and his daddy told us about being a policeman! We got Goldfish for snacks, and Jacob's daddy carried him on top of his shoulders when it was time to play outside."

Eliza's chest constricted from the image of Jacob and his dad that taunted her mind as Grace dangled the unwrapped cheese in front of Calvin. Snacks and a daddy—the highlights of the day as reported by Calvin. This was the third week of preschool and the fourth daddy she'd heard all about.

"Tell your mom about your art project," Grace prompted as Blitz moved to Calvin's side just in case the boy went against their house rules and gave the dog some people food.

Eliza only half registered the enthusiastic *yes!* and the description of the project he'd started but couldn't bring home yet because the glue was still wet. Her eyes met Grace's over her boy's head, and though they didn't say a word, it was clear they were thinking the same thing: Calvin was aching for a daddy, and suddenly Eliza had the ability to reach out to his.

"I can't wait until you bring it home and show us," Grace said. "And now, I gotta make like a tree and leave for work."

Calvin laughed at her *make like a* expression, as he always did, and Eliza couldn't help smiling at his easy joy.

"Have a good shift," Eliza said, standing, fighting through the paralysis that the photo on the table had brought on. She slapped the magazine closed and reached out for Calvin's hand as Grace picked up her bag, phone, and keys and darted out the door with a wave and a goodbye.

"Can we go to the park, Mama?"

"You want to swing?" she asked.

"And climb!"

With a glance at the clock, she decided they could get in some outside playtime and still have dinner at a reasonable hour if she made something quick like tacos. "Then swing and climb it is," she said as she hoisted him into her arms. "After another hug."

His little arms wrapped around her neck, and he pressed a clumsy kiss to her. She planted a noisy lip smack on him, making him giggle, then lowered him to the floor.

"Go get your shoes on, kiddo." She went to the hooks by the door and picked up Blitz's leash, which had the dog prancing excitedly. She attached the leash to his collar.

Calvin raced off to his room, making *vroom* noises, leaving Eliza alone with her muddled thoughts and that damn magazine, which, she noticed now, had a small photo of Mason on the cover as well.

"I gotta poop 'fore we go, Mama!" Calvin hollered from the other side of the house, making her grin and shake her head.

She looked at her eager dog and said, "Single parenting is not for the faint of heart, Blitz-o."

Because of Grace, the best friend God could give a girl—and Lettie, the dear soul next door who stayed with Calvin whenever they needed a third—Eliza had it better than a lot of single moms. She had a support system of steel.

But as much as she liked to believe their team of three women could be everything Calvin needed, there was no denying there were some gaps they would never fill. Take snakes, for example. Eliza could kill a spider as big as a quarter, but when a garter snake had slithered past her and Calvin at the park last week, she'd screamed like a girl and probably scarred her son.

And shoulder rides…though she could possibly carry him on her back right now, her boy was tall for his age and grew like a weed, and she would barely be able to lift him before long.

She tried to be both mom and dad to her son, but God knew she wasn't, couldn't be. Telling Mason North the truth scared the holy tar out of her, but if there was the slightest possibility of enriching her son's life by doing it, how could she not?

Though she wasn't swimming in optimism that it would produce a happy ending for her boy—she didn't know Mason well enough to have a clue how he would react—for Calvin's sake, she had to try.

CHAPTER TWO

*S*ome nights, the only thing that kept Mason North from staying at his office was the lack of a shower. Last night was one such night.

As he pulled up to the outdated corporate offices of North Brothers Sports, he glanced at the clock on the dash of his Audi R8, verified he still had fifteen minutes to finish prepping for the last-minute seven-a.m. meeting, and vowed yet again that last night's bad news would not stop them from building a new HQ in the next year—or, more importantly, from moving forward with all the other expansions in the three-year plan.

Without wasting a second, he grabbed his leather messenger bag and climbed out, noticing his brother Gabe had just pulled up in the spot next to his.

"Morning," Gabe said as he hopped out of his Tesla with a shit ton more energy than Mason had. That was due, in part, to the fact that this was Gabe's first week back after his honeymoon.

There was more to it than that, though. Always had been. None of the North brothers had ever felt the pressure of running their dad and uncle's legacy like Mason did, and that was the way he wanted it. It was his job to steer the ship, and though he needed every one of them and then some, a good leader carried the burden of ultimate responsibility. "How late were you here?"

Mason grunted and shook his head, knowing the truth—till

after midnight—would just back up the general consensus that he was a workaholic and needed to take a step back. They meant well. And they were probably correct about the workaholic label, but Mason did what he did because he thrived on it. If you took away his CEO position with North Brothers Sports, there wouldn't be much of him left.

"How's Lexie?" Mason asked instead.

"I left her with a smile on her face," Gabe said, leaving no room for doubt about how he'd done that, and Mason let out a half grin as he shook his head, as if there was no hope for his brother.

While romance wasn't in the cards for Mason and he was more than okay with that, he couldn't be happier for his brother —hell, *brothers*—finding love. Three out of five of them had hooked up permanently in the past year or so, and it had brought a deep level of contentment, a genuine happiness to each of them. He found people to be more productive at work when they were happy at home.

"So what are you thinking?" Gabe gestured vaguely toward the building, and Mason knew he referred to yesterday's end-of-month financials.

"Full-scale assault. We need to gear up on all fronts. All systems go. Full throttle."

"It sounds like you've been talking to Zane with all the battle shit."

"It's time for all-out battle," Mason said matter-of-factly. "We can recover from this and make the December deadline to ensure we get the funding we need. It's just going to take some extra strategizing and work."

They reached the main walkway to the building, and as they turned onto it, he noticed there was a tall dark-haired woman on the concrete bench to the side of the main entrance. She stood as they approached.

"Mason," she said in a melodic voice, "hello."

Between the voice, those rich dark-chocolate-brown eyes, and her long, tousled hair, Mason recognized her in an instant, and though he knew logically it wasn't possible, it felt like his heart caught, missed a beat. He kept any reaction from his face, wary. "Yes?"

"I don't know if you remember me…"

He hesitated, assessing whether there was a downside to admitting it. "I do."

In that moment, there was a tension-filled awareness that passed between them, as if she, too, had images of their night together flashing in her mind's eye.

"I apologize for showing up at your business," she said, her gaze shifting nervously between him and Gabe, her hands clasped and fidgeting in front of her. "I've been trying to reach you for over a week, but I haven't been able to get an appointment."

God bless Ruby and her protective instincts. It was just like Drake had said when the damn bachelor garbage first came out —people were crawling out of the woodwork. People from high school he hadn't seen for dozens of years, people he'd allegedly met and didn't remember, women, shit, so many women, and most of them he suspected he did not, in fact, know.

This woman, he knew. Well, knew of. Knew in a biblical sense. Remembered.

This woman, he hadn't been able to wipe out of his mind for all these years, with her quiet, sensual laugh, her miles-long legs, and that tattoo on her hip…

And wasn't that just fucked up like a soup sandwich.

Locking down on all of that, he said, "What can I do for you?" all businesslike. Formal.

She dropped any hint of her smile and stood straighter. "I need to discuss something with you in private." Again, she glanced at Gabe, and his brother took the hint, whether Mason wanted him to or not.

"I'll get the conference room opened up," Gabe said. With a brief nod at the woman—*Eliza*—Gabe headed to the door, swiped himself in, disappeared from sight.

"This isn't a good time," Mason said to head her off. Whatever she wanted, he wanted no part of, and he legitimately didn't have the time to waste.

"I understand," she said. "Could we set up a time to meet? I can come back here, or we could get a coffee or…whatever works for you."

"Call my assistant and set something up." He started to walk toward the door, forcing his mind back to the problem at hand, the future of North Brothers Sports.

Her hand on the sleeve of his suit jacket stopped him, though, not because it was a firm grip but because it was unexpected, and then the look in her eyes, the determination, had him turning to face her once again.

"Your assistant hasn't helped me so far, and it's important that I talk to you. Vital. It won't take long. Please," she said, and he saw the steel in her gaze that he didn't recall from that night so long ago.

Mason couldn't fathom what she might want from him, but it was best to nip this in the bud, hear her out, send her on her way.

When he saw his cousin Connor turn into the parking lot, he made a split-second decision, grasped her elbow to guide her, and said, "Come with me. I've got five minutes."

He ushered her back to the sidewalk and in the opposite direction from where he'd parked, toward the patio at the side of the building. They walked quickly, as he needed to avoid running into Connor with her at his side. The fewer explanations he had to make, the better. Gabe was already going to be all over his ass for this bizarre run-in.

When they were around the corner of the building and semi-hidden from the lot by a row of tall, skinny evergreen bushes, he faced her expectantly and not patiently. There were a half-dozen patio tables surrounded by chairs, but he didn't invite her to sit.

"This is awkward," Eliza said, then swallowed and looked at the concrete ground. "I'm not sure—"

"My meeting starts soon," he prompted.

"Yes." She took in a deep breath. "Sorry. There's no good way to say this, especially given your lack of availability, so I'm just going to say it."

Her eyes met his, and it stunned him more than a little to

realize that head-on impact was just as potent as it had been that night in the hotel bar when he'd met her. *Ka-bam!*

She swallowed nervously. "I… We… You have a son."

Not possible. This woman was crazy.

"A three-year-old little boy named Calvin," she said, the words rushed. "I don't want anything from you. I know what this looks like—an article comes out about you being the most eligible bachelor, and I'm betting all these women are trying to get a piece of you, but that's not what I'm doing. I just… I tried to find you. I thought maybe you lived in California and I didn't know your last name, didn't know…anything. But I tried to find you to let you know. So that's…that's what I'm doing."

Mason barely registered any of it, because as she went on, the truth sank in. He no longer believed she was lying. She thought he was the father of her son.

"What proof do you have?" he asked.

Her eyes narrowed ever so slightly, and if it was possible, that steel in them went cold. "The proof," she bit out, "is that I hadn't been with anyone for at least six months before you."

"And after?"

Her jaw stiffened as she stared at him, and though she didn't otherwise move, he felt her anger coming off her in waves, but what the hell did she expect? That he'd just take a paternity claim from anyone without question? Yes, he remembered her, but he also knew they'd used condoms. He always used condoms. So the chances she was right…

"Not that it's any of your business," she said in a low, measured tone, "but I haven't been with anyone since. Because I was dealing with the shock of a lifetime, pregnant and alone, and then I became a single mother." A lock of her silky hair fell across her cheek, and she shoved it back with a brusque motion. "I've felt bad all these years that you didn't know, but I didn't have any way of telling you. And then I saw you in that magazine and I thought…" She shook her head, looked away, and her voice came out even quieter. "I thought you might want to know you have a child."

Mason prided himself on his brain, on his sharpness, his

ability to take in a situation, assess, make a decision, and move forward. It was how he ran his life, how he ran a successful sporting goods chain. But right now, his brain was sputtering out, unable to absorb what she was telling him. He understood on the surface, but his normally reliable judgment had gone offline about three minutes ago.

Because a part of him believed her.

And part of him *could not comprehend* that he might be a father.

And yet another part was reeling just from the fact that he was standing face-to-face with this woman who had bewitched him…apparently four years ago. He hadn't been counting. He'd been trying to forget her.

"I can see I was wrong," she said just as his phone blew up with three different text notifications, undoubtedly his brother wondering why the hell he wasn't upstairs yet. "You better get to your meeting. Sorry to make you late."

She pivoted and rushed off, around the bushes and out of his sight. Mason knew he should stop her, knew this wasn't over, not by a long shot, but he couldn't seem to form words. Was struggling to latch on to a coherent thought other than the easy one: He had a meeting to get to. A damn important, do-or-die meeting.

He used his card to get in through the patio door and headed upstairs to lead his company, because that was what he did. And maybe by the time their business crisis was solved, he would have an idea of how to handle the unimaginable, life-changing disclosure that he might be a father.

CHAPTER THREE

*S*ometimes what a girl needed most was a reality check, Eliza thought as she speed-walked toward her SUV.

Reality check...*check.*

Mason North did not want to be a father.

Okay, she could work with that. She didn't need Mason North to be a father. She'd made it for three years and eleven months without him, as had Calvin. They could make it another thirty or so. Surely single parenting would be easier by then, right?

When she reached the driver's door, she let herself in, jabbed the key in the ignition, and backed out, not gunning it as she was compelled to do. Because he could be watching her, and he didn't need to know she was agitated.

With as much control as she could muster, she drove out of the parking lot of the North Brothers corporate offices, turned onto the street, and pulled into a coffee shop two blocks down. She parked in a spot facing the street and did not get out to get coffee. Though she was dying for another cup, she would wait till she got home and pour herself a cup from the coffeemaker on her counter instead of paying four dollars for one here.

As soon as she killed the engine, she picked up her cell phone, knowing Grace was waiting to hear how it'd gone. She pressed the button to dial her roommate, who picked up immediately.

"Well?" Grace said. "Did you see him?"

"I did more than see him. I told him."

There was a slight hesitation, then Grace said, "You've barely been there a half hour."

"He gave me five minutes."

"Jackass."

Tears filled Eliza's eyes at the single word of one-hundred-percent support. She brushed them away, though, because Mason North was not getting her tears.

"Tell me everything," Grace demanded, and Eliza could hear kitchen sounds in the background, as if the phone was on speaker on the counter as she made breakfast.

"Is Calvin up yet?"

"Seven a.m., like clockwork. He's in his room, playing with his fire truck until breakfast is ready."

Eliza smiled. Her boy loved that fire truck.

"Eliza, I'm dying here."

"Calvin shouldn't hear any of this." Not that he'd likely understand what they were talking about, but she couldn't risk it.

She could hear a change in the background noise, as if Grace took the phone off speaker.

"Spill."

"There's not a lot to spill. He took me over to a hidden patio to talk. I had no choice but to blurt it out. He questioned how I could be sure it was his child."

"Which I'd expect," Grace said. "Did he believe you?"

"I have no idea. I don't know him well enough to tell." And the Mason she'd known that night had been mostly absent from the Mason she'd just confronted.

"Well, what did he say?"

"Basically nothing. He just stood there with this awful look on his face. Mad, disgusted, I don't know. Definitely not *yay, I'm a father*."

"Be real, Eliza. Is that what you expected?"

No. It wasn't what she'd expected, but she'd be lying if she said she hadn't hoped. In fact... God, she felt like an idiot for how many times in the past seven days she'd caught herself envisioning a family of three, a mom, a dad, and their beloved boy.

For the past week, she'd tried everything she could think of to reach Mason, to set up an appointment, even a phone call, anything that would allow her to talk to him, to tell him the truth. His administrative assistant—Ruby, she knew because she'd talked to Ruby multiple times now—she was a steel wall who wouldn't let anyone she didn't deem to have a suitable reason through to Mason. Eliza had wondered more than once whether paternity was suitable enough. As frustrated as she'd become, she hadn't succumbed to laying that truth on the guard-dog woman.

Eliza and Grace had worked so hard since last Wednesday to track down the CEO that they were worthy of either receiving some kind of private investigator certification or being arrested as stalkers.

She'd found where he lived—a penthouse condo in a luxury building in Midtown, naturally one where she couldn't just walk up to his door and knock.

She knew not only where he worked but that he worked hellacious hours, and it had taken her getting up at five a.m. to make it to his office before him this morning.

She'd discovered that, unlike some of his brothers and cousins, he apparently didn't spend much time at the Harrison North Baseball and Softball Foundation—she'd tried not only calling there for info on him but also dropping by.

His father had died years ago, and his mother lived in town, but Eliza hadn't been able to find out where she lived. In fact, the rest of the family succeeded in keeping their personal residences secret. Probably for the best, because Eliza had had no intention of bothering his mom or brothers unless she exhausted every other possibility for reaching Mason.

"He was just..." Eliza shook her head, still processing the five-minute run-in even now. "I don't know. Like a brick wall."

"Are you seeing him again?"

"I don't think so. I did what I had to do. I told him. That's all I can do, right?"

"What if he contacts you?" Grace asked.

"He's not going to contact me. He could barely look at me."

"He's probably reeling, Eliza."

"Maybe."

Grace let out a harsh, husky laugh. "There's no maybe. He's reeling like a drunk guy on a boat in choppy waters. Think about it. You just told him he's a dad."

"I'm not sure Mason North is the kind of guy who reels about anything."

"I call BS. The man dotes on his mother." They'd seen photos online of him at her side at some fancy gala, and by all appearances, what Grace said was true. "You need to give him some time. Let him catch up."

"I don't need to do anything, Grace. I told him. He knows. Problem solved. Calvin and I are fine, thanks in no small part to you and Lettie being amazing humans."

"Pshaw," Grace said impatiently. "We're a family. You couldn't pry this guy away from me if you tried. Right, Calvin?"

"Right!" Eliza heard her son yell with fervor, which made her heart turn over a little. His life wasn't what you would call typical, but he was loved. Well loved.

"Which brings me back to, I don't need anything from Mason North. *We* don't need anything. We're good the way we are. And I'm coming home to get some coffee."

"Another pot's brewing as we speak."

"Best friend in the world," Eliza said with scores of unspoken gratitude.

"Likewise, sugar."

Calvin shrieked in the background and then Blitz barked. The sounds of home.

Grace continued, "No matter what happens, you said it yourself. You did what you needed to. Mission accomplished. Come home and let's eat pancakes. Forget about everything else."

"Plan," Eliza agreed and said goodbye.

As she started the car and drove toward home, she only wished she could forget about everything else. But the fact was, it'd been fifteen minutes since she'd driven away from Mason

North, and she was still shaking. It had nothing to do with his lack of response about Calvin and everything to do with merely laying eyes on that impossible-to-ignore man in person. Something about him, even in spite of his cool indifference to her and her news, rattled her on a soul level.

All the more reason it was for the best that she never saw him again.

———

THE SECOND he adjourned the meeting, Mason shot out of his chair at the head of the table and darted out of the conference room.

He hoped like hell Ruby had taken good notes, because his concentration level was shit.

As he strode down the hall toward his corner office, he blocked out everything around him, locking his eyes on his phone as he went, acting absorbed by the screen in case he passed anyone. As he walked by Ruby's empty desk, he heard Gabe behind him, calling his name.

Mason proceeded into his office, hoping his brother would get the message that he wasn't available.

No such luck.

Without a word, Gabe followed him in and closed the door.

"What the hell is going on?" Gabe demanded in a tempered tone.

Mason went around his desk and faced his brother without a word.

Gabe stepped between the desk and the visitors' chairs and tilted his head as he silently took in Mason.

Swearing to himself, Mason turned away, pointed his gaze out the window at the less-than-impressive view of the busy street. "Did you need something?" he asked.

Several beats of silence passed, and he felt his brother staring into his back, trying to figure out what was going on. It was a pointless effort. He'd never in a million years guess correctly.

"Who was the woman?" Gabe asked.

"A woman I met a few years ago. What'd you think of the meeting?" he diverted, his back still to Gabe.

Another long pause stretched between them before Gabe said, "I think you were only half there. Because of the woman. What did she say to you?"

Hands in the pockets of his suit pants, Mason rattled his keys, debating. It wasn't in his nature to share a personal problem. He was more comfortable with business problems and kept his personal life as drama-free as possible. Until now, evidently.

As much as he'd prefer to keep the bomb Eliza had dropped to himself, he recognized that this thing was big. Life-changing. The sooner he could gain some perspective and wrangle with the situation, the sooner he would be able to move forward with a plan. And so far, he was staggering, mentally, emotionally.

Mason lowered himself to his leather chair, pushed back from his desk, peered up toward the ceiling without actually seeing it. Gabe sat across from him, waiting.

"I met Eliza during the Business Leadership Conference four years ago at the Lewis Hotel. Remember the evening we had drinks in the hotel bar with Tony Biscane and Peter White? It was just after Uncle Ham died and the board approved me as CEO."

"I think I remember the night. You were staying in the hotel while you had your kitchen remodeled so you could put the place on the market."

Mason nodded. "You all left after a couple of drinks. I stayed, ordered dinner."

"And you met this woman. Eliza?" Gabe said.

As he'd finished eating, he couldn't help but notice the dark-haired woman who came in and took a seat toward one end of the bar and seemed to know the blond bartender well.

Both women were attractive. Beyond attractive. There'd been something more than surface beauty with the dark-haired one, though, something that had drawn his attention from the moment he laid eyes on her, and the longer he watched her, discreetly, from a distance, the more compelled he was to speak to her, know more about her. When the Cardinals, on the TV behind the bar, had scored a run and she'd let out a hearty cheer

—despite it being only a spring training game—his interest had pounded through him, enough that he'd gotten up and taken the stool next to her.

The word *bewitching* echoed through his mind again, because that's what she'd been. They'd gone into it knowing it was a one-night thing, and yet somehow, it'd been on a different level than all the other women Mason had been with over the years.

When he'd woken up alone the next morning, he'd tried to shrug the whole thing off and go on with his life as if his world hadn't been categorically rocked. He had a company to run. His father's legacy to continue to build. He didn't believe in magic and didn't have the luxury of letting sex distract him. And so he hadn't let it.

Much.

And now…

"She claims she's the mother of my three-year-old son."

Gabe's eyes popped wide open, and he leaned forward, planted his elbows into his legs, and covered his mouth with his hands as he gaped at Mason.

Mason leaned his elbows on his desk as his statement seemed to expand between them.

"Do you think it could be true?" Gabe eventually asked.

"I think I need to get a test. The fact that she said she doesn't want anything from me leads me to believe—"

"It could be true," Gabe finished as he sat up straight again. "Jesus, Mason. What are you going to do?"

"Hell if I know. I have to figure it out though, get it settled, because work needs my full attention. This couldn't come at a worse time."

Gabe let out a huff. "I don't think a kid is something you *settle* and move on from."

"It is if a paternity test comes back negative."

It was always a possibility, but something in his gut told him it wasn't highly likely. While Mason preferred logic to gut feelings, he'd learned over the years not to ignore his instincts.

"What would you do?" he asked his brother. Asking anyone for advice made Mason's skin itchy, but this was Gabe, the second-oldest North brother and someone he trusted implicitly, especially when it came to people and conflict and emotions. Gabe could read an interpersonal situation the way Mason could decipher a financial report or a white paper.

Gabe took several seconds to reply. "Where did you leave it with her? Are you supposed to call her? Meet again? Get a DNA test?"

Mason blew out all the air in his lungs, knowing his brother wasn't going to like his answer. "I fucked up. I let her walk away before I could get her contact info."

"We can track that down easily enough."

"We could if we had her last name."

Gabe's gaze shot to his face, his mouth open in disbelief.

"Don't say it. I know," Mason said. "There was no reason to know before, and this morning I was stunned stupid."

"Do you know where she works?"

Clenching his jaw, Mason shook his head. "Back then she tended bar somewhere on Broadway. I have no idea if she still works in the same place." As he remembered something she'd said this morning, he sat up straighter. "She's called here more than once. I'm sure she's spoken to Ruby."

"Ruby tracks everything. And if she didn't write down a phone number, I bet she'd remember a last name," Gabe said as a tone sounded on his phone. He pulled it out of his pocket. "Damn. I've got a conference call I can't miss in five minutes. Start with Ruby. We'll talk later."

"I'm fine," Mason said, which was a lie, but there was nothing Gabe or anyone else could do to make him any better.

As soon as his brother was gone, Mason shot up out of his chair and went to question Ruby. He didn't have enough info at this point to decide anything, but if there was, indeed, a boy out there who was his child, he was damn well going to be in that child's life.

CHAPTER FOUR

The Friday-night crowd was electric, raucous, and paying full attention to the music. Exactly the way Eliza and the four other musicians on stage with her loved it. If they were lucky, the enthusiasm of the packed-in bar patrons would translate to a hefty tip jar.

Jimmy Sanchez, the lead singer who'd brought her in on this gig, was one of the best when it came to working the audience for tips, and that was one of the reasons Eliza had approached him about playing tonight, her first live performance in more than a year.

She'd played with Jimmy countless times in her old life, before Calvin came along, and in fact, she had him to thank for the connections that had eventually allowed her to switch to being a studio musician. Though studio work was less fulfilling than performing live, it paid better, and if you could get yourself invited regularly, it was a decent way to earn an income, relatively speaking. The hours were more conducive to having a kid, and Eliza thanked the stars above that she'd landed where she had and was lucky enough to get studio work five days a week almost every week.

And still, extra expenses were tough to cover some months. *Most* months.

As the fiddle-heavy chorus of "Don't Be Stupid" started,

Jimmy, in typical Jimmy style, made sure Eliza was front and center on the small stage at the front end of the Broadway bar. She put everything she had into the lively song and didn't have to fake loving the tune, regardless of how many hundreds of times she'd played it before. It was a crowd-pleaser and the perfect end to their four-hour set, because it got people dancing and laughing and hopefully making a trip up to stuff a bill or two in the jar.

She took a couple of steps back when the next verse came on, giving Jimmy the spotlight, sharing a laugh with the guitarist, Rae Robins, at Jimmy's fervor.

After several more rounds of chorus and verse, with Eliza and Jimmy trying to outdo each other with every round much to the crowd's delight, the song ended, along with their set. Jimmy thanked each of the musicians by name and allowed them yet another round of applause, and Eliza let herself bask in it.

God, she'd missed performing live. She hadn't realized how much until this moment.

"You were fantastic!" Rae pulled Eliza into a side hug as Jimmy did his meet-and-greet thing over by the tip jar.

"You were too," Eliza said as they went to the corner where they'd left their cases and packed their instruments away. She'd met Rae roughly twenty minutes before they'd gone on stage together, not an uncommon occurrence. Eliza would happily play with her again if the circumstances arose. The guitarist brought her own energy to her side of the stage and had shown off some serious chops. "And so was the crowd."

"Jimmy's the best." The redhead, shorter than Eliza, was glowing with satisfaction, matching how Eliza felt.

"But not as pretty as you two." Dirk Preston, the drummer, who Eliza knew well and had played with countless times in the distant past, came up behind them and squeezed each of their shoulders affectionately. He, like Jimmy, was in his fifties and a respected, dedicated musician who thrived on this world of live shows. "Really good to see you on stage again," he said to Eliza. "You coming back to it? That baby of yours must be getting pretty old."

"He's turning four next month," she told him, which made him gasp.

"That can't be. So he's all grown up then, and you're coming back to this?" He laughed as he nodded to the crowd and the bar in general.

"I'm hoping to play a few shows so I can do his birthday right. If you'll have me."

"Jimmy's in charge but I'm sure we'll have you."

"He mentioned next weekend," Eliza said. "Will you both be here?"

"Count on it," Dirk said.

Rae was chugging the last of a bottled water and gave a thumbs-up. "The four of us have been playing pretty regularly," she said, including bass player Jed Pratt, next to Jimmy, who Eliza also knew from a few years back. He was maybe thirty now and always a favorite with the ladies in the audience. Eliza knew him as a big-time charmer who went home with someone different every night, whether it was a fan or a fellow musician.

Someone called Dirk away, and Eliza was dying of thirst, as she'd run out of water several songs ago, so, fiddle case in hand, she said goodbye to Rae and made her way to the bar, still riding the high of being on stage.

She'd set out to do this for her son's sake, but playing live was not a hardship. More like a treat. Maybe in a few years, when Calvin was older, she could get back to gigging a little here and there just for the fun of it.

For now, though, the goal was making some spending money. Calvin's birthday was next month, and he'd never had a party before. He hadn't had a long list of friends, because he hadn't been in daycare. It took three of them—Eliza, Grace, and their duplex neighbor, Lettie, who was with him tonight—to ensure Calvin always had someone to watch him, and it worked well. It just didn't allow for a lot of social interaction beyond a couple of neighborhood kids.

Now that he'd started preschool, her son was all about friends, and he'd already been invited to two classmates' parties. Naturally, he wanted one too, and Eliza was determined to give him one. That and the wooden train set he'd spotted in the toy store weeks ago. It was pricey, but she planned on surprising him with one of the medium-sized sets. It would be bigger and better than anything he'd ever gotten before, and she couldn't wait to see the look on his face when he unwrapped it.

When she'd called Jimmy two weeks ago about playing, he'd jumped at the chance, saying he'd been looking for a good fiddle player to join them. In the past, he'd told her it was easy to find someone good at playing the fiddle and harder to find someone who played well *and* got the audience going. He claimed Eliza was the best at it, and she did ham it up hard on stage, but Jimmy made it easy with his ongoing enthusiasm and infectious personality. At any rate, tonight was a great start toward Calvin's birthday.

The bar was so packed that it took some time to make the short walk between stage and counter, and several people stopped her along the way to compliment her playing. The gushing and appreciation were also things she missed. She was well respected in the studio, but there was nothing like a live show.

She was nearly to the close end of the bar, where there was enough space for people to slip between stools and place an order, when her gaze was drawn to a pair of eyes fixed on her a few feet away.

Her heart skipped a beat and she stopped dead in her tracks as adrenaline shot through her system.

What on earth was Mason North doing here? On a Friday night? Wearing a suit?

Here. On Broadway. Looking totally out of place.

He walked toward her, making his way through the crowd more easily than she had. Because he was big and determined and apparently wanted to talk to her?

She'd thought her mouth was dry before, but at the sight of him, every drop of moisture disappeared. When he reached her side, she couldn't speak.

"Eliza," he said with a slight smile, and damn, she really wished he wouldn't smile at all, because he was panty-dropping handsome without it. She was proof. Add the grin and her insides went to mush.

"Hi," she managed as someone budged in behind her and forced her into Mason's chest—his wide, perfect chest, she knew from personal experience. "What are you doing here?"

"Watching a hell of a show," he said, his large hand settling on the bare skin of her elbow as if to steady her. "You're incredible."

"Thank you," she said automatically, but inside, she went warm at the compliment. Just what she didn't want to do. She didn't know what he wanted, but as the seconds ticked by, she was more and more sure he did want something. This was no coincidence. "I need to get some water."

As she turned toward the bar to get through the last couple of layers of people, Mason kept his hand around her arm, gentle yet firm, and used his large body to get them closer to the counter. Thanks to his height advantage—she wasn't short but he had a good half foot on her—he raised his hand, got the attention of the bartender, and asked for a water "for the fiddle player." Before she knew it, she had an ice-cold bottle in one hand, and she was too thirsty to be annoyed at Mason's take-charge act. He twisted the cap off since she still had her fiddle in her other hand, and she drank half the bottle in one go.

Once the liquid started to rehydrate her body, her brain seemed to work better. "Why are you here?" she asked again, loudly enough to be heard over the crowd roar, not buying for a second that he happened to be on Broadway by himself on a Friday night just for fun. Most locals stayed away from downtown, knowing it tended to be overrun by tourists.

"We have things to discuss," he said simply as he peered down at her. "You didn't give me your phone number."

"You didn't ask for it." She'd realized later she hadn't given him any contact info, not even her last name. "How did you find me?"

"My assistant," he answered. "She remembered your last name. A quick search online took me to your website. I thought you were a bartender, not a musician."

"I used to be both."

A short woman with long dark hair passed close, leaned into Eliza's ear, and said, "You were amazing. Great show."

"Thank you," Eliza said graciously to the stranger and was grateful when the woman kept walking.

"How often do you play?" Mason asked.

"I haven't played live for over a year. Mostly I do studio sessions because they work better with being a mom, but there's nothing like playing for a live audience. It's a great way to earn some extra cash for some upcoming expenses." She couldn't bring herself to admit the expenses were *his son's* birthday.

"I'm impressed. My understanding is that gigs aren't easy to get."

"I've built up a lot of connections over the years."

Behind her, a couple of guys shoved through too small a space, and she was pushed into Mason's chest again. He caught her with a hand on her waist, holding her up against him as he shot a look over her shoulder, then focused his intense attention back on her.

"Can we go somewhere and talk?" Mason asked.

She lifted the water bottle to her lips again, to quench her thirst but also to buy herself a few seconds.

Since she'd confronted him yesterday and told him about Calvin, she'd thought they had no more to talk about. He'd practically shoved her away so he could get to his meeting and given her no indication he wanted to know anything more about Calvin—or that he even believed she spoke the truth.

She'd started to make peace with that. Started to accept that, after all these years, the mystery of Mason was gone, and now that he knew he had a son, nothing was going to change. He didn't want to be in Calvin's life.

So much the better, she'd told herself.

If he didn't want to know his incredible boy, that was his loss.

But now she wondered if he'd changed his mind, and she didn't know how to handle the emotional whiplash.

"Where did you want to go?" she asked. Another stall.

Nothing on Broadway was conducive to the kind of talk they would likely have. It was all crowded, loud, and chaotic.

"There's a coffee shop about three blocks over. Probably pretty quiet at this hour. Are you up for walking?" He glanced down at her cowboy boots.

"That's fine. I need to get my bag and let Jimmy know." It would take a while for him to settle up with the bar and get the tips figured. Normally she'd wait around and listen to the last set of the night, but she trusted Jimmy and could either catch him after she talked to Mason or track him down tomorrow.

"Where's your bag?"

"A tiny room in back." She pointed and then sent off a quick text to Jimmy. There were approximately five hundred people directly between them and the room. It was going to take a while.

Or so she'd thought.

Mason took her hand, and before she could decide whether that was okay or not, he was leading her through the throngs as if he was used to taking charge and having people acquiesce. Which, as a CEO, he probably was. And maybe she should be irritated by it, but truthfully, after four hours straight of playing, she was exhausted and totally okay with ducking behind him and letting him fight their way.

Beyond the restrooms, just before the back exit, Eliza guided him into the private room where her bag was in a locker. She set her case down and worked the combination on the lock, took out her bag and shouldered it, and picked up her fiddle, fully conscious of Mason's eyes on her the whole time. She avoided looking at him, in a hurry to get out of that tiny room where the two of them together barely fit.

Once in the narrow hall, she went to the back exit and pushed her way out into the September night, the fresh air a relief, as was the sudden decrease in noise when the door closed behind them.

Eliza breathed.

As much as she loved performing, she was still, at heart, an introvert, and being around so many people, expending so much outward energy for so long drained her.

"The coffee shop is this way," Mason said with a gentle hand on her lower back, jolting her from her moment of respite.

She'd dressed for a packed bar where the crowd and the performance itself kept the musicians on the toasty side. When she'd arrived for the six-p.m. gig, her shorts, flowy tank, and boots had been sufficient, but now, just after ten o'clock, the temperature had dropped with the sun.

The goose bumps that rose up and down her shoulders and arms were strictly from the cool air hitting her flushed, over-heated flesh, she told herself. They had nothing to do with the man or his touch.

Lying to herself was okay if it helped her get through a moment.

They were three doors away from the street and walked in silence along the side of the alley, then turned right.

"How long have you played?" Mason asked as they moved away from the chaos of Broadway.

"I started on the violin in first grade." She got the question all the time and was used to answering, so she continued with the rest of the condensed version. "When I was in third grade, I discovered 'The Devil Went Down to Georgia' and was determined to play the fiddle part."

"What's the difference between a violin and a fiddle?" Mason asked. "I've always wondered."

"They're basically the same instrument. The difference is in the type of music they're used for."

"So did you learn to play 'The Devil Went Down to Georgia'?"

"I did." She'd been obsessive about it. "It turned out that my violin teacher, Mr. Senegal, had been into the country music scene here in Nashville in his younger days, and he was thrilled with my interest. We had a deal that if I kept up on the violin and playing in the orchestra, he'd keep teaching me fiddle music on the side."

"How long did you keep up on the violin?"

"Until I graduated from high school."

"You must be pretty decent at it too," he said, his voice low and whiskey smooth now that they didn't have to shout to hear each other.

With a half grin, she said, "I can hold my own on Vivaldi's *Four Seasons*."

"Do you ever play violin music anymore?"

"Sometimes I get calls for musical scores, for movies or ads."

"Impressive," he said as they took a left, and she saw the sign for a coffeehouse about halfway down the block.

"It's just what I do. Like CEOing is what you do. I could argue that's at least equally impressive."

She wasn't out to flatter him, but she'd be lying if she said she wasn't still reeling over finding out exactly who was the father of her child. Just as she'd not talked about being a musician during their night together, he'd not breathed a word about leading a large, successful company. They'd had better things to do.

"I'd just been named CEO that night I first met you," he said. "It was a tricky thing, because I moved into the position when my uncle died. It didn't feel right to celebrate. The night I met you, though, my brother and a couple of friends who were at the conference insisted on drinking a low-key toast to my promotion."

"You have four brothers, right? And some cousins in the family business?"

"Four brothers and three cousins. My dad started the company in the seventies with his brother. My mom and aunt eventually got involved. As the oldest of all the kids, my goal was always to someday take the reins, and I worked my ass off to get there."

Even though it was a totally different side to the man she'd known for mere hours, she could easily see it. He was intense and intent—that night his attention had been on her, and it'd disarmed her in about three heartbeats. He seemed like the kind of guy who determined what he wanted, went after it single-mindedly, and got it.

"What about you? Any siblings?" he asked as they neared the door to the coffeehouse.

"Only child. A couple of cousins on the West Coast but I don't know them well. Our family's small and not very close."

Mason opened the door and let her precede him into the cozy but not very busy coffeeshop. There was a group of college-age girls at a table in the back corner, a handful of couples, and a sprinkling of singles with laptops. There was no line, and a few minutes later, Eliza headed toward a table for two away from the other customers. Mason followed, carrying a tray with a peppermint tea, a slice of chocolate cake, and another ice water for her and a black coffee and a cinnamon roll for him.

"Caffeine doesn't keep you up all night?" she asked once he'd gotten rid of the tray and sat across from her.

"I've got some work yet tonight, so sleep is a ways off."

"On a Friday night?" If they only sat here for half an hour, it would still be close to midnight by the time he got back to work.

"Let's just say my break to see you play was spur-of-the-moment. I've got a few hours' worth yet to get through."

And she thought she worked her ass off. Of course, he didn't have a little boy at home taking precedence. She nearly laughed aloud at the thought, because technically, he did have the same little boy. He'd just never known it.

"I'm sorry to take you away from your work," she said.

"You didn't. I could have tracked you down another way," he said as he forked a bite of gooey cinnamon roll. "I was curious."

About me or your son? she wondered. She didn't have the nerve to ask out loud. She wasn't sure she wanted to know the answer. Then she forgot the question because of what he said next.

"Eliza, I want a paternity test."

CHAPTER FIVE

he bite of cake Eliza swallowed seemed to get stuck in
her throat, making her cough. She swiped up her
water bottle and swigged some down, her eyes watering.

"That can't come as a surprise," Mason continued, his tone
matter-of-fact, as if he were sitting at a business meeting. "I have
to protect myself and my family's interests."

There was a part of her that realized that must be true, what
with his likely net worth, his family's business, and other assets
at stake. Especially when it came to her, a woman with almost
nothing to her name. But she couldn't help being insulted that he
would think she'd claim something she wasn't absolutely certain
of. There was zero question that he was the father.

"I'll cover the cost, of course."

"How nice," she said, biting down on a few other things that
wanted to pop out. She had expected he would want proof. It
didn't make the situation any easier to swallow.

He set his coffee down abruptly. "Look, you have to understand that the article in the *Nashville Heat* brought out scores of
people trying to contact me for a myriad of reasons. And yes,
paternity claims included."

She gasped. "You have other children you didn't know
about?" Who the hell was this man she'd been romanticizing for
four-plus years?

"No," he said firmly. "That's my point. People lie. The article brought out the worst in a lot of them. It's why Ruby wouldn't let you talk to me. There've been women calling daily trying to meet me or 'reconnect' with me, most of whom I have no idea who they are."

She sat back in her chair, a little horrified that she was lumped in with the lying, money-grubbing masses. "I'm not after your money."

"I'm not saying you are," he said. "Just that I need to have proof he's mine. To protect my family."

Eliza nodded. On a rational level, she got it. So she would give him what he needed as far as a test was concerned. "That's fine. I can tell you right now what the results will say, but I understand you need it documented." She swallowed hard, having lost the appetite for her chocolate cake. "I'll say it again, though, I'm not out to get anything from you. I thought letting you know you have a child was the right thing to do."

"It was," he said gravely, his gaze going off into the distance. She turned to see what he was focusing on, but there was nothing there.

"Do you have any pictures of him?" he asked, surprising her with the sudden hint of gentleness in his voice.

To herself, she laughed. Did she have any pictures of her adorable only child on her phone? Only a few thousand. She kept a straight face, though, nervous for some reason as she took her phone out and unlocked it.

She tried to maintain as much privacy for her child as she could, especially since her career required her to sometimes have a spotlight on her. She wasn't used to showing off her boy to people she barely knew. Obviously, it was different when the person she barely knew was the father.

Mason shoveled another bite of cinnamon roll into his mouth as she swiped through her photos, trying to find the best one. *Why the best one?* she wondered. *A first impression shouldn't matter when it's his own son.*

She settled on one from just before preschool started, of Calvin on the play equipment at the park. He was standing at the top of the slide and yelling at the top of his little lungs, the joy on his face unmatchable. She spent an extra moment taking it in, tried to see it from the perspective of someone who'd never met Calvin. With a lump in her throat, she held out her phone and Mason took it.

"My God," he said as he set eyes on his son. She saw him swallow, watched the expressions that crossed his face—disbelief, shock, and finally, his eyes lit up and there was a mix of good stuff too. Affection? Happiness? "When was this taken?"

"About a month ago. Early August."

He was quiet for a few seconds, just staring, and then he said, "He's a dead ringer for Drake at that age. My youngest brother," he added. He put one hand over his mouth, pinching it, as if he was in shock. "Are there more?"

This time she did let out a quiet laugh. "There are more."

He handed her the phone back. They spent the next few minutes passing it between them, with her swiping from one Calvin pic to the next and Mason studying what she showed him, asking questions.

After a couple dozen, he met her gaze with a piercing one and folded his hands in front of him, elbows resting on the table. "I want to meet him."

Eliza tried to keep her expression neutral, but inside, she froze with fear.

She'd known, of course, that there was a fifty-fifty chance he'd want to meet his son, but hearing the words come out of his mouth made it real. Terrifying.

What if he tried to get custody?

What if he tried to spoil Calvin with all his money?

What if Calvin liked him better?

What if… What if… What if…

She squeezed her eyes shut and ran her hands over her face, fatigue rolling through every cell in her body. She couldn't deny him the chance to meet Calvin. She had no reason to believe Mason had nefarious intentions. All he was asking for was to meet his son.

Lowering her hands, she studied him. His arresting ice-blue

eyes, square jaw covered with just enough scruff to be sexy, dark brown hair with a tousled style that was long enough to run fingers through, and a set to his jaw that spoke of determination and grit.

It must be intimidating to sit across a boardroom table from him.

Who was she kidding? It was no picnic to sit across a coffee shop table from him with him wanting something she was scared to give.

"I don't want him to know you're his father yet," she said.

As Mason narrowed his eyes, she rushed to add, "I have to do whatever it takes to make sure he's okay. Dropping a bombshell like *hey, kid, I'm your daddy* will rock his entire existence, especially if he doesn't know you. That's a lot to handle at any age, but he's only three years old."

His gaze remained fixed on her, scrutinizing her hard, as if trying to determine whether to accept her arguments.

"I'm not saying no to you meeting him," she added. "I'm just saying we need to take this slowly."

"How slowly?"

"I don't know. One step at a time? How do I know you're not going to meet him, tell him you're his father, and then lose interest?"

A glint of ice flashed in those blue eyes. "I'm not going to lose interest."

She saved the internal debate of whether that was a good thing or a bad thing for later, because sitting across from him, seeing the intention in his eyes, she believed him.

"Please," she said in a quieter voice, hoping to appeal to that side of Mason that apparently catered to his mother. "This isn't easy for me either. I'm trying to do what I've done for four years and that's whatever's best for my son."

"*Our* son."

"Yes," she conceded. "We'll eventually tell him who you are, but can you give us time to get used to you, to get to know you better? I've trusted very few people when it comes to Calvin—"

"Thank you," he said gruffly, catching her off guard, and she stared at him, her mouth open.

"What are you thanking me for?" she finally asked.

"For taking good care of our son all this time. For protecting him. I can tell you put his needs first."

She nodded once, such a small outward gesture when the gratification that rushed through her was big and overwhelming. It was as if all the years of trying to do what was best for Calvin, all the thousands of decisions she'd had to make regarding his welfare were somehow being acknowledged by this man she barely knew, and it rendered her unable to speak for a few seconds.

And, yes, it softened her toward him ever so slightly, but that could also be because he was so damn good-looking. Who wouldn't want to give him at least a little of what he wanted?

The fact was, Calvin came first no matter how compelling this man was, and in the long run, if Mason was a good man as he appeared to be, it could be positive for Calvin to have him in his life. But for her sake and Calvin's, they would have to take baby steps.

Before either of them could say more, Mason's phone rang. He took it out of his pocket, checked the display, and stood abruptly. "I need to take this. I'll be back. Hey," he said into the phone as he went toward the door. "How'd the meeting come out?"

She watched him walk out, and even in her distressed state, it didn't escape her how well he wore that suit, from the front, back, any which way. He'd been wearing a suit the night they'd met, until he wasn't wearing anything, and she wondered if he ever wore anything else.

The front of the coffeehouse was windowed, and she kept her eyes on him as she tried to sort out everything in her head, from Mason's unexpected appearance at the bar to his demand to be introduced to Calvin to the fact that it was—she checked her phone—two minutes after eleven at night, and if she wasn't mistaken, his call was business-related.

His dedication to work… She couldn't lie. It was a big, fat red flag. She knew all too well what it was like to have a workaholic father, one who put his job above his family, and that was something she emphatically did not want for her son.

The phone call appeared to be short and to the point, and Mason came back through the door with confident strides.

"I need to go," he said when he was in front of their table. He picked up his mug and swigged down the rest of his coffee.

Eliza stood, feeling the sting of being pushed aside and wishing she wasn't so sensitive. She grabbed the water bottle and left the cake half-eaten and the tea mostly gone.

"I'll walk you to your car," Mason said.

"You don't have to do that—"

"It's Friday night and eighty percent of the people downtown are drunk. I'll make sure you get out of here safely. Where are you parked?"

She told him as they exited the coffee shop. Though she'd gotten to her car without incident hundreds of times, she felt safer with him by her side, particularly as they walked by a group of boisterous, rowdy college-age guys.

"The phone call must have been important," she said as they got closer to Broadway, fishing for more information, still wondering if the late-night call was business-related.

"It was my brother Cole," Mason said, his hand landing on her waist as they neared an intersection that was crowded with pedestrians.

"So not business?"

"He had a dinner meeting tonight regarding one of our new stores in Colorado."

So business. "Bad news?"

As the light changed and the crowd surged into the street to cross, he said, "Potentially good news after a week full of bad."

"Oh?" She looked up at his profile as they walked away from the busiest part of downtown.

"It's nothing that can't be fixed with some hard work."

She considered herself to be a hard worker, but his statement made her uneasy.

"Do you always work so much?" she blurted out.

With an almost grin, he said, "My family will tell you I'm a workaholic."

Her gut knotted. "Are they right?"

He sobered and hesitated. "Probably. But I don't think they stop to consider the extreme pressure I'm under to not fuck up my dad's legacy. He put everything he had into North Brothers Sports, and it's ultimately up to me to make sure the company not only makes it but thrives, when the market is more competitive and online sales are overtaking traditional retail models left and right. I have a top-notch team, but at the end of the day, if something goes wrong, it's on me."

"That is a lot of pressure," she acknowledged, still uneasy. "My dad was a workaholic."

"Was?"

"He died of a heart attack at age forty-four."

Mason expelled a gust of breath. "I'm sorry."

Eliza nodded automatically, unwilling to let her thoughts get too mired in the past.

"Were you close?" Mason asked.

Eliza shook her head. "My dad was never really a family guy." She locked down on the quagmire of emotion that threatened to surface. Her general rule of thumb was to waste as little energy as possible on her childhood, her parents, her disappointments.

"Is your mom still living?" he asked.

"She is. In Minneapolis, where I grew up."

"It must've been hard on her to lose her husband so young."

Like Mason's mom had, she realized. From the little she knew, based on what Mason had said about his dad's legacy, Eliza guessed his family and hers were complete opposites. She heard love and admiration in his voice when he talked about his dad, and just the fact that most of his brothers worked together said they were likely close-knit.

"I'm not sure," she said as they turned on a side street lined by parked cars. "I'm sure she was sad, but I don't think my parents loved each other by then. Maybe they never did." She shrugged.

"That's sad. What did he do for a living?"

"He was a lawyer. Always worried about billable hours. It seemed like his mantra was *more, more, more*. Nothing was ever enough."

"I know that feeling well. All except the billable hours," he said, and she couldn't quite make herself respond with empathy.

Her old, tired car came into view. She saw it through different eyes tonight. His eyes. The eyes of a guy who undoubtedly had a pretty new car that cost more money than she'd see in a decade.

Well…welcome to reality. They might have connected on a deep, sensual level the night they were together, but in real life, they had nothing in common. Nothing except a three-year-old child.

That connection made her uneasy in light of his over-dedication to work. If his family accused him of being a workaholic, then he probably was.

The signs were there. It was likely true that a CEO worked long hours regardless, but was Mason the type of man who would miss his child's high school graduation because his head was too buried in work?

If he was, what could she do to prevent Calvin from getting hurt? Because she would do everything in her power to spare her son the kind of unwarranted hurt she'd experienced repeatedly growing up.

"This is me," she said, not apologizing for her seen-better-days Corolla.

"I'll have my assistant contact you about when I can meet Calvin," Mason said, one hand in his pants pocket, rattling keys.

"No," Eliza said without hesitation.

"No?"

"If you want to meet your son, you can contact me yourself. Calvin is not a business deal. He's a little boy."

"You're right. I'm sorry," he said, surprising her a little. "I'm new at this. Ruby takes care of just about everything, and it's become a habit as much as a necessity. I'll call you. Give me your number."

He took his phone out, typed in her name, and held it out for her to add her phone number. Then he sent her a message so she'd have his as well.

"Thanks for walking me back," she said, in desperate need of escaping so she could maybe start processing everything about tonight and Mason North.

"Goodbye, Eliza," he said before she shut her door and started the engine.

Fantasy Mason had been perfect. Reality Mason was not, and she was beginning to wonder how she would make everything okay for her son when and if Mason pursued a relationship with him.

CHAPTER SIX

*M*ason had been blessed—or cursed, depending on who you asked—with a killer ability to focus single-mindedly on work. Tonight, as he rode the private elevator to his penthouse condo at nearly midnight, he was twice as thankful as usual for it, because, one, it allowed him to block out his personal life and all its uncertainty, and two, if there was ever a time when he needed all his attention on North Brothers Sports, it was now.

He unlocked his door and stepped into his foyer and soaked in the usual quiet that welcomed him. Without turning on a light, he glanced out automatically at the distant lights of downtown Nashville through the floor-to-ceiling windows, taking comfort in the fact that the chaos of the big-city night went on nearby, both downtown and at Vanderbilt, his alma mater, a block away.

He made his way through the seldom-used double living room, divided by a two-sided fireplace, to the stairs and up to the second floor, where he spent most of his time. With a quick stop in his bedroom, he kicked off his shoes and hung up his suit jacket but didn't change from his suit pants and dress shirt. Then he took his messenger bag into his study to get to work.

When he'd taken the reins of the company four and a half years ago, it had been a family-owned business with five locations, all in Tennessee, that was holding its own, barely, in a rapidly changing market. While its sales had increased modestly most years, its market share had been declining, and it hadn't taken an MBA from Vanderbilt to see that the company's longevity was at risk.

The company's longevity, in Mason's mind, was paramount. His entire family depended on North Brothers Sports, as did hundreds of other employees, and he didn't take that responsibility lightly.

As he'd gained confidence and experience at the helm, he'd known it was vital to make some changes, and he'd set aggressive goals to build the company into a serious contender in the national sporting goods industry. A crucial part of that plan was expansion.

Last year, they'd begun with some cautious movement into markets outside of the state, and when those had proven successful, he'd convinced the board they needed to step up their plan. It was no longer enough to just hold on.

That had resulted in securing financing from a private investment company for NBS's aggressive growth plan. There were certain benchmarks NBS had to meet this year in order to receive additional funding for years two and three of the plan.

Mason monitored sales, along with a thousand other data points, like a hawk, an obsessed, starving hawk. While the company was meeting several ongoing goals, it was in danger of not making the biggest, most significant one—company-wide sales for the year. They had a number, a magic number they needed to meet by December first, and at the end of July, they'd been missing the year-to-date goal by two percent.

Two percent was not detrimental. The company could right itself and make up for that easily in a good month.

The problem was that August had not been a good month, and the report Mason had received two days ago showed they were now down by more than five percent. Making up that deficit would be a bigger challenge, but the more concerning aspect was the trend.

They needed to not only stop the monthly shortfalls but make up for the low months enough to meet the annual goal. If they didn't, the company's future was at risk. The lifeblood of Mason and his brothers and cousins and so many others was in danger. Worst of all, if they couldn't succeed with their ambitious growth goals, his father's legacy could be lost.

If that were to happen, Mason would never forgive himself.

He flipped on the lamp on his desk, sat in his top-of-the-line ergonomic chair, and ignored the floor-to-ceiling windows to his right. His mind was in it now, and very little could drag him out of work mode.

He shoved down the image of Eliza, her dark hair swinging along with her sexy hips as she played the hell out of her fiddle on the stage tonight.

With determination, he took his laptop out, opened it, waited for it to find the network, then opened his inbox.

Cole's email waited for him as promised, and he clicked on it, becoming engrossed in the challenge of opening the Colorado store a month earlier than planned, November first instead of December.

As he refigured schedules, details, and all the people who needed to be brought in on the change, Mason started to wonder about the feasibility of doing the same with the under-construction Westside Nashville store. If they could open both stores two to four weeks early, it would impact sales in a positive way. They'd have a much easier time of making up for the shortfall and getting ahead on the annual goal.

When he finally looked at the clock again, it was close to four a.m. His eyes burned with fatigue, and he'd sent out emails to a dozen and a half people and was at a standstill now until he heard back from them. That would be several hours, best-case scenario. His leadership team was good about checking email, and he would likely hear back on the weekend, but for now, the best thing to do was try to get some sleep.

As he walked down the hall and through the upstairs den, he felt every one of the seventeen hours of his workday, live music break not included.

Once in his expansive master bedroom, he shed his shirt, pants, and underwear, tossed them onto an armchair, and slid between the covers, all without turning a light on. He set the alarm on his phone, plugged the device in on the nightstand, and let his head fall to the pillow.

The second his eyes closed, he again saw Eliza's pretty face in his mind, remembered the look of maternal pride and love when she'd showed him pictures of Calvin.

His *son*, Calvin.

His flesh and blood, who looked so much like Mason's little brother had as a child that Mason knew in his heart he didn't need the paternity test.

He was a father. He had a little boy.

It blew his fucking mind.

He flipped to the other side, knowing he needed to sleep in order to handle the company's latest crisis, but damn if he could get his mind clear of the child he didn't yet know. The child he *would* know. Soon.

He would indeed contact Eliza himself to make arrangements. Lying there in the dark, he shook his head as he remembered the feisty look in her eyes when he'd stupidly told her his assistant would call her. The more he thought about it, the less he could blame her. His admiration for her grew because of it. It was clear she would fight for whatever she believed their boy needed, and damn was he grateful for that.

He tried to imagine what the past four years had been like for her as a single mom. He tried to envision what he'd missed. All the things he'd missed.

Shit.

He didn't have any experience with newborn babies as an adult, only as the oldest brother in the family, and now maybe he never would. He'd missed it all with Calvin.

Eliza hadn't shown him any pictures from that far back, only recent ones, but now Mason was dying to see what his little boy had looked like seconds after his birth. He wondered what it would've been like to witness Calvin's first smile, his first step, his first word.

Swallowing hard, he tried to accept that there was no way to remedy this, that even if he got ahold of photos from Calvin's birth on, he would never know what it had been like, never have those moments in his memory bank.

Regret gutted him, and he punched the pillow, squeezed his eyes shut, aching to block out the pain and helplessness that the inability to fix this, to change history, brought on.

He couldn't do anything about the past, and fixating on that was making him miserable, so he forced his mind to what he *could* do.

He could meet Calvin. He could hug his boy, pick him up, play with him. Learn what he liked, find out if he was a picky eater, see if he was quick to laugh and shout, like Drake had always been, or more introverted, like Cole. Or somewhere in between, depending on the situation, like Mason himself. In business, he was an extroverted, socially adept leader, but privately, he liked peace and quiet and a dose of being alone.

Was Calvin like him in any way? Did they share interests or personality quirks? And what effect did being an only child have on his boy? Gabe was only two years younger than Mason, and Mason had no memory of being the only North child. Did being the only kid make his son more creative, more introspective?

There was only one way to find out.

After endlessly tossing and turning, both physically and mentally, Mason checked the clock. It was nearly six thirty, which was when his alarm would go off. Ignoring his fatigue and his determination to plow through a bunch in the office today, he sprang out of bed and headed to the shower. The office would wait for an extra hour or so.

He was going to see about meeting his son.

CHAPTER SEVEN

*L*ettie Robertson, who lived in the other side of Eliza's duplex, was a perpetual godsend.

Not only did she graciously serve as one of Calvin's surrogate mothers by watching him whenever Eliza or Grace couldn't, but she looked after all three of them like a mom would. Eliza's mother lived in Minnesota, and they'd never been that close, so Eliza loved that Lettie had become a member of her nontraditional little family. The woman, who was in her mid-seventies, retired, and lived alone, adamantly refused to let Eliza pay her for childcare. Eliza now understood that including her in their life was the best way to "pay" her.

Saturday morning, at quarter till eight, Lettie had knocked lightly on Eliza's back door, bearing fresh-from-the-oven apple cinnamon coffee cake, knowing full well that Calvin would've woken Eliza up nearly an hour before.

She also knew firsthand how badly Eliza needed to make a grocery run, as Lettie had stayed with Calvin last night while Eliza played her gig and went with Mason to the coffee shop. Eliza had left a frozen pizza for their dinner, but there wasn't much else in the house.

Though the older woman didn't mention it, she had to be well aware that breakfast this morning was going to be hard to come by.

"This is yummy!" Calvin said with all the enthusiasm and volume of a boy who had to constantly be reminded to use his indoor voice. He shoveled another bite of coffee cake in his mouth.

"Shh," Lettie said. "You don't want to wake up Grace."

"She's not here," Eliza said with a meaningful look at the older woman.

"Reed?" Lettie asked, her brow furrowing, and Eliza nodded.

"I thought she was *disenchanted*." Lettie's gray brows rose on her light brown forehead as she used the very word Grace had used herself just a few evenings ago regarding her boyfriend of six months.

"I think she's trying hard to be *re*-enchanted," Eliza said sympathetically.

When Eliza's coffee cake was gone, she hopped up to get a refill of coffee and offered the same to Lettie, who refused.

As she made her way back to the table, the doorbell rang, startling her, sending Blitz into a barking frenzy as he shot into the living room. A glance at the clock on the stove told her it was two minutes after eight.

Who in their right mind would ring her doorbell that early?

"Are you expecting someone?" Lettie asked.

Eliza shook her head as she glanced down at herself. She hadn't showered yet, had pulled her tangled hair up into a messy bun, and had thrown on some cotton shorts and a tank top when she crawled out of bed. Not an outfit she normally wore in public, mainly because it did nothing to hide the eight to ten pounds of baby fat she still hadn't managed to lose.

"You look just fine," Lettie said. "Everything's covered. Better see who it is. I'll get this one another small serving."

"Thanks." Eliza caught up with the excited pup, hurrying toward the front door. Before she could get there, the person knocked. "Impatient much?" she muttered to herself.

She looked out through the peephole and sucked in a breath at the sight of Mason North on her front stoop.

Oh, God.

What was he doing here?

What would happen if she ignored him? Just walked back out to the kitchen? Sat back down at the table?

Both Lettie and Calvin would question her, that's what.

Before he could knock again, she unlocked the door and braced herself as she eased it open, scolding Blitz to get back just as Lettie called the dog into the kitchen with a biscuit.

"Good morning," Mason said before she could utter a word, and that low, whiskey-smooth voice…

She shoved down the effect it had on her. She wasn't in the mood to be charmed. Not when he'd dropped by without an invitation, without her even giving him her address, come to think of it.

"How did you find out where I live?" Eliza asked.

"Easy. Too easy. I tracked you down online, or technically, my cousin Logan did. It took him less than five minutes. We need to talk about privacy, some precautions you should take. It's not safe to have your information out there."

Frowning, she said, "I don't have my information 'out there.'"

"It's something about how your website is registered," he said. "I can help you fix it."

She disliked that she would probably need to take him up on that offer, but right now there were more pressing matters.

"What are you doing here?" She glanced over her shoulder toward the kitchen, thankful that Calvin was in the corner chair at the table, out of her sight. Out of Mason's sight. To be sure it stayed that way, she stepped out onto the stoop and closed the door behind her, running a hand over her hair as if she could make it look okay.

"I want to meet my son."

Eliza froze, then lowered her arm to her side. She stood there, staring up at him, waiting for more.

Like, *I want to meet my son next weekend.*

Or *I want to meet my son when we can properly arrange a first meeting.*

Mason simply peered down at her, waiting her out, the intensity in his blue eyes piercing.

"And you thought it was okay to just drop in?" she said,

keeping her volume low but not hiding her disbelief. "For something so significant? When I specifically asked you to contact me first?"

Her heart was racing, palms sweating. She locked her arms tightly across her chest, as if putting up an impenetrable barrier between him and her son.

Their son, she silently corrected before he could.

"We don't have to mention who I am today. Like you said."

She broke eye contact, hearing the arguments running through her head and knowing they weren't reasonable. They were fear-based and insecure. She glanced up and down the street to see if anyone was around to overhear, as if any of her neighbors, who she mostly didn't know, would care about her baby daddy drama.

Last night, as she lay in bed, worrying about Calvin meeting his dad for the first time, she'd constructed a plan. They could meet at the park. A neutral place, so Mason wouldn't be encroaching on Calvin's home territory. Okay, Eliza's home territory. Mason wouldn't see that their duplex needed paint on the outside and an overhaul on the inside. They might only be renters, but it was their home, and while Eliza and Grace had made it comfortable and cozy, she couldn't help but be aware of all the flaws he might see, being accustomed to his luxury condo.

Eliza had worked hard for everything, and she was proud of what she was able to do for her boy, but standing here, face-to-face with a man who was likely at least a millionaire, she couldn't help but wonder if he'd see this as not good enough for his child.

"I couldn't sleep last night," Mason said quietly, yanking her attention from her thoughts. "From thinking about him. Wondering. Seeing photos of him made it real." He let out an unsure half laugh. "Well, more real than it was. I'm still trying to absorb it all. That I'm a father."

"So you believe me? That he's yours?"

"After seeing photos? I can't deny there's North DNA in him." One hand was jammed into the pocket of his black business pants, and he jingled his keys, his frown deepening. "My son is nearly four years old and I've never met him. Never even laid eyes on him. I don't know what he likes to play with. Don't know his favorite food. Don't know what his voice sounds like."

She saw him swallow hard as he looked away, and when his gaze met hers again, she recognized what she was pretty sure very few people ever saw in Mason North. Vulnerability. Insecurity. Just a flash—

A *thunk* hit the other side of the door, and as Blitz's barks started up again, the door opened and Calvin shouted, "Mama, where are you?"

"Calvin!" Lettie hollered from the kitchen. "Let your mama be. Come back in here."

All that happened in a flash, and Eliza's heart simultaneously skipped a beat or three and her lungs failed to inhale.

"Hi, baby," she said on autopilot, and she put her hand on Calvin's shoulder and pulled him close to her side as she glanced back at Mason.

The expression on his face stunned her silent for a few more seconds. Mason gazed down at Calvin, his overwhelm evident as his eyes widened.

"This is Calvin," she said.

Mason's face lit up, his eyes taking on a sparkle and his smile spreading wide. "Hello, Calvin. It's nice to meet you."

"Who are you?"

Eliza cringed at her son's lack of manners. He knew better, but of course, he *would* slip right now.

"Calvin," she chided gently.

Her son craned his neck to look up at her. "I'm 'posed to say *Pleased to meet you*, but I didn't meet him yet."

The door opened again, and Lettie was there, her gaze veering between the three of them as she took in the scene. "Calvin Thomas, you have sticky hands. Come back to the kitchen and let your mama be."

"It's okay, Lettie," Eliza said. "I was just introducing Calvin to my friend Mason."

As Calvin held out his sticky hand to Mason and said, in his little-boy voice, "Pleased to meet you," Lettie's attention shot back to their guest.

Lettie knew all about Mason, had been in on discussions with Eliza and Grace for the week they'd unrelentingly tried to track him down, offering them support and ideas through it all. Now she searched Eliza's expression for a sign of how to handle the moment. Was he friend or foe? Welcome or unwanted?

Eliza sent her a subtle nod, even though she herself felt anything but sure.

"Mason, this is my neighbor and dear friend Lettie Robertson."

"Pleasure," Lettie said.

"Likewise," Mason said with a charming smile that reached all the way to Eliza's insides without her being okay with that.

"You should invite him in for coffee cake," Lettie said, mother hen taking over. "We've got plenty."

"I'm sure Mason is in a rush. Heading to work?" she asked him. With the dress pants, he wore a wine-collared button-down shirt and a tie. The most relaxed she'd ever seen him. This must be his version of casual Saturday.

"I've got time. Thank you, Lettie. Coffee cake sounds good."

"It is good!" Calvin repeated, and the enthusiasm in his voice set off Blitz again, somewhere behind Lettie.

As Lettie gently scolded the dog, Calvin zipped inside at full speed. Lettie was next, then Eliza led Mason inside, and Blitz fed off Calvin's energy, barking and doing circles around him.

"Welcome to chaos," she said, glancing around the living room, taking inventory of every little thing they'd left out of place —Calvin's toy drum and a pile of Matchbox cars, Grace's hoodie, Eliza's earbuds, and no less than three of Blitz's chew toys.

As Mason followed her over the threshold, she felt his hand at her waist, and it surprised her enough that she paused, looked up at him again.

"Thank you," he said in a low but meaningful tone.

She forced a smile to convey that it was nothing, but that was a lie. She was tied up in knots.

"Here's our kitchen," Calvin helpfully explained from the doorway between the living room and the cramped eat-in kitchen a few feet away.

"Thank you," Mason said in an entirely different tone from the private one he'd used with Eliza, this one making Calvin puff up with pride.

"I have to skedaddle," Lettie announced. "I've got to get my dinner in the Crock-Pot."

Scheming woman, Eliza thought without true rancor. "Thanks again for the coffee cake," she said. "You're the best. I'll bring you the leftovers later."

"Save me one piece. That's it. Grace will need some and Calvin likes it. Don't you, child?"

"Mm-hmm!" Calvin had climbed back up on his chair and kneeled, his elbows on the table, and once again, Eliza wondered why he chose today to ignore every lesson in politeness she'd ever given him. "Bye, Miss Lettie."

Lettie let herself out the back door with a goodbye to everyone.

"Butt down," Eliza said to Calvin as she cut a large piece of cake for Mason. "Do you take anything in your coffee?"

"Black," Mason said and thanked her when she set both in front of him.

"Can I please have some more, Mama?" Calvin said, eying Mason's plate.

Well, at least he'd found his manners at long last.

"You've had two pieces already, mister. That's enough sugar for one morning. How about a glass of milk?"

Calvin nodded his head less enthusiastically and watched Mason dig into his cake.

"Your mom told me you're three years old," Mason said as Eliza tidied up the kitchen, mainly to burn off her nervous energy—and avoid sitting down at the table with her son and his father. She stacked the dirty dishes in one side of the sink for later.

Calvin held up three fingers, struggling to straighten his

index finger as he usually did, and then he said, "I'm having a birthday."

"Really?" Mason said as he forked a bite of cake, but even as he did it, his attention was ninety-five percent on his son and five percent on the food. "When is your birthday?"

"October twenty-first," Calvin said proudly. "I'm turning four. Mama said I might get a party if she can get some money."

Eliza had her back to them, thank God, as her face burned with embarrassment. "You're getting a party," she said with conviction. Jimmy had texted her late last night. It'd been a good night for tips, and he wanted her to play with them for as many Fridays as she wanted.

"Yippeeee!" As Calvin shot his arms up in celebration, he knocked over his milk, and his joy disappeared instantly as his eyes widened, watching the liquid drip off the edge of the table between him and Mason. "Sorry, Mama."

By the time he said it, Eliza was at his side with the roll of paper towels, tossing a wad of them onto the puddle. She pulled him to her side and kissed the top of his head. "It's okay. Accidents happen. Go wash your hands and then you can play."

"Okay." Calvin was more subdued, likely embarrassed in front of Mason. He got down from his chair and zipped toward the only bathroom.

"Did he get you?" she asked Mason as she moved Calvin's chair out of the way and bent to mop up the milk on the floor, glancing at his pants leg to make sure there were no spots. No doubt those were dry-clean only.

"Missed me," Mason said, standing, taking another several paper towels from the roll and swiping at the table.

"Sit," Eliza said too abruptly. It felt far too intimate, too family-like to have him help her clean up after their son. She scrambled to soften her command. "I've got this. You finish your coffee cake."

After a slight pause, he sat again, setting the wad of wet paper towels at the edge of the table. "Lettie baked this?" He jabbed another big bite on his fork and ate it.

Eliza nodded as she collected the soaked paper towels and took them to the trash. "That woman is a blessing and a half."

"She seems to care a lot about both of you."

She came back to the table with a damp towel to get rid of any stickiness. "It takes an army to raise a child. Lettie's part of ours. She watches him whenever Grace and I can't. She's like a grandmother but one who isn't afraid to discipline him when he needs it. Which is usually," she said with a laugh.

"Definitely a North trait," he said lightly, but she didn't miss that it was the second time he'd made such a claim since he'd been here. While she was relieved there wasn't a battle to convince him, it also somehow felt threatening. Not as if he was threatening her outwardly, but she felt it all the same. She was used to being Calvin's world…well, she and Grace and Lettie.

"Mr. Mason, want to hear me play my drum?" Calvin hollered from the living room.

When Mason met her gaze, his eyes brimming with amusement, she cringed with exaggeration. "We don't have many quiet moments here."

"He must have inherited your musical talent." To Calvin, on the other side of the wall, he said, "I'd love to, kiddo. Give me just a minute to finish."

He scooped in the last bite of cake, then washed it down with some coffee. Next, he stood and carried his plate to the sink, not realizing how many points that won with Eliza, and headed out to the small living room.

"I'll be there in a couple," she said.

It would take her five minutes to wash the few breakfast dishes. She ran the water and started scrubbing as the sink filled, welcoming a small break from Mason's impossible-to-ignore presence.

Behind her, she heard her son's voice intermingled with Mason's but couldn't make out their words over the running water and the clinking dishes.

There was pounding on the drum, both Calvin's and Mason's, she suspected, and then Calvin turned on the toy microphone Eliza's mother had sent him for Christmas last year—proof that she didn't know her grandson well. If she did, she would understand he didn't need anything to amplify his voice or his drums or anything else.

As she finished up, Mason's voice came through the toy microphone. "Is this thing on?"

Calvin giggled and then said, "One, two, three, four," and at the signal, they began a duet, with Calvin banging on his drum, keeping a beat, and both of them singing "Twinkle, Twinkle, Little Star," Mason with the mic.

Eliza's eyes popped wide open as she dried off her hands, and then she stood for an extra second with her back to them, her hand covering her mouth.

Mason had a chill-inducing singing voice, and so help her God, it was sexy even as he belted out the annoying, worn-out children's song.

With trepidation, she went to the living room doorway. Just as she'd expected, the sight of them, father and son, with Mason sitting right next to Calvin on the seen-better-days carpet in his fine, high-dollar dress pants, punched her in the gut and nearly brought her to tears.

She didn't want to be moved by this man. Not as a father to her child and not as a hella good-looking guy. It would be far too easy to fall for him, and that would be messy, ugly, and end with her getting her heart crushed—and possibly Calvin's too.

By the time they reached the last note, Eliza had leaned against the doorjamb, unable to yank her gaze from them. Forget about Mason's allure as a man—he was twisting something even deeper inside of her with his connection with Calvin.

"You're incredible," Mason said as Calvin ended his final drum "roll," which consisted of him beating on the drum with both sticks as fast and as hard as he could, with zero finesse but full-on fervor.

"*You're* incredible!" Calvin hollered, chortling, then he stood and danced in a circle as Mason pulled himself up off the floor.

Mason sobered, and Eliza thought she read flashes of both astonishment and overwhelm in his expression. When he caught her watching him, he flashed his grin again, all confidence and happiness, and she wondered how much of it was blustering.

He checked his wristwatch, switched off the mic, and set the toy on the drum. "I have to go, but maybe we can jam again soon," he said to Calvin.

"'Kay!" Calvin said as he continued his gallop-dance around the living room.

"Do you usually work on Saturdays?" Eliza asked, trying to keep her tone conversational.

With a nod, he said, "Lots going on," and judging by the slightest tic of a muscle beneath his eye, she'd guess it wasn't good stuff going on.

Calvin did another lap, singing the same song again, this time at the top of his voice. A visit to the park to burn off his energy would be a necessity today, especially considering he was going to be subjected to a grocery store visit.

"Tell Mr. Mason goodbye, then you can pick one show to watch while I shower." Eliza went to the front door and opened it, waiting for Mason.

"Bye, Mr. Mason!" Calvin shouted, still dancing.

"Bye, Calvin. I'll see you soon." Mason lingered for an extra second, taking in his son, looking…gobsmacked, Eliza thought, and then he went out the door.

She followed him, pulling the door closed behind her after making sure it was unlocked. Mason stopped on the stoop and faced her.

"Wow," he said on an exhale. "Your son is exuberant."

"*Our* son," she corrected automatically.

There was that tic again, and he shoved a hand into the front pocket of his dress pants. "He seems like an amazing child."

"He's a good kid," she said humbly.

"Thanks to you."

"Or in spite of me." She shrugged. "Who ever knows?"

When you were a mom, you did what you needed to, moment to moment, for your child. You made the best decisions you could, questioned whether they were the right ones a dozen or a hundred times, and lay awake at night worrying, but you didn't do it for any kind of thanks or rewards. If you did, you were likely going to be shit out of luck.

"Being a single mom isn't for the faint of heart," he said, his intensity back and his gaze zeroing in on her face. She remembered that his father had died young, and although Mason had hit adulthood by then, some of his brothers must have still been teens or preteens.

Feeling twitchy under the scrutiny, she looked away, noticed the weeds that were taking over the flower bed.

Mason nudged her chin up with his finger to make eye contact. The stoop wasn't very big, and there wasn't a lot of space between them. The ice blue of his eyes sparked with emotion, like an exclamation point on everything he seemed unable to put into words.

Then he said, "I can tell you're a good, devoted mom, Eliza." He shifted his hand to the side of her face and held it with a gentle, enticing touch. "*Thank you* seems inadequate."

He gazed at her another powerful second, and then he leaned toward her. She watched as if he moved in slow motion, as if she was paralyzed, couldn't do anything but stare. She saw his eyes dip to her lips, took in his clean-shaven face, could tell it would still feel slightly rough against her skin. Then her eyes closed automatically as he pressed his lips to hers, his large hand still cradling the side of her face.

The kiss lingered for two heartbeats, three, more, and there was a familiarity to him that surprised her. His utter confidence, his talented mouth, his masculine scent... It all enveloped her, made it seem as if she'd kissed him yesterday instead of more than four years ago.

She savored it, breathed him in, barely registering the boy-and-dog racket on the other side of the door, and then Mason ended the kiss abruptly, as if he'd snapped to his senses, realized what he was doing.

"I need to get going," he said, jolting her the rest of the way back to reality. "I'm sorry."

For needing to leave or for kissing her?

Eliza decided she didn't want to know. Didn't want to spend

any time thinking about it or wondering about his intentions. Because she had hers, and they did not include getting entangled with him.

"That can't happen again," she said, averting her gaze as her heart thundered into a near panic at how easily she'd been drawn in again. How quickly she'd weakened.

She couldn't be weak, couldn't succumb to attraction. Not now, not with this particular man. As tempting as it would be to throw caution to the wind and pursue the chemistry that apparently was still alive and pulsing between them, that wouldn't be in anyone's best interest.

"We're in agreement," he said, and he glanced at that damn watch again. "Thank you for letting me meet Calvin." His voice had gone formal and chilly. "I'll be in touch soon."

In spite of his vagueness, she believed he would be back in touch, and she would be ready, with all her defenses in place. If she let them down again, she didn't know whose heart she'd be putting at greater risk—her son's...or hers.

CHAPTER EIGHT

To say Mason was off his game was an understatement.

Meeting his son yesterday had been a mind fuck, pure, plain, and simple.

It was almost embarrassing how fast he'd run out of Eliza's place after spending a half hour with Calvin. He'd been managing to maintain an even keel, had kept a lid on the maelstrom of emotions pretty well...*until he'd gone and locked lips with Eliza.*

He still didn't know what the hell that'd been about, other than him losing his careful control for an instant and grasping on to a moment of gratitude.

It turned out gratitude was easier to navigate than meeting one's three-year-old son for the first time.

His vanishing act to work had been legitimate, but whereas his job had always allowed him to escape mentally and emotionally—even when his dad had died, Mason had missed three days and then been back in the office the day after the funeral—yesterday it hadn't offered any kind of solace or distraction. Rather, his mind had veered repeatedly to the giant implications of fatherhood.

He'd forced his way through his to-do list, worked until the early-morning hours again, though he should've been finished by dinnertime. Then, though he'd been bone-tired, he'd lain awake for ages, mind racing, for the second straight night. Before the sun rose, he'd rolled out of bed to do it all over again.

Finally, midafternoon, keeping his eyes open had been a battle, and he'd succumbed, stretching out on the leather sofa in his home office. He'd slept so hard he hadn't remembered what day it was or that he was a father when he woke up.

Until he had.

Now he was late for Sunday dinner at his mom's, and he'd never hear the end of it.

Though he made record time between his place and the home where he'd grown up, he braked to the speed limit as soon as he turned down his mom's street and calmly pulled up to the curb, trying to summon an unbothered facade.

Everyone was already here, even perpetually late Drake, gauging by all the cars in the driveway and on the street. With a gritty curse, he ran a hand over his hair and realized he'd neglected to comb it after waking up on the couch. He pulled a Cardinals cap out of the glove compartment, stuck it on his head, and climbed out.

Mason let himself in the front door and was immediately hit by the raucous noise of his family, laughing, trying to talk over one another, debating, more laughing. He walked through the entry hall and turned the corner into the living area, which was open to the dining and kitchen, and there they all were. Drake, Mackenzie, Aunt Liz, and Cole sat around the large table, and his mom, Gabe, Lexie, and Sierra were in the kitchen.

"What the hell happened to you?" Drake asked as soon as he laid eyes on Mason.

"Nothing happened to me. I've been working around the clock."

"That would be status quo. You don't look status quo," Drake said.

"You're never late," Gabe said.

"You're wrinkled," Cole added. "And casual."

"It's family dinner," Mason said. "I didn't know we had a dress code."

"I've never seen you wear a T-shirt," Mackenzie, Drake's

fiancée, said, sounding truly perplexed, and Mason laughed at the absurdity of the situation.

"I wear T-shirts," Mason said, and there was an edge to his tone that he hadn't intended.

Reel it in, he coached himself as he let the confused looks and comments roll off and made his way into the kitchen. He gave his mom a side hug and kissed the top of her head. She wiped her hands on a towel before returning the hug, then she gazed up at him, her eyes narrowed, as if she saw too much.

Mason smiled at her, going for distraction tactics. "Why don't you let me finish that?" he asked, nodding toward the apples she was slicing into a fruit salad.

She studied him for a moment longer, then handed him the knife, handle out. "I need to check the mac and cheese."

He didn't kid himself that he'd avoided her third degree, merely put it off. When he accepted the knife, she stepped across the roomy kitchen to the oven.

"What's the latest on the Colorado store?" Gabe asked.

"Roberson wants to confirm with a couple people tomorrow, but it looks like we'll be able to push the opening up by a month to November first."

"A whole month of extra sales, plus a Black Friday," Drake said. "That'll make a big difference in numbers."

"That's the hope." Mason finished slicing the last apple into the salad, then picked up a banana. "We're also in the early stages of trying to move up the opening of the new Nashville store."

"There's no way," Gabe said, and there was more than a little heat in his voice.

"We're exploring." Mason was momentarily taken aback by the negativity coming from Gabe, who was normally an ally in most things North Brothers Sports, and then he saw the look Gabe exchanged with his wife, Lexie, who was slicing bakery-fresh buns, and it hit him. "Lexie's a key consideration."

The westside store was their original location, and after nearly fifty years in the same building, they'd outgrown it and were constructing a brand-new location to take its place. They were slated to open December first, and Mason had thought from the beginning it was unfortunate that they'd miss the start of the holiday shopping season. Until their recent financial panic, he'd let Connor, VP of Operations, convince him to let it be. Now he was determined to explore whether they could move it up even a couple of weeks. If they could roll out their grand reopening sale in conjunction with Black Friday, they could likely generate extra vendor support and offer some incredible deals to generate record-setting sales.

While they might be able to double up on construction crews to speed things up, Lexie's part of the project would be a bigger conundrum. She'd already begun work on the first of eight murals on the interior walls. There was only one Lexie, so moving up her deadlines would mean she would have to work longer hours.

"She's already working close to fifty hours a week," Gabe said, and Lexie put a hand on his arm as she pegged him with a quelling look.

"It was the first week, and I got carried away with the sketching and lost track of time, Gabe. It had nothing to do with Mason or anyone's demands."

They weren't paying her by the hour but a flat fee with multiple benchmarks where she would get another installment.

"That's one of the aspects we're keeping an eye on," Mason said. "We don't want you overworking yourself. There are other possibilities if we move up the date. The most important mural is the main hidden pictures one. The departmental ones don't all have to be done before we open."

"The store will be more of a showpiece if they're finished," Gabe said. "We had a plan, and I don't think we need to be in panic mode over anything."

"Speak for yourself," Mason muttered as he threw away a pile of banana peels.

As much as his brothers were invested in the company and its success, none of them understood what it was like to be in the driver's seat. They hadn't been in on his conversation with his father when Mason was seventeen years old. They didn't know how all-encompassing the pressure to succeed was. If anything ever happened to the company, Mason would be gutted and unable to face himself in the mirror.

"The brats and burgers should be about ready to come off the grill, shouldn't they?" Drake asked. He, more than any of the Norths, was ruled by his stomach. He was late joining the NBS corporate team—just a few months ago as the director of the new Home Fitness Division—and though he was proving a valuable addition to the company, it wasn't a big surprise that he was more concerned about his dinner than business, at least on the weekend.

"Go check them," Gabe said, sliding a clean plate toward Drake across the counter that separated the dining area from the kitchen. Drake took it and disappeared out to the grill in the backyard. "All I'm saying is you need to step back and breathe before switching everything up," Gabe continued to Mason. "Untwist your boxers and keep your emotions out of the decision."

Mason's brows shot up his forehead as he set the knife down and turned toward his brother. "*You're* accusing *me* of being run by my emotions? I'm the most analytical, the least subject to emotional reactions of any of us, and you know it."

That was likely why Calvin and Eliza had him so fucked up, come to think of it.

"Boys," their mom said, "it's Sunday. Mason, I can tell by looking at you, you need a break. You can argue this out in the office tomorrow. Let's set it aside and have a pleasant dinner." Her words were underlined by her *or else* tone that had always gotten results from her five sons, and this time was no exception.

———

AN HOUR AND A HALF LATER, dinner had been devoured, the kitchen cleaned, and the nine of them sat around the table with beverages and cookies-and-cream pie that their aunt Liz had made. Mason's whiskey had mellowed him out a bit, as had a full stomach, and for the most part, he sat and tried to listen, tried to get the hell out of his head.

The latest topic was weddings, something Mason didn't have much to say about anyway. With one of his brothers just hitched and two more engaged, everything lately was about weddings.

"Twenty-four more days," Mackenzie, who sat next to Mason, said, beaming. Her copper-tinged brunette hair was longer than he'd seen it before, and she'd explained she was growing it out so she could put it up for the wedding. It didn't make a lot of sense to Mason, but then weddings and women's hair weren't the most logical things. "In less than a month, we'll be on a beach in Malta, saying I do."

"Getting on a plane even sooner than that," Drake added, grinning as widely as his fiancée. He was holding Mackenzie's hand under the table and raised it to press his lips to her fingers. Love was making most of the family lose their minds.

Kind of like he had yesterday with Eliza, Mason thought. Not because of love—hell, he barely knew her—but those moments when he'd kissed her definitely fell into lost-his-mind territory.

Drake and Mackenzie had decided on a destination wedding and had invited the whole family plus a couple of close friends to join them on the island in the Mediterranean. Though Mason wouldn't miss such an important family event, he couldn't help thinking about the challenge of being away from work at such a critical time for the company. However, Malta was better and more convenient than Jiva, in the South Pacific, which had been their second choice. The travel time alone would've doubled.

"And how much longer for you two?" Aunt Liz, who was sitting to Mason's right, asked Sierra and Cole, at the other end of the long table.

"Four months, give or take," Sierra answered. "And we still have so much to do. I'm trying not to freak out. We'll get to it as soon as we get back from Malta."

"We will," Lexie said. She and Mackenzie were both brides-maids for Sierra.

"You've got the big decisions made," Mackenzie said. "Every-thing's reserved, including the honeymoon. Most important part, in my opinion." That elicited a laugh around the table, because high-end honeymoons were Mackenzie's business, and she'd booked their trip to New Zealand herself, as well as the private yacht cruise that would serve as their three-day-long wedding reception for the entire wedding party. "You're going to be just fine."

"And then the real race is on," their mom said. "The grand-baby race."

Sierra let out a sputter as she was taking a drink of her wine. "Do you think we could find your mom a nice man to keep her occupied?" she asked Cole with a laugh. "I'm so not ready for babies yet."

"I'm even less ready for a 'nice man' than you are for babies," Faye said. "We can give you a few months to get you married, I suppose."

"Mom," Cole said sternly, ready to jump in and protect his future wife.

Faye held up a hand. "I'm only kidding. You have to be ready. And I've got two other immediate chances for grandbabies."

Gabe narrowed a look at Mason from across the table, clearly thinking exactly what he was—that their mom was already a grandmother but just didn't know it yet.

Mason had been going back and forth in his mind about when to share the news with the family. On the one hand, it was big, and he knew his mom would be over the moon, so he wanted her to know. On the other, he was still grappling with the truth himself, trying to get his head around it.

"What was that look for?" Drake said too astutely. His gaze skittered over Mason and then went from Gabe to Lexie and back to Gabe. "You two have something to tell us?"

Lexie shot a confused look up to Gabe, but Gabe put his arm around her, drew her close, and said, "*We* do not."

Maybe Mason imagined the emphasis on *we*, but then Gabe's gaze connected with his again, and soon the rest of the table was looking between him and Gabe, as if trying to interpret their silent exchange.

Mason could've diverted the attention, but maybe telling his family about Calvin would help it sink in for him.

He expelled a breath and leaned his elbows on the table. "I have some news."

Searching for the right words, he glanced around the table at each person, meeting with confusion and curiosity and wide, expectant eyes.

"Just say it, Mason, whatever it is," Aunt Liz said, placing her hand on his forearm supportively.

He summoned his courage and sat up straight, as if he was talking to his board of directors, and went straight to the point. "Last week, I found out I have a child. A three-year-old son."

His mom's reaction was the first and the loudest—a sharp gasp as her hands flew to her mouth.

"What the hell?" Drake said.

"Oh, my God, Mason," Mackenzie said. "That's huge."

"Holy shit," was Cole's addition from across the table.

"All of the above," Mason said. "It's still sinking in."

His mom still had her elbows propped on the table and her hands covering her mouth as she stared at him with shocked eyes. He couldn't tell what she was feeling beyond that, but he was hit with the thought that maybe she was disappointed. Not with the grandchild in general, but that he hadn't known for the first three, almost four years of his child's life, which meant that not only had *he* missed out but she had as well. He wasn't accustomed to being the screwup of the family.

"We're going to need more info than that," Drake said.

"All the info, mister," Liz added. Though her words were a demand, her brown eyes were warm, kind.

"I met him yesterday. His name is Calvin." There was so much more, so many emotions that came over Mason yet again just thinking about the moment he'd laid eyes on the boy, and he pinched his thumb and forefinger over his eyes, as if that could help him hold it all in.

"Calvin," Sierra said. "That's a good name. Cute for a little boy but strong."

"Adorable name," Lexie agreed.

"He's…" *Amazing, exhilarating, spirited, loud, incredible…* "He's got a lot of North in him." Remembering the photo on his phone —the one of Calvin on the playground, which Mason had asked Eliza to forward to him—he stood abruptly. "I've got a picture."

Demands to see it broke out around the table, but Mason went to the head, where their mother sat, her eyes damp. He unlocked his phone, then swiped to the photo Eliza had sent, the one that looked so much like Drake as a child, and held it out to his mom.

"Oh, my heavens," she said, her voice filled with wonder and awe. One hand flew to her mouth again as she studied the photo. She craned a look up at Mason, stunned quiet for a second, then said, "He's looks just like Drake at that age."

Drake, next to her, leaned in, and his eyes popped wide open, then narrowed. "Where'd you get that?"

"From his mother," Mason said.

"Which brings up all kinds of questions," Cole said. "Who is she? Why did she keep him from you? Can you trust her that he's yours—"

"He's Mason's," Drake said with certainty, still leaning in and gawking at the photo. "Unless he's mine. Damn. Who's the mom?"

Mackenzie swatted him.

"Her name's Eliza and she has better taste than that," Mason said, hating the thought of his brother, any of his brothers, with Eliza, past, present, or future. It didn't mean he wanted her for himself; it was his protective instincts surfacing. He'd do anything to protect Calvin, and that meant also protecting Calvin's mother.

His own mom reached out for Mason's hand and held on to it as she continued to stare at Calvin's photo, and Mason swallowed hard to fight down a surge of emotions—still a big, ugly mix of them, from love and wonder to anger and regret that he'd missed so much.

She handed off the phone to Drake, stood, and threw her arms around Mason. He held on to her, soaked in her unconditional love, which he understood was for both him and her grandson even though she hadn't yet met him. When she finally let go, it was to gaze up at him, and her eyes were more than damp. She smiled, patted his cheek, and shook her head, obviously speechless, before lowering herself to the chair and glancing toward the photo again.

"Quit hogging it," Cole said to Drake a few seconds later. "Pass it on so we can all see him."

Mackenzie gasped as she got a better look. "I've seen pictures of you as a kid. This could be you," she said to Drake.

While they passed the phone around, Mason went around the counter and busied himself pouring more whiskey, then remained there, watching his family's reactions to Calvin.

"So what's up with the mother? Eliza?" Drake asked, his tone hinting of censure.

As succinctly and tactfully as possible, Mason explained his minimal history with Eliza and the reasons she hadn't been able to tell him about Calvin. His family shot questions at him, and as he answered, their tones became calmer, more accepting, more sympathetic to a situation that was difficult to accept.

By the time everyone's questions had been exhausted and his brothers and their significant others started leaving, Mason was wrung out and relieved to have the scrutiny over with. And then, as he straightened from a hug from his aunt, eager to escape to the peace of his condo, he caught the look his mom gave him.

"You'll stay for a while so we can talk?" She said it as a question, but he knew it was more of a command.

Mason eyed the cabinet where he'd put the whiskey bottle away, and his mom said, "We'll have some water."

He acquiesced, only because if he had much more liquor, he'd need to spend the night here, in his childhood bedroom, and with the hours he'd been keeping lately, that didn't appeal.

He fully intended to go home and bury himself in work some more. Taking action had always been preferable to sitting around and ruminating.

When it came to his son, though, knowing the best actions to take was even more of a dilemma than how to raise NBS sales by six to eight percent in a month.

CHAPTER NINE

While his mom saw the rest of the family out, Mason went out the back door to the patio, wishing for an escape. Not from his mom, necessarily, but from the shit fest going on inside of him.

The sun had set, but the temperature was warm. The wind had picked up, and the humid air told him a hell of a late-summer thunderstorm was brewing. Suited him just fine.

As he stood at the edge of the patio and watched as the wind bent the branches of the giant elm tree that was older than him, the back door opened behind him, and he heard his mom come out, then felt her at his side.

"It must've been quite a dramatic few days for you," she said, leaning her head on his upper arm as she put an arm around him and squeezed.

He closed his eyes and sought out the comfort his mom had always delivered with her hugs and the right words, but so far, nothing was comforting.

"Want to sit down?" she asked.

Sitting down was the last thing he wanted to do, but if he sat, she would too, and he'd feel better if she rested after cooking for all of them.

"Let's sit," he agreed, and they went to the pair of patio chairs near the house. They were Adirondack chairs, and the damn things made it impossible to do anything but sink all the way back.

Once she'd settled into the blue chair his dad had given her for her very first Mother's Day, she asked, "What's going through that head of yours?"

He popped out of his chair as if it were on fire. No matter how hard he'd tried to fight off the negative shit and focus on the positive—a little boy named Calvin who was truly amazing—his emotions were not all sunshine and roses.

"I'm pissed," he said in a low voice, not proud of himself at all but unable to deny the truth. Again, he paced to the edge of the patio, his back to his mom. "I can't stop thinking about everything I missed—almost four years of his life. His birth. First smile, first word, first steps. Birthdays, Christmases…" He stopped and breathed in, got control of himself. "That boy has gone through every day of his life without a dad. Even at thirty-nine years old, it sucks not having a dad."

His mom was quiet for a few seconds. "Regret is a tough pill to swallow," she finally said. "Do you believe Eliza's explanation? That she tried to find you but couldn't?"

"There's no way she could've found me. She didn't have the resources." He squeezed his eyes shut and wondered for the thousandth time how things would've been different if only they'd exchanged last names or phone numbers or any goddamn piece of identifying info.

What the hell had he been thinking to be so circumspect?

"I'd just been approved as CEO," he said. "Discretion was on my mind."

"You've always taken your responsibilities with the company very seriously. That's an honorable trait, Mason."

"I'm pissed at myself," he blurted out as the truth hit him. "Myself, the circumstances… It'd be a hell of a lot easier if I could blame her, make her the bad guy."

"But she's not." His mom didn't make it a question. "I know you, Mason. I don't know everything you do or who you do it with, and believe me, I don't want to, but a mother knows her children, and you've never been attracted to the bad-girl type."

He wasn't going to discuss details with his mom, but she was right. Mason rarely took time out for women, but when he did, it was usually a one-night thing, mutually, and never with someone he couldn't have an intelligent, civilized conversation with. Not that he needed conversation with his sex, but he had standards. High standards. If he was going to the hassle of hooking up, it would be with the right type of woman, and Eliza had been that in every way.

"From what I can tell, she's been a devoted, loving mom. He's a well-adjusted kid." A smile pulled at his lips as he thought back to yesterday, to every second he'd spent with Calvin. The memories put him more at ease, and he turned back to his mom, joined her in the Adirondacks again, told her all about Calvin's enthusiasm for coffee cake and music and befriending Mason.

"He might have a future as a drummer," he said. "And not only does he look like Drake but he's got that charm factor to him. I don't know how a person couldn't like him. Maybe someone who doesn't like noise, I guess."

"He sounds special."

"Damn straight he is."

"Focus on that, Mason. I know how much it hurts to think about the past and all the what-ifs, but you need to let that go. There's no way to change it. Think instead about moving forward. What do you want from the future?"

Without hesitating, he said, "I want to be in my son's life. To be a real father to him. Not just the fun guy who visits on Saturdays."

His mom reached out and took his hand. "I'd expect nothing less from you."

"I can't wait for you to meet him, Mom. You'll need a nap afterward. He's so full of energy—"

"He comes by that naturally," she said, her voice dripping with affection and memories. "There were days I thought my little boys would kill me with all the nonstop energy."

"The twins were a handful." Mason had been eleven when they were born and remembered how much work they were.

"I had you older boys to help, and your dad pulled his weight with them whenever he wasn't working. Bless that man. He was a good father from day one."

"The best," Mason agreed.

There was a voice that kept popping up in his mind, one that insisted he didn't know the first thing about being a dad. It was raw fear, he knew, and it reared its head especially at night, as he lay there trying to sleep. In the light of day, he was able to shut it down by reminding himself he'd had a hell of a role model for the first twenty-four years of his life.

Harry North had had his faults, but Mason barely remembered them. The man had not only built up a business that had—and would continue to, if Mason didn't fuck it up—sustained the family financially but he'd been *present*. More than present. He'd been such a part of their lives, especially through baseball, that his death had left a gaping hole, even for Mason, who'd no longer lived at home.

"Eliza must be a strong, capable woman. Single motherhood is quite an undertaking, and it sounds like she's doing a good job."

"He's undeniably a happy kid."

"That speaks volumes about how secure and loved he feels."

"I don't know how she manages it, to be honest. She's trying to make it in the music industry, which can't be an easy road. I don't think she makes much money, and yet she's provided a comfortable home for Calvin, and he seems to have everything he needs. I think her roommate and neighbor lady help out by watching him when she works."

"A lot of motherhood is figuring out what needs to be done and then finding a way to do it," his mom said.

"I suspect she excels at that."

He thought about the way Eliza had interacted with Calvin, coaching him on manners, not jumping on his case when he'd spilled milk, cutting off his sugar intake, and doing it all good-naturedly. Though their home itself was somewhat run-down and Mason itched to take care of that, it was inarguably filled with love.

"You care about her," his mom said as she studied him from the side.

"I don't know her well enough to care about her." The implications of that were damn awkward to admit to his mother, but it was the truth.

She continued to eye him in the darkness. He could feel it, even though he kept his gaze fixed straight ahead, to the swaying tree branches.

"It sounds like you have the opportunity to get to know her."

"To be in Calvin's life, yes, I imagine I'll become better acquainted with her."

"There must still be some attraction there?"

Hell yes, there was still some attraction. But he could handle that. He *would* handle it. "I'm focused on becoming a father. The last thing I need is to try to navigate something with his mother at the same time. Especially right now. It's going to be a challenge to carve out as much time for Calvin as I'd like."

"Because of work," she stated rather than asked.

"You know me well." He allowed a half grin to surface.

It quickly fell from his face when she said, "Mason Joseph North, how can you be so dense? You have a child with this woman, a child whose life you want to be heavily involved in, *and* you're attracted to her. But instead of letting anything develop, you want to fight it off so you can work more? You could put that energy and effort into building a family that's already half-built. How many chances at that do you think you're going to get in this lifetime?"

"It's the worst possible timing, Mom. The stakes are too high. It wouldn't make sense to get involved with someone right now." He'd never succumbed to a relationship even in smooth times. Why would he think he could nurture one now?

His mom let out a low laugh. "Love doesn't usually make sense."

Mason scoffed. "There's no love involved. Not for a woman I barely know."

Silence fell between them for several seconds as she apparently changed gears. "I admire your drive at work, Mason. You know I always have. And I understand, more than a lot of people, how important this expansion is to you."

She paused, and there was a big *but* coming. He could feel it. He sat quietly and waited, lining up his arguments even before he knew what he was arguing.

"What would happen if you don't hit the benchmarks and the financing for next year doesn't come through?" she asked.

He propelled himself out of the chair again, his jaw clenched with tension, and paced to the edge of the patio. "Is that rhetorical?"

Faye North was thoroughly, intimately acquainted with the inner workings of NBS, as she'd been the VP of Merchandising and a member of the board for years and years. Even when she'd retired, she'd stayed involved as a consultant for some time.

"It's not rhetorical," she said. "I want you to tell me the worst thing that could happen if expansion plans get put on hold."

He pivoted to face her. "The worst thing? We lose our tenuous foothold in the market, market share declines over the next couple of years, and we can no longer compete with other national chains and online retailers. North Brothers Sports dies a slow and painful death, and we're out of business."

She eyed him across the darkness, the light from inside the house illuminating her enough that he could see her raised brows. "That's a worst-case scenario, to be sure, but the likelihood of that happening? Not high."

"You don't know that," he snapped, turning his back to her again.

"I do. Because even if you don't get funding to build another dozen stores and a new HQ next year, I know my oldest son, and he doesn't just quit."

"I wouldn't quit," he said, "but I can't let this opportunity slip away." His voice went lower as so many emotions swept in and thickened in his throat. "I can't let Dad down."

The sound of the wind whipping through the trees had become loud enough that he didn't hear his mom stand up and approach. She appeared beside him, startling him as she wove her arm through his. "You could never let him down, Mason. He'd be so proud of you."

He swallowed hard and squeezed his eyes shut. The wind covered the sound of him expelling a heavy breath, and then he told her a story he'd never told anyone else. "At the end of my first day as a full-time employee in the corporate office, right after I finished my MBA, Dad pulled me into his office." He paused, hesitant to let the memory in, knowing it would bring a tidal wave of bittersweetness with it. "Everyone else had gone home, even Uncle Ham, and it was just him and me. He opened his bottom drawer and took out his bottle of whiskey and poured us both a finger."

"I can see it in my mind's eye," his mom said, her voice full of love. "He saved his whiskey for celebratory moments."

"As we sipped it, he told me how proud he was of me and how he'd built NBS for his family and that he had every bit of confidence that one day it would be mine to run. He said he trusted me completely and suspected I would take it in directions and to heights he couldn't even imagine."

When he paused, he realized he was gazing up at the skies, as if his dad was up there somewhere, looking down expectantly. "I grew up with dreams of being the CEO, but that day, that conversation turned everything from a dream into an imperative."

"You're a strong leader, Mason. Look at everything you've accomplished in less than five years. When you took over, North Brothers was a Tennessee company. You expanded it to be a regional and now a national company. You've taken it from five stores to more than twenty in less than two years. You've moved it into the online retail world successfully and are building it into an industry trend setter with the Home Fitness Division." She tightened her arm through his and faced him, peering up at him now. "I'm indescribably proud of you, my dear son, and your father would be as well. You've already taken the business in directions and to heights neither he nor I could imagine back then."

"So you're saying I should just give up? Let the financing challenge go?"

"Of course I'm not saying that. I'm saying you're meeting your father's expectations every single day, year after year, and he would respect and admire you to pieces, Mason, but he would never, ever want you to sacrifice love and a family life for business."

"I don't have love," he reminded her.

"But maybe you could."

"It takes time and energy to pursue that. Just like becoming a dad to Calvin will take time and energy. I'm about maxed out as it is, Mom."

"But you're going to become a dad," she said with confidence. "I'm not saying you should actively court Eliza, but if you'd just open yourself to the possibility instead of being determined to fight any feelings off, who knows what would happen."

He knew very well what would happen if he didn't fight it. He'd end up sleeping with Eliza again. What he didn't know was how that would work with Calvin in the mix, the logistics or the rules she would set, but he knew just as sure as his suits would be ready at the dry cleaner at five p.m. tomorrow that their chemistry would end them up in a deeper mess.

"Mason?" she said when he didn't answer for several seconds.

"Yeah, Mom."

She sighed, as if he was her most exasperating son, a role he wasn't at all accustomed to being. "Will you promise me you'll try to open your mind to the possibility?"

"What possibility?" he asked with an ornery grin, knowing full well what she was talking about.

"That your attraction to your son's mother could be a good thing, something that would enhance your life, make it fuller." She shook her head. "Forget that. Just...let things happen with her instead of trying to control every little thing. Can you do that?"

Just the thought of it, of giving over his control to something as potentially powerful as Eliza's allure, scared the hell out of him, but he had to give his dear mother something.

"I promise I'll try."

CHAPTER TEN

The ancient, towering tree in Eliza's backyard had crashed through the roof of the duplex at 6:07 a.m.

Nearly two hours later, Eliza was cycling repeatedly through calmly taking charge, panicking on the inside, and gawking yet again in disbelief at their ruined home. Panicking on the outside was a constant threat, but she did her best to keep her cool in order to not scare Calvin any more than he already was.

She, Calvin, and Blitz were sitting in her car, which had thankfully been spared, parked on the street a couple of houses down, a safe distance from the commotion and first responders, waiting. When the crash had finally ended and she'd figured out it wasn't, in fact, an earthquake, she'd called 911. The dispatcher had advised her to get them out of the house ASAP, and she had, with the exception of taking forty-five seconds to tear her pj's off and yank on leggings and a sweatshirt. It had been instinct, before she'd truly understood the danger they could be in, but she was glad she wasn't stuck wearing boxers and a tank.

Firefighters had been there since shortly after the ferocious wind had uprooted the tree, sending it smack into the center back side of the duplex. Thank God Calvin and the dog had already been huddled beside Eliza in her bed, scared of the storms that had raged all night long. Double thank God that Grace had been at Reed's all night and Lettie had already been up and about, puttering in her kitchen. If either of the two of them had been in their beds…

Eliza squeezed her eyes shut and slammed her thoughts off abruptly, but the cold fear of the what-ifs sliced into her anyway.

Thank God, she silently repeated another dozen times.

Lettie was okay, physically anyway. It was hard to be emotionally okay when your house had a tree running through it and a gaping hole the size of a semitruck. Lettie's son, who lived on the other side of town in a one-bedroom apartment, had driven off with his mom in tow just ten minutes ago. Even though they'd be crowded, Lettie could stay with him for as long as she needed to.

Grace still had no idea there'd been a catastrophe, as she hadn't answered her phone the two dozen times Eliza had called and texted. It wasn't unusual for her to sleep late on days when Eliza didn't need her to take Calvin to preschool, though how anyone could sleep through that storm was beyond Eliza. She'd lived through plenty of storms in her life, but she'd never, ever seen anything like last night's.

She'd waffled between taking Calvin to school to distract him and keeping him by her side to reassure him and ultimately decided to keep him with her. She still wasn't sure if she'd chosen the better option.

The neighborhood was like a war zone, with trees and power lines down everywhere, branches and debris strewn across yards and the street, and chainsaws buzzing. Though nearly everyone on the block had damage to some extent, Eliza and Lettie—and Alan Simmons, their landlord—were the jackpot winners of the biggest and worst of it. Several people had stopped by to make sure they were okay and to get a better look. It definitely wasn't her favorite way to get to know her neighbors.

Mr. Simmons had been by earlier but had soon rushed off to another property he owned, which had lost part of the roof. As he'd explained, that seemed more fixable than Eliza's home. After multiple conversations with firefighter Brock, she couldn't disagree. So far, he hadn't allowed her to go in, even to get a toy or a book or a Pop-Tart for Calvin.

In a pinch, she'd found two Fruit Roll-Ups in her purse for him and downloaded a couple of games to her phone, which her son was currently bent over in the passenger seat, while Blitz was sprawled out in the backseat, sleeping off all the excitement of the morning. Calvin was subdued now, but he'd been scared to death, in tears, shaken until she'd distracted him with the new apps.

"Mama," Calvin said, holding her phone up as it rang, interrupting his ABCs game.

She took it from him, hoping Grace was finally responding, but that wasn't the name that showed at the top of the screen.

Why was Mason calling at 8:05 on a Monday morning?

After hitting accept, she said, "Hello?"

"Good morning, Eliza," he said in that low, alluring voice, and in spite of the all-out stress of the morning, it affected her, soothed a tiny bit of her frayed nerves. "How are you doing?"

She held back a half-hysterical laugh. "Oh, you know, not too bad considering there's a tree in my kitchen." And Grace's room and the bathroom and a corner of Calvin's room, which she could not even *begin* to let herself think about.

"What? Did you have some storm damage?"

"Some," she said dryly, because if she didn't try to keep her sense of humor, she'd likely start bawling, "or a lot. The oak tree in the backyard crashed through the roof at six this morning—"

"Is everyone okay?"

"Yes," she said simply, suspecting that if she went into detail, she would lose it. "The people are fine, if shaken. The house is… The firefighters won't let us go in. They have to make sure it won't collapse further."

"Shit. Where are you?"

"Calvin and Blitz and I are in my car. We're okay," she repeated, but he likely didn't hear her because he talked over her.

"I'm coming over. I'll be there in twenty minutes."

"Don't you have work?"

She herself did, fortunately not until one this afternoon, no morning session scheduled, and she only had a few hours to figure out...well, everything before she had to leave for the studio.

She could *not* miss her session today, not only because she needed the money but because one of the reasons she got so many calls to work was because she was always reliable, always showed up when she was supposed to.

When Mason didn't reply, she pulled the phone away from her ear to see that the call had ended.

Okay, then. She guessed Mason was on his way, but there wasn't a thing he could do to fix her house.

———

MASON RUSHED OUT of the office as if it were on fire, telling Ruby only that he had a personal emergency. As he hauled ass to his car, he checked his calendar on his phone to figure out what would need to be rescheduled for the morning and what he could tackle on the drive to Eliza's. He could make a couple of phone calls before he got there.

First on his list was Roberson, the contractor in Colorado, to ensure he would seal the deal on moving up the store opening. Though Roberson was an hour earlier and he hadn't yet finalized the details, he insisted it would be a done deal later today. They agreed to touch base late afternoon, and Mason texted Cole an update, then allowed himself to put that worry aside for the time being. Cole would handle any crises that arose while Mason was out of the office.

When Mason turned down Eliza's street, his jaw gaped and his swear words grew progressively cruder and louder as he steered between branches and kept his speed at a crawl to ensure he didn't drive over any power lines.

Whatever the hell blew through here appeared to be ten times worse than what he'd seen at his condo.

He spotted the fire truck in front of her duplex from down the block and realized, as he got closer, he'd have to park a few houses away.

As soon as he stopped the car, he killed the ignition and

jumped out and took off down the street on foot. So far, he hadn't laid eyes on Eliza's Toyota, and his alarm ratcheted up. As he neared her house, he tried to assess the situation. From the front, he could see branches jutting out from the top of the one-story house—thick, solid branches—but he couldn't get a real sense of the damage.

When he walked past the fire truck, finally he spotted Eliza's car down the way. She sat in the driver's seat, and in the passenger's seat was a blonde woman with Calvin on her lap. Grace, he guessed. The two women were wrapped up in conversation.

Before heading their way, he walked up her narrow driveway to get a better view of what had happened. There were a handful of firefighters calling out to each other in the backyard, still out of his view, and then he made it far enough to see the backyard.

Jesus. His adrenaline spiked and his heart raced. It was no small miracle that no one was hurt—or dead.

The tree was a giant, with a diameter that had to be close to three feet. It had crushed not only the roof but the back wall of the house, shattering at least one window. If anyone had been in the direct line of it, they would not have survived.

Mason had trouble getting a full intake of air as it hit him how close he'd been to losing the son he'd only just met.

"We need you to stay back, sir," a firefighter said as he came around the root ball that was taller than him by several feet.

With a nod, Mason turned and headed back down the driveway, toward his son and Eliza, his heart still hammering.

Eliza noticed him as he approached, and she got out of the car and came toward him, meeting him a couple of car lengths from her Toyota. Calvin remained in the car with the blonde.

Still shaken, Mason took in every inch of her face, noting the stress and fatigue in her eyes. "You're both okay?"

She tried to smile but it looked closer to a grimace, and she nodded. "Physically." When she opened her mouth to say more, she stopped herself, closed her eyes, averted her face, bit her lip, as if she couldn't get more out without breaking down.

Mason pulled her into his chest and wrapped his arms

around her, aching to ease her mind. He heard her suck in a breath, and then she grasped him tightly and buried her face.

Without letting go of her, he asked, "How's Calvin?"

The breath she expelled into his dress shirt was shaky. "He's calmer now but still scared. Grace just got here a few minutes ago and that's helping. She's telling him how brave he is. I'm sure he's hungry. All he's eaten are the old fruit snacks I found at the bottom of my purse. They won't let us in to get anything."

"We need to get you out of here. It won't be safe for some time." Days, he thought, best-case scenario.

She straightened and took a step back, out of his embrace, as if she realized it was odd for him to hold her. To him, it felt both natural and strange at once.

"We don't... I don't..." She eyed her house and pressed her lips together.

He snapped into take-charge mode. "You can stay with me, for as long as you need. We'll buy you whatever you and Calvin need."

She shook her head. "It's not just Calvin and me. We have Blitz and Grace too. We'll figure out something—"

"The dog and Grace can come too. I've got plenty of room." He wasn't sure exactly how they'd work it, but they'd figure that out later. "The sooner we get Calvin away from the site, the sooner he can start feeling more secure. And you too."

As if on cue, the car door sprang open and Calvin raced toward them.

"Mr. Mason, a tree fell on our house!" Calvin's eyes were wide with incredulity.

Mason wanted nothing more than to pull his son into his arms and make everything okay, but he wasn't sure how either the boy or his mom would react. He crouched down to Calvin's level, rubbed the boy's upper arm, and said, "I'm so glad you're okay, buddy. That must've been scary, huh?"

"I was a brave boy," he said, obviously parroting one of the adults. "Our stuff isn't important."

"Stuff is replaceable. People are what's important. Your mom said you might be hungry."

With an earnest nod, he said, "I'm starvated."

"Starved," Eliza corrected distractedly. "I should've taken him somewhere to get food, but I kept thinking we'd get word from the responders."

"You mean the firefighters?" Calvin said, craning his neck to look up at her.

With a nod, Eliza leaned down and hefted him up into her arms, pulling his cheek in for a kiss. "That's right." She closed her eyes as she held him close, and Mason suspected she was thinking how lucky they were that they were okay.

He couldn't stand to let that line of thoughts go too far. He put his hand on Calvin's back. "How would you like to stay at my place?"

"You mean your house?" Calvin asked.

"Well, I live in a condo. It's on the top floor and you can see the skyscrapers out the windows."

"Can we, Mama?" He squirmed, and Eliza let him slide down the side of her body just as the car door shut and the blonde woman walked toward them. Calvin darted toward her without waiting for an answer. "Grace, we're going to stay at Mr. Mason's condo."

"Oh?" The woman joined them, holding Calvin's hand as her blue eyes went to Eliza before landing on Mason, and he realized she was the bartender the night he and Eliza had met at the hotel bar. "Hello," she said to him. Her voice was slightly husky, like a seductress, and yet it did nothing for Mason other than to catch his attention because of its uniqueness.

"Grace." He nodded politely at her, then extended the invitation. "You're welcome to stay at my place too."

"You probably want to stay with Reed," Eliza said.

"Reed and I are no longer speaking," Grace said with a distracted scowl. "Which is why it took me so long to see your messages. But I don't want to intrude—"

"You're not intruding," Eliza said before Mason could. A look passed between the women, and he suspected Eliza was silently pleading with Grace. He wasn't sure if she wanted her roommate to join them or leave them alone, and for the first time since blurting his offer out, he realized it might be uncomfortable if it was just the three of them and Grace went somewhere else. Too cozy and family-like.

"I have two extra bedrooms with queens in both," Mason said. "Calvin can sleep in Eliza's room or we can set him up in my study."

Grace's expression eased a little. She glanced back at Eliza for a moment and then nodded. "We don't exactly have a lot of options."

Eliza nodded once, not looking at all at ease. She eyed their home for one more lingering moment, then seemed to snap into everything'll-be-okay mom mode and addressed Calvin. "What should we say to Mr. Mason for the generous offer?"

Calvin looked up to her for a moment, then seemed to take the cue. "Thank you, Mr. Mason! Can we have breakfast too?"

"We should stop and buy groceries on the way," Eliza said.

"I've got a stocked pantry, and we can have whatever else you'd like delivered this afternoon."

Eliza looked doubtful, so Mason asked Calvin, "Do you like waffles?"

"I *love* waffles."

"I just happen to have some in my freezer. Let's go get some waffles." Mason's phone was on vibrate, and he'd felt it a half-dozen times since he'd been here. He continued to ignore it as it buzzed again, but he couldn't help but wonder how much was piling up at work. He'd check in with Ruby on the way to his place and make sure nothing needed his immediate attention.

"I have to—" Eliza sucked in a gasp. "My fiddle!"

"It's in the house, isn't it?" Grace asked, seeming to instantly grasp the problem.

"In my room." Eliza glanced at the house. "They won't let us in."

"But I bet I can get a big, heroic firefighter to get it. I've got this. You get Calvin buckled in. I'll go charm a firefighter." Grace darted off toward the house.

"If anyone can, it's her," Eliza mumbled. "Let's go, kiddo." To

Mason, she said, "Text me your address please? And let me know where I should park."

The three of them walked to her car together. As she got Calvin situated in his booster seat, with Blitz having woken up and standing at attention at the boy's side, tail wagging, Mason sent her his address, and then she straightened and shut their son in.

Ignoring the activity up and down the street, a fire truck, chainsaws, pickup trucks, and a few cars coming and going, Mason zeroed in on her as their gazes met. She looked utterly exhausted, and an uncharacteristic urge to make everything okay engulfed him. A strand of her dark hair had escaped her ponytail, and he swept it away from her face, tucked it behind her ear before stopping to think whether he should do something so intimate.

Her eyes dipped. "I'm so sorry you got dragged into this," she said.

"I didn't get dragged into anything. I marched in by choice."

"True," she said with a hint of a grin. "Bet you're regretting that."

"The only thing I regret is not being there for you and Calvin for the past four years. But I'm here now, and I have plenty of room for you all to stay as long as you need to."

When she peered up at him again, as if measuring whether or not he was sincere, he was sucker-punched with the urge to lean down and kiss her.

That would not make everything okay.

That would make everything complicated to the nth degree.

He took a step back, mentally scolded himself, pushed himself into practical mode. "There's a parking garage. Follow me in and the visitors' spots are first. You can park there until I can get you both an assigned spot."

And once he got there, he'd be sure to have his defenses in place. Even so, he couldn't help thinking, as he walked toward his car, that it would've been much smarter to pay for them to stay at a good hotel rather than inviting Eliza and her brood into his personal space.

CHAPTER ELEVEN

There were times, as a mother, when you were forced to shut down hard on emotion and fear and somehow fake that life was okay.

This was one of those times.

Eliza followed her phone's directions to Mason's as Calvin chattered about firefighters and Mr. Mason's condo and whether there'd be a doghouse for Blitz—something they didn't have at home, so she wasn't sure why Calvin believed it was important now.

Grace followed in her own car, and even though Grace also had the address entered in her phone and likely listened to the same cues, Eliza checked the rearview regularly as she spouted appropriate responses to Calvin.

Holding it together, she thought. *Name of the game. Don't think about the fact that you're basically homeless, without access to any of your belongings.*

Except her fiddle. Goddess that she was, Grace had indeed convinced one of the firefighters that Eliza's livelihood depended on her fiddle, and it was now in the trunk, safe from Blitz's excited prancing and nonstop barking in the backseat. He must've sensed her stress.

When they arrived, Eliza pulled into the parking garage and spotted Mason leaning against the back side of his expensive little sports car, engrossed in his phone. She parked one spot over, as if leaving a little room would allow her to breathe better, then fielded Calvin's nonstop questions about parking "tunnels," condos, and race cars.

Grace parked between them, and Eliza bolstered herself with a deep breath, then realized she hadn't even grabbed a leash for Blitz. It turned out that wasn't top of mind when you were afraid your house was going to collapse on your child.

By the time she opened Calvin's door, he was unbuckled and slid out of the backseat.

"Blitz, you'll have to stay here until we're ready to go in. Then I'll carry you. Remind me to buy him a leash," she said to her son.

"Mama says we need to buy Blitz a leash," Calvin trumpeted to the others, and it echoed through the garage.

Mason frowned, as if he hadn't yet thought about the leashless dog problem either. "How good is he at heeling?"

Grace answered by laughing. "Does potential count?"

"We haven't been great about training him," Eliza said.

She barely had time to get her son to school, fed, cared for as it was. Dog training? They'd not planned to get a dog, had taken him in as a stray, and she figured she was doing well to keep him in kibbles.

"He can sit!" Calvin said.

"That's important," Mason said to him. "I'll carry him up. Then he won't run loose or pee in the elevator."

"I can carry him," Eliza said.

"I'm sure you can." Mason went to the side without the car seat, opened the back door, and leaned in. When he stood, Blitz was in his arms, and as Mason came toward them, her traitor dog had snuggled his head onto Mason's shoulder as if it was true love. "Let's head in."

Mason went first so he could use his key card for entry, and when Eliza, holding on to Calvin's hand, followed Grace into the lobby, she had to fight to keep her jaw from dropping. Grace shot her a raised-eyebrow glance.

It reminded her of a fine luxury hotel, one that she could

never afford to stay in. The walls were a combination of charcoal tile and ivory paint. The decor was black, gray, and ivory with red accents. There were couches, chairs, and love seats in small groupings, multiple slate fireplaces, and a curved bar with a quartz countertop, all of it deserted at the moment, save for a gentleman at a desk in the corner. The man nodded at Mason with a smile and no comment about the dog.

This was the kind of place she dared not let Calvin roam free, for fear he'd do thousands of dollars of damage just by sneezing wrong.

Maybe they should've found a way to pay for a motel for a couple of nights.

At a corner, Mason stopped and gestured to them to precede him to the elevators.

"You have an elevator in your condo?" Calvin asked him.

"Not inside of it, but we have to take one to get to the top floor. Push that top button."

Calvin did it, watched it light up, then smiled up at Eliza. She thanked God for his innocence and ability to be distracted from life-altering events.

When one of the cars arrived and the doors opened, they all stepped on. As the doors slid shut, Blitz let out a little whimper, then barked, and Eliza stopped to think if the dog had ever been in an elevator before or…

"Shi— Shoot," Mason said. "How long since Blitz did his business?"

"Oh, my God," she said, knowing instantly she'd screwed up. "Did he pee?"

"My arm is warm and wet."

Grace's hand shot to cover her mouth, and her eyes sparkled with amusement. "Does that count as peeing in the elevator?"

"Oh, God," Eliza said again, mortified on top of everything else. "I was so preoccupied I didn't even think to let him out of the car to go. I'm so sorry."

And she'd been worried her son would cost them thousands of dollars' worth of damage in the lobby. Mason's suit had to have cost at least as much as a designer couch.

Again with the motel. It would've been so much smarter and less humiliating.

"It's okay," he said as the speedy elevator car came to a stop. "Calvin, take my card and wave it over that black square." He nodded toward the buttons.

Calvin again followed directions. "Why do we have to use a card?"

"That's a magic card that lets us out on the top floor."

Eliza tried to brace herself to see where Mason called home, but even so, when he let them in and set the dog down, her eyes went huge as she took it in.

"Wowsers," Grace said quietly as she did the same. "This place is incredible."

"Woooow," Calvin said, his voice full of awe. "Look at all the buildings!"

Buildings indeed. Straight ahead was a wall of floor-to-ceiling windows that looked out toward downtown Nashville. As she stepped farther in, she realized the wall of windows wrapped around the corner, so that the two outer walls were completely glass. Twelve floors up, there wasn't anything that blocked that view.

It took several full seconds for her to wrench her gaze away from the vista. The kitchen, dining area, and living area were all one big open room, with a staircase along the back wall of the living area that led to an upper level. In the center of everything was a large granite island with a sink and four stools on the opposite side.

Grace had wandered toward the glass corner on the opposite end. "You have two living rooms?"

Eliza could see her through a two-sided fireplace that apparently split the sitting area down the middle.

"It's good for entertaining," Mason said. "Which I don't do frequently, but when I need to…"

"It's perfect for a cocktail party," Grace said.

"I need to change clothes. Feel free to look around. There are two bedrooms on this floor, and you can decide who sleeps where." Mason went toward the stairs.

"Can I have some waffles, Mr. Mason?"

Mason halted. "You bet. If it's okay with your mom."

Eliza nodded. "I'd apologize for his forwardness, but that's my fault too, just like Blitz's accident. I should've gone somewhere to get breakfast."

"It's fine, Eliza. Feel free to help yourself to the freezer and the waffles. The toaster is on the counter there. And you and Grace are welcome to have some too. I'll be back down in a few."

Once he was up the stairs, out of sight, Eliza exhaled, exchanged a look with Grace, who was still prowling around the main floor, looking everything over. Her roommate said, "So this is what a luxury condo is like. Sugar, you are moving up in the world."

"As if," Eliza said, sending her a message with her eyes to remind that little ears were present.

She went to the double-sided fridge that was big enough to hold food for a family of twelve. She was surprised to find the freezer half-full. Beneath several labeled plastic containers, she located the family-sized box of frozen waffles and pulled them out.

"Godsend," she muttered to herself. She, too, was hungry, but she would wait. "One or two waffles?" she asked Calvin.

"Two."

"Two what?"

"Two waffles, silly."

"Two waffles what?"

Calvin's brows dipped, and then he brightened and hollered, "Two waffles please!" and giggled.

Grace came up behind him, hugged him, and kissed the top of his head as Eliza put the waffles in the toaster.

"You want some?" Eliza asked her roommate.

"Not right now. I'm dying to look around."

Eliza found orange juice and syrup in the refrigerator and put them both on the island. She felt weird about looking through the cabinets for a plate but did it anyway.

Grace had wandered into a room on the other side of the stairs and then reappeared, with Blitz trailing her. She walked across the main floor to the open doorway on the left of the dining room and poked her head in. "I'll take the back bedroom. You and C-man can have this one. There's a walk-in closet big enough to be his own bedroom, so he could sleep in there on the floor."

"That's fine." She was only half paying attention, her mind still swirling over the trauma of the morning and the irony that they'd ended up here. The last place she would ever feel comfortable.

As Grace ambled toward the windows in the dining area, Calvin zoomed by her and smacked his hands on the glass with no regard for, well, anything.

"Calvin!" Eliza said. "Hands off the windows. They're for looking through."

"Lord, you're messy," Grace said, her voice full of affection and amusement. "I wonder where he keeps the glass cleaner."

Sure enough, there were two handprints smeared on the glass about three feet up, and Eliza groaned, thinking this place was anything but three-year-old-boy-friendly.

She checked under the kitchen sink, where normal people stored cleaning supplies, but it was neat and uncluttered and lacking any supplies. Then she spotted a door that might be a pantry. When she opened it, though, she discovered a wine storage room with floor-to-ceiling dark wood wine racks, more than half-full, and a small serving counter built in.

"Good God," she muttered as she closed the door.

"Hold the phone," Grace said. "Is that what I think it is?"

"Wine," was all Eliza said. Hundreds of bottles, and she was inherently certain none of it was her kind of bargain wine.

Eliza spotted another door and opened it, finding a spacious pantry with cleaning supplies and some dry goods. "He has more wine than food," she said to herself. After the morning she'd had, maybe that wasn't a bad thing.

She located glass cleaner, and as she came out of the pantry, the waffles popped up from the toaster, and Grace exited the wine closet.

"His wine collection is worth more than our house. *Before* the tree fell on it," Grace said dryly.

Eliza didn't know whether to laugh or cry. Instead, she grabbed a paper towel and went to the window to clean it while Grace served Calvin his waffle and poured the syrup.

As she scrubbed, she noticed the balcony that ran along the entire side of the building. The railing was glass, so that the view was unobstructed. She'd have to make sure Calvin knew not to go out there alone.

When she turned back toward the interior of the high-end condo, it hit her like a brick to the head—this was insane. What were they doing in a place like this?

It was a bachelor pad and it dripped with money. Nothing was child-proofed. Everything was in danger of Calvin or Blitz inadvertently getting it dirty or worse. Leather sofas, glass everywhere, no yard for a boy to play in or a dog to pee in. Add in the emotional complexity that Mason represented... This was a bad idea all around.

Yet she couldn't think of a single other solution. If it were only going to be a couple of nights, they might be able to swing a motel, but the more the situation at the duplex sank in, the clearer it became that their home was not going to be livable in a couple of days. If they were lucky, they'd be able to go in and get some of their belongings in a couple of days, but even best-case scenario, they needed a new roof and an exterior wall.

She swallowed down despair and tried to tune in to Grace and Calvin's discussion about the best kinds of waffles. Was there such thing as a liquor-laced waffle?

"I'm going to check out the bedroom," she said, needing to be alone for a couple minutes to get her shit together.

"Take your time. We're good," Grace said as she put waffles in the toaster for herself.

As Eliza entered the bedroom, she let out a breath. There was a nearly empty walk-in closet that was as big as their kitchen, a queen-sized bed with a luxurious-looking thick pale gray comforter and a nest of throw pillows, and a flat-screen on the opposite wall. The room had a private bath, with a deep tub, separate shower, and sparkling granite counters.

A door opened out onto the balcony, and she exited it, thinking maybe fresh air would make her feel better.

It didn't.

She told herself it was the wind that made her eyes tear up, but truthfully, there wasn't much more than a breeze today. It was clear, and the view was amazing, but she couldn't truly appreciate it. Her mind was too busy, trying to sort through the situation now that the initial emergency was over and she had a moment to herself.

The privacy didn't last long, as Grace joined her a couple of minutes later.

"Hey," Grace said.

"Does Calvin need me?"

"I left him with Mason. The kid wanted more waffles so I gave him mine, and Mason is sitting with him, talking about race cars."

"That started as soon as he saw Mason's car."

"You doing okay?" her roommate asked.

A laugh burst out of Eliza. "Define okay."

Grace sidled up next to her and put an arm around her, pulled her in for a side hug as they faced the view. "Well, not dead seems like a start." Grace shuddered. "I can't even think about how bad it could've been."

"Thank God you were at Reed's."

Grace nodded. "The asshole."

"What happened? What was the fight about?" Eliza welcomed the different topic, one that wasn't directly her problem, because most days it seemed everything was her problem.

Grace shook her head. "Not worth talking about. He's just… I don't know. I told him about a guitar gig I heard about last night at work, and he said he might call about it, and then he turns around and complains about always being broke. He has the ambition of a dead cat."

"He's younger than us, right?"

"Twenty-eight, but I'm starting to think there's no hope that he'll grow up."

"Did he get a side job yet?" It was nearly impossible to make enough with music, especially if you weren't all about the hustle.

Grace merely shook her head. "So Mason is kind of incredible, huh? Scrumptious to look at, loaded, and generous on top of it."

"In other words, too good to be true," Eliza said. She thanked God for Mason's generosity, she did, but now that she had a minute to think, she couldn't help but wonder about his motivation. "Did he ride in to rescue us out of the goodness of his heart, or is he hoping to get closer to Calvin?"

"You know he's hoping to get closer to Calvin. He just found out he's his son. Does that make him a bad guy?"

Question of the hour.

"I already felt like he was rushing me. Now…he's going to be on me about telling Calvin the truth."

Grace let out a husky laugh. "I can think of worse things than having a man like him on me."

A thought had been poking at Eliza for days, and it finally exploded to the surface. "What if he's angling to get custody?"

That Grace didn't immediately negate the thought told Eliza she wasn't crazy to be concerned about it.

"I don't think a judge would give him full-time custody," Grace said. "And Mason doesn't seem like he'd be stupid enough or hateful enough to try for full-time."

"Not making me feel any better."

"You're jumping way ahead here. He only just met Calvin."

"And by moving us in here when we're desperate, he'll speed everything up. Telling Calvin who he is, getting to know him, filing for some kind of custody… Grace, he's my little boy." Tears popped into Eliza's eyes again. "I can't…" She closed her eyes and shook her head, and her chest ached.

"I know." Grace hugged her from the side again. "I can't stand it either. You know it's like he's half mine."

All Eliza could do was nod.

"Maybe you should ask him what his intentions are," Grace

said. "That way we know what we're dealing with and whether it's time to lawyer up."

"With what money?"

Grace shrugged. "We'll figure it out. Just remember judges like moms. You're a good mom, Lize."

"He's got enough money to buy Calvin everything he needs and then some. I'm working extra just to give him a birthday party."

"But you're doing it. That's worth a lot. You'd do anything for that boy."

"So would you," Eliza said.

"Damn straight. We'll figure it out, whatever happens."

Eliza nodded, dabbing at the tears in the corners of her eyes as she looked again at the skyline. "I have to get to the studio by one. Will you still be able to stay with him?"

"Of course. I don't work till six."

"Better question, will you be able to keep him from breaking through all the glass and plummeting to his death?"

"Piece of cake."

They stood there in silence for a couple of minutes, Eliza's mind going five hundred miles per hour as she tried to find something, any little thing, to make her feel better about…anything.

"It might be a long shot, but tonight I'm going to search for some kind of short-term rental," she said. "We can't commit to more than that until we figure out the status of the duplex and our lease, but we can't stay here any longer than we have to."

"Whatever you need to do," Grace said. "I'm flexible. Although I have to say…this really doesn't suck." She gestured around them to the condo and the view.

Maybe if there wasn't so much at stake, Eliza would agree.

CHAPTER TWELVE

*S*omething had to give.

Four days into knowing he was a father, Mason was failing the juggling act between coming to terms with that and doing his damn job.

He knew without a doubt it wasn't that simple, that finding out he was a father was life-altering, but his work was suffering, and he couldn't afford that.

After leaving Eliza, Calvin, and Grace at his place, he'd had a semi-productive half day of work, but his mind wasn't fully on it, wasn't sharp and focused as it usually was.

That's why he'd left the office at a record early time. When he'd strode out at five thirty with his work bag, the fear on Ruby's face was clear.

"Did someone die?" she'd asked.

Which had hit home the realization that he needed to fill her in about Calvin. Outside of his family, she was one of the people he trusted most.

He'd pulled her back in his office, given her the bullet-point version of the story that had been his life for the past four days, and found the fifty-nine-year-old woman who'd worked for his family for nearly thirty years wrapping motherly arms around him in congratulations, tears filling her eyes.

That, in turn, had made an emotional freight train roll over him, but he'd managed to keep his cool for the most part then sworn her to secrecy until he was ready for his new family status to become public knowledge.

Now here he was, exiting the elevator on the top floor of his condo while the sun was still up for once. He could admit it—he was eager to see how Calvin liked the gift he'd had delivered. What he wouldn't acknowledge was the kernel of anticipation at seeing Eliza again.

When he let himself in, the aroma of dinner cooking—tomatoes and garlic—enveloped him as he took in the scene.

Blitz barked a welcome and ran over to him from the living room, where Calvin was, his claws clicking on the hardwoods.

Eliza was at the stove, stirring something, her hair up in a high ponytail, with strands wisping around her face. She must have gotten some spare clothing, because she wore short denim cutoffs that showed off her long, gorgeous legs and a black tank with a graphic he couldn't make out. Her feet were bare, cheeks slightly flushed, and his gaze got caught up on her for longer than it should have, considering Calvin had hollered his name the second he'd come in the door.

"Down, Blitz," Eliza said to the dog, who was excitedly jumping up on Mason's legs.

"Hello," Mason said to her, then forced himself to look away just as Calvin thundered toward him. That excited the canine more and sent him into a louder barking frenzy.

"Mr. Mason! You got me a train set! 'Zactly what I've always dreamed of!"

As he bent down to his son's level, he glanced at Eliza in time to catch her clenching her jaw, as if she wasn't as happy as her son about the present.

"Come see!" Calvin tugged at his arm, and he followed the boy and the dog, making a mental note to question Eliza in private later.

"Calvin, let Mr. Mason get in the door and breathe."

"He's fine," Mason said, unable to hold in a smile as the reality of the situation sank in—his *son* was happy to see him.

The train set, of course, had something to do with that, but the moment was surreal.

As they walked into the living area, Mason took in the little-boy mayhem. There was wooden train track everywhere, some of the pieces connected, some strewn about. Toy engines and train cars were scattered across the room, from the windows on one side to the stairs on the other. The connected track formed a partial circle around the center fireplace, as if he was attempting to build a route that went all the way around, through both halves of the room.

Calvin talked ten miles a minute as he showed Mason every single engine and explained all the plans for the track and the hills and bridges. Mason wondered how Eliza and Grace could have an ounce of energy left at the end of a day with this energetic child and his dog.

"I didn't expect you home so early," Eliza said from the kitchen as Calvin went quiet, intent on assembling a single long train out of all the cars and engines.

"I'm usually not," Mason admitted. "I wanted to make sure you have whatever you need."

"And then some," she muttered as she ducked toward the oven to remove a loaf of garlic bread. "Thank you for the grocery delivery. There's plenty of spaghetti and marinara for all of us."

That was the best news he'd heard all day. Coming home to a home-cooked meal that smelled like heaven was not a hardship. "I'll change clothes and help you get it on the table."

"Calvin's job is setting the table. Come on, kiddo. You can play for a few more minutes after dinner, but you're going to have to take down your tracks and put them away before bed."

"Aww," Calvin said, looking crestfallen.

Mason was about to say it would be okay for him to leave out the track, but he happened to catch the look Eliza zinged his way that said, *Don't you dare.*

There was a faint suspicion building in his mind that maybe she thought he was overstepping. He filed it away to come back to later as he went up the stairs.

After stripping out of his suit and pulling on dark jeans and a navy polo, he went back down and found Calvin setting out silverware next to three plates at the dining table.

He couldn't remember the last time his dining table had seen use, but the idea burrowed into him. Appealed. It felt like a traditional family dinner, the kind he still had each week with his brothers and mom.

As they ate, Eliza was tense and quiet. Her morning had no doubt been traumatic, and she probably hadn't had time to begin to recover from it, what with Calvin by her side every minute, plus working this afternoon. But instinct told him there was more going on, and that he might be the cause of some of it.

Dinner passed with Calvin filling up what might have been an awkward silence, chattering about preschool as well as more about the train set. As his son kept him on his toes, darting from one subject to another, Mason registered how good the food was. His housekeeper prepared meals for him once a week and stored them in the freezer, ready to cook, but they didn't compare to Eliza's freshly prepared meal.

Once dinner was over, the three of them cleared the table, and Eliza told Calvin he could play with his train set while she and Mason cleaned the kitchen. Boy and dog headed into the living area and got busy. Mason offered to take care of the kitchen, but Eliza insisted on helping.

"It's the least I can do," she said, "with everything you're doing for us." She bit down on the words, as if overcome by emotion, and he narrowed his eyes at her from the side.

Eliza turned away abruptly.

He had the water running to wash the pans, and he shut it off, watching her from behind. Moving in close, he said in a low voice, "Hey."

She squeezed her eyes shut tight for a second and let out a shaky exhale, then bent to pull out the bottom rack in the dishwasher.

"Eliza."

After pausing for a moment, she straightened and faced him. Her face was so wrought with restrained emotion that he had to fight not to pull her into his chest, aware their son could see them. Mason didn't have any motivation other than comforting her, but he still had the sense he was fucking up more than he was getting right tonight, and he suspected she wouldn't want Calvin to see him hugging her. There seemed to be a bunch of unspoken rules that he needed to figure out.

She was still fighting for control over herself, and since he couldn't comfort her the way he wanted, he tried a different tack.

"You've had a hell of a day. Why don't you go take ten minutes to yourself. Let me handle the kitchen and Calvin. Just for ten minutes," he insisted when she looked like she was going to argue. "Wash your face or breathe or punch a pillow or whatever."

He gently took her shoulders and guided her a few steps in the direction of her bedroom and was shocked when she acquiesced. "I've got this," he told her, and she nodded, her back to him, then disappeared into her room.

"Where's Mama going?" Calvin asked.

"She's going to have a few minutes to herself. It's just you and me."

"And Blitz."

"And Blitz. The lucky thing for you is that it'll take me a little longer to clean the kitchen by myself, so you get a few extra minutes."

"Cool!" Calvin bent back over his track and started singing to himself.

Mason got busy on the kitchen, his mind occupied with what he could do to help Eliza solve her problems. Problem-solving was one of his strengths, and he refused to believe there wasn't a solution to just about every challenge.

Cleaning went quickly, as it appeared Eliza had tidied up as she cooked, and all that was left were the dishes from dinner and the pans.

"Okay, C," he said after drying his hands. "Time for us to clean up this train yard."

Instead of complaining, Calvin stood, looking sad, and then confusion twisted his little-boy features. "Where are we gonna put my stuff? I don't have a toy box here."

The kid had a point.

What would Eliza do? Mason wondered. *Make it fun.*

He looked around for the box the set had come in but didn't see it. Probably in the recycling bin downstairs. For tonight, he'd improvise.

"Do you like games?" Mason asked.

Calvin nodded, eyes big.

"This is a sorting game. We're going to sort the track pieces into piles of the same kind, so long straights go here." He picked up two of the long, straight tracks and stacked them up against the wall formed by the fireplace. "Curve pieces go here." He started another stack.

"Short straights here!" Calvin said, buying into the game and searching out a short piece.

Within five noisy minutes, they had all the track pieces in stacks, all the engines lined up together, all the cars in another section, and the extras like signs and trees in their own area. The pieces were out of the way, as put away as they could be without a bin or shelf.

Blitz had "helped" them with the task, but now the dog was at the door, and he let out a bark.

Eliza's bedroom door whipped open, and she came out to look at the dog. "He needs to go," she said and went back into her room, probably to get shoes.

"Calvin and I can take him." Mason grabbed the leash that was on the island, which he'd had delivered along with the train and groceries, and started toward the dog.

"I can take care of it," Eliza called out from her room. "He's not your responsibility."

"We can handle it just fine," Mason said, attaching the leash to Blitz's collar. "Right, C?"

"Right!"

Eliza came to her doorway and looked between them, hesitant, and Mason stood from where he was squatting next to Blitz and went toward her.

"Ten more minutes for you," he said in a low voice. "We'll stick to Blitz's business and be right back."

Finally she nodded. "You stay right next to Mr. Mason," she told her son.

Mason said, "Get your shoes on, Calvin," not willing to give Eliza the chance to change her mind.

Calvin did one better than stay right next to Mason for the short walk. He held on to Mason's hand.

For the first half, the boy was talkative and inquisitive, asking about the fenced-in park across the street and the man at the desk inside and elevators and stairs and fire hydrants. Once they turned and headed back toward the main door, the questions slowed, and Mason suspected Calvin was getting tired.

"You've had a big day, huh, C?"

Soundlessly, Calvin nodded, craning his head to watch a woman who walked past them in the opposite direction.

"How about a ride?" Mason asked his son.

Calvin switched his gaze to him, puzzled. "In your car?"

Shortening the slack on Blitz's leash, Mason squatted and said, "On my back," and motioned toward it. "Piggyback."

A grin split Calvin's face, and then his eyes lit up. "Can you carry me on your shoulders?"

"I sure can. Can you duck when we go through doorways?"

"Yes!" Calvin did a little gallop dance in place as Mason lowered himself even more and took one of Calvin's hands.

"Hold on to my head but don't poke my eyes out," Mason said as he rose slowly with Blitz looking on.

When Mason was to full height, Calvin giggled and Blitz barked.

"Don't let go," Mason said.

"Okay. I can see everything from up here!"

With Blitz's leash in one hand and Mason's other arm locked around his son's leg, they made their way back to the main door, laughing all the way.

In the elevator, Calvin had to lean down a few inches, and Mason watched in the mirrored walls as his son leaned his head on his, both arms wrapped loosely around Mason's neck.

The sight, the feeling of having his son hold on to him, happy, content, and trusting, took Mason's breath away and shot warmth and fatherly love through him like he'd never known possible.

And yet Calvin had no idea Mason was his dad. It diminished the moment.

Mason was doing his best to be patient with the situation, but his patience was waning. Maybe it'd only been four days, but his heart was making up for nearly four years, and every second counted. He would never take a minute with his son for granted.

He had to bring it up with Eliza again soon. Tonight, after Calvin went to sleep, if he wasn't too high up on her shit list for whatever it was he was on her shit list for.

When the elevator doors opened and they stepped into the high-ceilinged hallway, Calvin straightened and laughed again. "I can almost touch the ceiling!"

At the condo, Mason let them in and dropped the dog's leash as soon as he'd shut the door.

"Mama, look at me," Calvin said. "Just like Jacob!"

Eliza came out of her bedroom, a smile on her face—until she laid eyes on Calvin, still perched on top of Mason's shoulders. She shuttered her expression in a millisecond.

Mason didn't know who Jacob was or what he'd done now, but he knew without a doubt, instead of taking a part of her burden off her shoulders, he was somehow responsible for adding to it.

CHAPTER THIRTEEN

*E*liza had reached her limit with this day two hours ago—
or maybe twelve. Then Mason had waltzed in and
pushed her even further.

Her fault, not his.

She and Mason had tucked Calvin into the bed she'd made
him on the floor of the walk-in, making it his own separate room,
close to Eliza but with a door between them so she wouldn't
wake him up with noise.

Mason had just rushed out to answer his ringing phone, and
Eliza closed herself in her bedroom in relief. The half hour he'd
arranged for her to have to herself earlier had been appreciated
but barely a drop in the bucket as far as what she needed to
recover from this day.

The lights of the city skyline beckoned to her, as did the fresh
air. After grabbing a throw blanket from the chair in the corner,
she headed outside to the balcony. To the right of the door was a
metal chair. She curled up in it, wrapping the blanket around her,
knees pulled into her chest, and let her mind go back to Mason,
who seemed to be rocking the fatherhood gig without breaking a
sweat.

She should be ecstatic. Grateful. Relieved.

Instead she was raw and oversensitive. Feeling thoroughly
inadequate. And dammit, it pissed her off that she could let him

make her feel that way. She'd been trying to fight it down since the moment she'd walked in after work and found Mason had sent over the deluxe version of the train set she'd planned to buy Calvin for his birthday. The train set she'd been playing Friday night gigs in order to save for.

The deluxe version, which was twice as expensive as the one she'd been saving to buy. No doubt, he hadn't even blinked at the price tag.

Before she could get a full breath, the door from the living area out to the balcony opened, and she closed her eyes. Coming outside to be alone had clearly been a tactical error.

Without speaking, Mason picked up a matching chair from farther down and carried it closer, then sat in it.

After several seconds, he said, "These aren't at all comfortable."

Eliza glanced toward him to confirm he meant the chairs.

With an attempt at a smile, she said, "You haven't noticed before?"

"I don't think I've ever sat out here."

That was sad, but telling him felt judgmental, and God knew she had no room to judge anything about him or anyone.

More seconds ticked by, and Eliza worked up the fortitude to swallow her pride and show some gratitude. "Thank you for getting the train set for Calvin. He loves it."

She felt Mason studying her from the side in the darkness, but she kept her gaze pointed straight ahead.

"You're welcome. I figured he'd need something to keep him occupied until you can get some of his toys."

"He did." And the train set far surpassed what she'd picked up for that purpose during their Target run before she'd had to rush off to work—two Hot Wheels cars, three books, and a stuffed otter, which her son had inexplicably named Poopy.

"It seems like," Mason started, then hesitated, his low voice an alluring rumble, "you're not happy with me for some reason. For buying the train?"

Hearing him say it out loud hammered home how petty she was

being, not that she needed it hammered. She'd done her best to fight it down while Mason and Calvin were walking Blitz, but then when they'd walked in with Calvin on his shoulders, the daddy bond was in her face and impossible to ignore. It raised all kinds of insecurities.

Yep, petty.

Of course she wanted her son to have a strong, positive relationship with his dad. That was why she'd ultimately taken the chance of tracking down Mason. But being on board with it didn't mean she wasn't struggling to catch up emotionally.

"Calvin's wanted a wooden train set for months," she said quietly, her voice rough with the emotions she was trying to keep in check. It wasn't easy to admit the rest, but after growing up in a home where passive-aggressiveness was the primary means of communication, she couldn't stomach not being direct. "I was planning to buy one for his birthday."

"Shit. I'm sorry. I didn't think of asking, just wanted to surprise him and help him get over a rough morning."

"Oh, you did. And there was no way you could've known that's what I've been saving for." It didn't make it any easier to swallow.

Mason was quiet for a while, and Eliza took the time to build up her control, because the tears were right under the surface, just waiting to gush out.

"Damn," he said, leaning forward, resting his elbows on his knees. "That's why you've been playing Friday nights, isn't it? For Calvin's birthday?"

And there were the tears, popping up in the corners of her eyes.

She dropped her blanket, stood, and stepped to the railing, not needing to answer. Calvin had told him she was "getting money" for his birthday the other day. That had been embarrassing enough.

The tears welled and spilled over the edges of her eyes in a torrent, and she fought not to give in to the shudders that threatened to rack her shoulders or the need to wipe at her cheeks, not wanting him to notice she was silently losing her shit. She focused on sucking in air, letting it out in a controlled exhale. In, out, as the tears would not freaking stop.

And then he was at her side, his arm rubbing against hers, and she squeezed her eyes shut, as if that could hide her meltdown.

"Eliza," he said in a low, concerned growl of a voice.

Next thing she knew, she was wrapped in his arms, her face hidden in his chest, tears drenching his shirt, and then the soundless sobs came. No longer able to hold them off, she burrowed into him, let her arms wrap around him, and had to acknowledge how good his wide chest and strong shoulders felt, as if she'd been craving this kind of comfort for four years, or her entire life, but hadn't realized it.

A few minutes later, when she felt cried out and wrung out, she sniffled and started to breathe more evenly, even if there was still a shakiness in each breath.

She felt him skim his lips over the top of her head, and all she could do, other than try to breathe right, was close her eyes and soak in his concern. She'd spent too many years alone, trying to handle it all.

Yes, she'd been so blessed to have Grace and Lettie, but she'd always endeavored to wrestle with the tough decisions and the stress of parenting herself. Calvin wasn't their child, and they shouldn't have the burdensome side of parenting on their shoulders.

Turned out her shoulders were tired.

"Talk to me, Eliza."

A few more breaths later, she wiped her cheeks and eyes with her tank top, still not daring to meet his gaze. His arms were still at her waist, and she couldn't make herself move away just yet.

"It's just…his birthday's a big deal for me," she said. "I wanted to make this one special, with the train set and a party… He's never had a party before"—a lingering shudder escaped her—"and we always get him presents but never anything so big…"

"And I ruined all your plans in an afternoon."

"You make it all look so easy, but it's never been easy for me."

"I don't know much about parenting, but I know it's anything but easy."

She sniffled again. "And then when you came in with him on your shoulders…"

"I wasn't going to drop him," Mason said.

"I know."

That wasn't it at all. It was more that it had caught her off guard, and that image of father and son connecting, laughing together… It stung because that's what Calvin should've had all along. It was the one thing—well, two if you counted money—she couldn't provide for him.

"It made it hit home how much he's been missing with just me." That he was aching for a father in his life.

She pressed her lips together, thinking before she said the next thing on her mind, making sure it was right, because once it was out there, there'd be no going back. "It's probably time to tell him you're his father."

Mason's hands were still on her back, and one of his thumbs had been caressing her, back and forth, but now he went completely still.

"Are you sure?" he asked.

She let out a gust of a breath chock full of emotion. "No, I'm not sure at all."

"What are you afraid of, Eliza? You're his mom. He's never going to stop loving you."

Working up her nerve to voice what she needed to, she put space between them, backing up until his hands slid off her. She gazed up at him, ignored how damn attractive he was, and said, "I'm afraid you're going to file for custody."

He held her gaze, and her heart raced as she waited for him to confirm or deny.

"I'd never take him away from you."

"But you want to be involved in his life."

"I do. Absolutely. It kills me that I've missed so much."

Her mouth went desert dry with fear. "Then what are your plans?"

"I haven't thought through the specifics—"

"Have you contacted a lawyer?"

"Not yet."

"But you're going to." The hysteria was building up inside of her again.

"Of course I am. For everything from how to get my name on his birth certificate to setting up a trust for him to figuring out how to handle years of backdated child support…"

"I don't need backdated child support. I just need you to…" *Not go after custody.*

But she knew that wasn't likely. Maybe he wouldn't go for full-time, but he would never be satisfied to simply visit his son for dinner a couple of times each week. If she tried to set the emotions and the panic aside for a minute, she could admit that, in his shoes, she would never, ever settle for that, either.

The thought of watching her little boy walk out the door with a backpack of clothes to stay with Mason for a weekend or more…

If there'd been any tears left in her, they would've rolled out now, but it seemed she was cried out.

"Let's start with telling him who I am," Mason said, as though wanting to soothe her. "You're staying here for a while, and we'll all be able to get to know each other better. With that will come trust."

"I'm trying to find us a different place to stay," she confessed. She'd done an initial search for apartments with short-term leases when she'd taken refuge in her bedroom earlier.

He frowned. "Why?"

"I heard from our landlord this afternoon. The engineer can't get out to assess the duplex until Wednesday, and that's only the start. He's sure it'll be at least a month, maybe more, to repair the damage."

"I told you you're welcome as long as necessary."

Her eyes fluttered shut for a moment. "Thank you. I'm truly grateful, but this isn't an ideal place for a little boy. He needs to be able to run around. Blitz needs a place besides the elevator to pee."

"There's a private park across the street."

"A private park. Of course there is."

"With a fenced-off dog area. I'll leave you the key card to get in."

She returned to her spot along the railing, shaking her head, inwardly rolling her eyes.

"What did I say?" he asked from behind her.

"You just…seem to have all the answers." She bit down on anything else before it could pop out. "Forget I said that. The park will be a godsend."

A quiet rumble of laughter sounded right behind her. "I don't have all the answers. Not even half. Eliza…" He touched her upper arm and gently tugged at it. "Look at me."

After a moment of hesitation, she faced him, took her time in making eye contact, because every time she did, she melted a little on the inside, even when she was this upset. There was no denying the physical draw between them.

Mason grasped both of her hands, and the feel of his warm, strong hands against her own flesh was impossible to ignore. Her attraction to this man was impossible to ignore.

"I know you don't know me very well," he said. "Barely at all. But the night I met you, I felt a crazy connection like I've never felt before. I think you felt it too."

She nodded, unable to deny that. All this time, she'd figured it had just been her.

"Based on that alone, I care about you." He let out a gust of breath and averted his eyes, seeming nervous. "I never forgot about you. Thought about you a lot. For four years."

Her heart raced, and for a moment, she felt lighter than air. "Really?" She couldn't help the skepticism.

"I wouldn't make that up," he said with a self-conscious half smile that turned her inside out and made her almost forget her insecurities. "And I never planned on telling you. Never thought I'd have the chance. But here you are. And here I am. I'm not a big believer in fate or destiny, but I can't help wondering if maybe our son is giving us another chance to get to know each other."

She got lost in his gaze for a few seconds, felt a reaction down to her lady parts. The practical side of her was clawing and reaching for reason and suspicion, because life had taught her that if something seemed too good to be true, it probably was. And yet she couldn't deny there was *something between them.* Something powerful and irresistible.

He cradled her cheek in one hand and studied her, all signs of insecurity vanishing as his gaze became more intent. Then he leaned down and kissed her.

His lips were sure and insistent, but she didn't need any convincing and darted her tongue out to let him know. He plunged his tongue inside her mouth, the chemistry between them that she'd been trying to deny all day rolling into an inferno of need.

She clasped the front of his shirt, clinging for balance as her insides plummeted into a free fall. Everything around them—noise on the street below, the city lights, the breeze that rustled her hair—disappeared as all of her senses zeroed in on Mason. Virile, sexy, tempting Mason.

He moved his hand to the back of her head, bracing her as he kissed her hard. She felt his other hand at her waist, on top of her tank, and she longed to feel the heat of him directly on her skin.

What she wouldn't do to have one night like they'd had before, with no worries, no hard stuff hanging over her, nothing but what was happening between him and her.

A battle raged within her…lose herself or fight to keep her wits about her?

His kiss was waking up parts of her that'd been in deep hibernation for ages, making her come alive, making her long for things she hadn't allowed herself to so much as think about.

Sex. Intimacy. Partnership.

And wasn't that asinine?

It was only a kiss.

A kiss that, if Calvin wasn't twenty feet away, could turn in to sex.

Just sex.

It wasn't intimacy and it wasn't partnership and she needed to remember that.

With a surge of willpower, she ended the kiss before she slipped any further toward the *losing herself* side of the line. Her heart raced and her body cried out for more, and she took in a shaky breath to try to come down from the high of kissing Mason.

"We can't…" she said. "Calvin…"

"He's asleep."

Nodding, she said, "I mean in general. You and I can't… Especially if we're…" Her brain was still scrambled from his kisses. She tried to mentally shake herself out of it and make sense. "Calvin wants a normal family, with a dad and a mom, even more than he wanted that train set. It's already a complex situation with us staying here at your place when he learns you're his father. I don't want him to think we're getting married and going to be a traditional family."

"Maybe we should get married," Mason said.

She narrowed her eyes at him for a moment, decided he was insane, and said, "We're not getting married. It's confusing enough as it is." For Calvin *and* for her.

"Maybe that would make it less confusing."

Once again, she found both her hands in his, their palms touching, fingers interlocked.

"I barely know you. You barely know me. We're not getting married," she said.

He looked down at her with an expression that said he was getting all kinds of ridiculous ideas.

"Mason. Be real."

"It could solve a lot of problems."

"And cause even more," she said, refusing to entertain the idea.

"Think about it." He let her hands go, as if he was getting serious, going into CEO mode. "I could be a full-time father at the same time you remain a full-time mom. No two-residence back-and-forth life for Calvin. You'll have a partner in parenting, and we could pool our resources—financial, emotional, logistical."

"A marriage of convenience," she said, shaking her head. "I don't want to get married out of convenience."

"It makes sense, Eliza. It's a win-win-win."

"A *logical* marriage is not what I want Calvin exposed to."

"It's not as though we're enemies. We like each other," Mason said, gathering steam instead of losing it, in spite of her objections.

"Mason," she snapped, "Calvin and I are not a business deal."

Call her old-fashioned, but if and when she ever got married, she wanted it to be for love.

Could she love Mason? She had no idea. She still barely knew him, and what she'd learned of him was that she and he were from different worlds, lived entirely different lives.

He pierced her with an assessing look, as if gauging whether he could win this debate today or if it was time to retreat. Finally, he inhaled and nodded once, as if relenting.

"How about this?" he said in a gentler, quieter, less determined tone. "You agree to stay here until your home is livable. That way you don't have to worry about a roof over your head or search for a short-term place or move. I can get acquainted with my son, and you and I can get to know each other better."

It was the getting to know him better that scared her most. But that was better than having him pester her about something as ridiculous as getting married.

"What about Grace?" she asked.

"She's part of the package, right?"

"She is."

His understanding of that, that she would say no if Grace wasn't welcome, eased her mind, but only slightly. Because the more worrisome element was whether she could think rationally if she was living, even if only for a month or so, with Mason.

If she could, then his living arrangement proposition was a no-brainer. Low-risk and a solution to several of her problems.

Mason and Calvin could spend time together, and either she or Grace would be present all the time. Though she didn't believe Mason had any intention of harming Calvin, she didn't know whether he could microwave a hot dog or pull out a splinter or set limits on screen time. This way, she could oversee, well, everything. Either directly or indirectly. At least until she knew him better.

The question that had ruled her life for the last four-plus years was, what was best for Calvin? And though there were a lot of unknowns where Mason was concerned, she had to believe that letting her son get to know his father better would be to his benefit—until it wasn't.

Eliza swallowed down on her fears, then nodded. "Okay."

"Okay? You'll stay?"

"Until our home is ready for us, we'll stay."

CHAPTER FOURTEEN

s Mason walked through the lobby of his condo, he squinted against the bright reflection of the late-afternoon sun on the white marble floor. He couldn't remember the last time he'd come home from work while the sun was still shining, other than three days ago, when Calvin, Eliza, and Grace had moved in.

That he was tonight was nothing short of a small miracle and a shit ton of determination, and in his bag was a thick stack of work to address later on, after Calvin went to bed. That inconvenience was inconsequential in the grand scheme of things, because this evening was of the utmost importance. It was what he'd been anticipating for a full week—since the day Eliza had rocked his life with the news he had a son.

Tonight, they were telling Calvin the truth about his paternity.

After securing Eliza's agreement Monday night to stay put at his place until her duplex was livable, he'd submerged himself into work, both the ongoing crisis that threatened the company's future and the day-to-day issues that came up. He'd thought of Calvin from time to time, Eliza too, if he was honest, but he'd barely seen them for forty-eight hours. The exception was this morning, when he'd been able to enjoy a champion's breakfast of frozen waffles with his boy before rushing off to a day jam-packed with meetings and conference calls.

Along with a handful of other people, he walked into the elevator, hit the button for the top floor, and turned to face the doors. As he did, a woman—Eliza, he realized—came whipping around the corner and scrambling toward the elevators.

"Hold the elevator, please!"

He stuck his hand out to stop the doors from closing and took in her appearance as she rushed forward without making eye contact. In one hand was her fiddle case and from the other shoulder hung a large canvas bag. She wore a loose sleeveless fuchsia top, cropped jeans, and shoes that turned the outfit from girl-next-door to eye-catching—heeled sandals with three bands that wrapped around her ankles in a hue that matched her shirt.

What caught his attention even more than the sexy shoes, though, were the fatigue and stress etched across her face.

Her head down as she fumbled with her phone, Eliza hopped on, apparently still not noticing it was him.

"Thank you," she said. When she finally looked up at him, recognition registered and her smile became less forced.

"You're welcome."

As the elevator began its ascent, Eliza took in a deep breath and let it out slowly, almost inaudibly, and Mason likely wouldn't have been aware of it if he hadn't been tuned in. It was a weary breath, as if she carried the weight of the world on her shoulders.

The desire to help her shoulder that burden or, better yet, carry it for her washed over him.

"Something wrong?" he asked quietly.

"I'm late. My car wouldn't start when I came out of the studio. Grace has a gig at six, so she needed to leave fifteen minutes ago. Usually Lettie covers any gaps but..." Leaving it unspoken that Lettie was no longer right next door, she clicked her phone to check the time and glanced at the elevator panel, where the numbers for three floors before theirs were lit up.

As the car stopped on the first one and the doors slid open,

Mason pulled Eliza close to his side to let a fifty-something blonde out.

"How'd you get here?" he asked.

"Davis—the bass player—jump-started me."

"Do you need a new battery?"

"I just got one two weeks ago," she answered distractedly as she typed in a text message to Grace.

Almost there, he read from her side, thinking her car clearly had something deeper than a battery wrong with it.

"Does this happen a lot?"

"Not since I got the battery," she said, "so I thought it was fixed."

"We need to get that checked out."

With a frustrated half laugh, she said, "Yeah. As soon as I have time." Her tone said that might be sometime before Christmas if all went well.

As they reached another floor and the others disembarked, Mason pulled out his phone and opened his contacts. "You parked in the visitor section of the garage?" he asked as he scrolled to his car guy's personal cell number.

She nodded and checked her phone when a notification tone sounded. At the same time, she put space between them, moving to the other side of the otherwise empty car. He swiped his key card to open the doors on the penthouse level as he waited for his call to be answered.

When the doors slid open, there were Calvin and Grace, sitting on the settee opposite the elevator. Calvin hopped up and hollered, "Mama! We were waiting for you."

Roy Marks answered the call, and Mason greeted him. He watched distractedly as Grace dashed to the elevator, grasping Eliza's hand for a quick, affectionate squeeze on the way.

"I gotta make like a banana and split," Grace called to Calvin, blowing him a kiss as she hopped on and the doors closed. The boy laughed and blew a kiss back.

"Hi, Mr. Mason," Calvin said, taking his mom's hand.

Mason ruffled the boy's hair and mouthed, *Hey, buddy*, and then launched into an explanation to Roy of what was going on with Eliza's car as the three of them walked toward the condo. He was vaguely aware of Eliza telling Calvin he could talk to Mason more when his phone call was finished.

They reached his door. Still conducting his call, he let them in, and Blitz met them, tail wagging, legs dancing. They each got an individual welcome/sniffing from the dog, and Mason stopped in front of the island, intent on his phone discussion.

When he ended the call a couple of minutes later, Eliza and Calvin were in the living area, with the boy showing her the track configuration he'd completed earlier in the day.

"My car guy's going to come by and take a look, see what he can tell," Mason said to her.

"Tonight?" She sounded scandalized.

"On his way home from work. Hey, C," he said to Calvin as he joined them trackside. "You've been busy."

As Calvin began Mason's "tour" of today's track, with Blitz on alert, as if he was waiting for a treat, Eliza said, "Your guy doesn't need to do that."

"He knows I'll make it worth his while," Mason said as he squatted down to see into the engine house, as Calvin requested.

He lowered himself all the way to a kneel as his son sidled up right next to him and told him all the must-know details of the setup, his enthusiasm never once waning.

Mason grinned without reservation. A week ago, he probably would've said something like this would be an unwelcome distraction from his demanding day. But as Calvin sat down on top of Mason's knees, still talking nonstop and so avidly, the truth burrowed into Mason's chest. This was the best kind of welcome home after a high-pressure day at the office. He leaned forward and caught the shampoo scent of Calvin's head.

He thought for the hundredth time about his marriage proposition three nights ago and still didn't regret it. It was the right answer.

Was he in love with Eliza? No, and she didn't love him either, but they both loved their child.

Love had never been a priority for Mason. He believed in it, had grown up with a front-row seat to his parents' love, and now his brothers seemed to have found the loves of their lives. Mason was all for it for others, and wasn't opposed to it someday for himself, but he'd been nose to the grindstone with his life goals from college on—learning the business of North Brothers Sports inside and out, from the bottom up, and eventually stepping up to the helm. NBS had always been the priority.

He wasn't stupid though. Calvin hadn't been in the plans, but part of running a successful business was being able to pivot when a situation changed. A wife might not have been in the plans, but here was Eliza. They had the most important goal in common—raising Calvin. And it wasn't a stretch to think love could develop between them eventually.

He saw no reason to wait around for that to happen.

"Calvin," Eliza said, "why don't you go get Blitz's food out?" Calvin zipped off, the dog following him. To Mason, she said, "I was planning to get an appointment for my car later this week."

"You can't have a car that won't start. What if the same thing happens tomorrow after work? Or before?"

"I'd call an Uber," she said without thought, and he sensed she'd in fact had to do that before.

"We need to get it addressed right away. Roy will probably need to take it in. If so, we'll get you a loaner."

"Mason," she said on an exhale, sounding frustrated, which he didn't understand. This was a problem he could fix. "I can't afford a loaner. And I don't want you to pay for it for me," she added, having correctly anticipated what he was going to say next.

The sound of crunchy dog food spilling all over the hard floor near the entryway, where they'd set up Blitz's dishes, drew their attention.

Calvin stood there with a bag of food almost as big as he was, staring at the mess with an exaggerated cringe that made Mason smile.

"Sorry," Calvin said as Mason and Eliza went to help him clean it up and Blitz overzealously chomped down the food on the floor as if he hadn't eaten for a month.

"We have a bin and a scoop at home," Eliza explained to Mason. "It makes it easier to manage."

"Then we'll get one for here."

The three of them finished cleaning the mess, and Eliza told Calvin to wash his hands in the bathroom, where there was a stool to reach the sink.

She turned to Mason, pushing her long dark hair out of her face, her jaw resolute and her gaze direct. "Look, I appreciate you letting us stay here, truly, but I don't need you to fix my life."

That wasn't what he'd expected her to say, and he peered down at her in surprise. She had so much mettle flaring back at him in her gorgeous brown eyes, and in that moment, he saw the essence of how she'd provided for Calvin, not just financially but in every way he needed. Whatever the challenges life threw at her, she barreled through, never thinking *if*, only thinking *how*.

"Your life doesn't need to be fixed," he said. "Just your car."

"And I planned to get it fixed, Mason. I don't need you trying to take over all the 'man' tasks in my life. I can handle them on my own schedule."

"I have zero doubts you can," he said, stepping closer, grasping her hands in his, maybe for the pleasure of touching her, maybe to prevent her from stomping off. Maybe both. "Eliza, when I look at you, I see a woman who's probably not had an easy time of it. I can't imagine everything you've been through since finding out you were pregnant, and you did it all alone."

"I had Grace."

"And I'm so fucking glad you did, but now you have me too, at the very least as a willing partner in parenthood. I'm just trying to make one thing easier for you. Can you let me do that?"

Her gaze darted down to their interlocked hands, and then she pulled hers away as she nodded. "Yes. Thank you."

He wasn't used to having to work so hard to get someone to accept something from him meant in kindness. He had a long way to go in understanding this bewitching, hardheaded woman.

"How are you feeling about this evening?"

"Telling Calvin?" She exhaled strongly enough it blew a

strand of her hair. "Freaking out," she admitted. "But I'll get over it. No time to dwell on it. I need to take the dog out, then get the kid some food."

"Ruby, my assistant, had a picnic dinner delivered," he told her. "I thought we could all go to the park to eat, and we can talk to him afterward."

She stopped with her hand on the refrigerator handle, about to open it. "Really?"

"Full disclosure, it was Ruby's idea to do something special and fun for Calvin."

A hint of a grin tugged at her lips. "I'd like to meet this Ruby sometime."

"She's been with the company for about thirty years. She was my father's assistant, then my uncle's when he was CEO." He'd flounder without the woman, professionally and sometimes even personally, especially now.

Eliza opened the fridge, and there was a reusable grocery bag on the top shelf. She removed it, and Mason located another shopping bag on the counter, also thanks to Ruby.

"This," he said as he opened the bag and pulled out its contents, "is an insulated picnic bag with everything we'll need. Why don't we both go change clothes and then we can go. Think Blitz can wait that long?"

The dog had disappeared into the dining area, where Calvin was now up against the window, peeping at the view, his hands pressed against the glass.

"Hands, kiddo," Eliza called out, and Calvin whipped them away from the glass but kept gawking. "Blitz will be fine if we hurry," she said more quietly to Mason. "By the way, Calvin's staying overnight at Lettie's son's house tomorrow night. Grace and I both have to work."

"I can stay with him."

She shook her head without hesitation, without giving his suggestion any thought. "You have work," she said.

"I can come home when you need me and work from here."

"Watching Calvin is a full-contact sport on a good day. He's not really compatible with working at home."

"Then I'll work after he goes to sleep."

"With your workload, you'd be up all night," she said, and he heard a hint of disapproval in her tone. Because he had to work long hours? "Besides, I already promised Lettie some Calvin time."

"If you're sure…"

"Hundred percent. Calvin's excited for a sleepover."

Mason suspected it wasn't just about Lettie or Calvin's excitement. In her eyes, he wasn't up for the task. It was going to take some time, but he would work to convince her otherwise.

Before he turned to go upstairs, he saw her glance at Calvin again and suck in a slow breath, her worry obvious.

"Hey," he said, nudging her chin upward so she would make eye contact. "Everything's going to be all right."

She peered up at him, still looking drained from the day, her eye makeup a little smudged under one eye, hair tousled, and yet her beauty even now spoke to him on a primal, cellular level.

"Sometimes you make me think so, and I have to be honest," she said quietly, "that scares the crap out of me."

She turned and went to her room, leaving him standing there, wrestling with how to convince her to let him take some of the challenges off her shoulders. At the very least, the ones that concerned Calvin.

One thing at a time.

CHAPTER FIFTEEN

To anyone who saw the three of them together in the park, four if you counted Blitz, stretched out on the plaid picnic blanket, eating cold fried chicken, grapes, and chocolate chip cookies, it would appear Eliza, Mason, and Calvin were a tight family unit.

Beneath the surface, though, a storm of conflict raged through Eliza.

Mason North was hard to resist on a good day, with his dark-haired, blue-eyed good looks, his sexy low-pitched laugh, and his fascination with his son. Throw in his thoughtfulness and knack for taking care of things—he'd even had Ruby include a chew toy for Blitz to keep him calm while they ate—and he seemed like the catch of a lifetime.

His job was a problem though. Or rather, his devotion to his job. She couldn't deny it was an important, demanding position, but three days into staying at his place so he could get to know Calvin, and his usual time to come home so far was after nine p.m., after Calvin went to bed.

She'd give him credit for making a point of FaceTiming Calvin in time to say good night, but she was having all kinds of flashbacks to her own childhood, her own workaholic dad, her own wounds caused by her dad's choices.

She did *not* want the same for her son.

If Mason was choosing work over Calvin this soon after finding out about him, what would it be like in a month? A year? Five years? Was there any way it could get better? Could Mason learn to balance work and his child better than he was?

Time would tell, she supposed, but the truth of the matter was that she was skeptical and worried for her son.

Every nerve in her seemed to be on edge with anticipation, the stressful, draining kind, of telling Calvin Mason was his father. They'd just finished eating, and it felt like there was a ticking time bomb counting down.

As Blitz settled down on the corner of the blanket after a wiener dog had waddled out of sight, Eliza wiped Calvin's mouth clean of melted chocolate from the cookies, only half listening to his ongoing chatter about the moon and spaceships and astronauts. Thankfully, Mason was fully engaged with him and carrying on the conversation, with all its three-year-old twists and turns. It gave her mental space to work up her courage.

She'd been the one to decide this was the right thing to do, after all. And she believed, deep down, it was. Now that she'd found Mason and told him the truth, there was no turning back.

"Calvin," she said when there was the slightest pause in the space discussion. "We have something important to talk to you about."

"'Kay!" Calvin had stood up and now had his hands planted on the blanket in front of him, bent at the waist, and was kicking his legs up behind him, one and then the other, donkey-style. God knew why, and most days, it would make Eliza grin and shake her head at the wonder of little boys.

"You need to sit down while we talk," Mason said, gentle and firm at once, surprising her in a good way. It was a fatherly order, the first she'd heard from him, as so far, he'd been Mr. Mason, Eliza's "friend."

In one motion, Calvin went from foot up in the air to sitting on his butt, grinning widely at his "trick" and staring up at them with big, eager eyes.

After a fortifying inhale and a glance at Mason, who gave her an encouraging nod, she said, "Remember when I told you your daddy lived far away and wasn't part of our family because of that?"

"Mm-hmm. He lives in Californie."

"California," she corrected automatically.

She'd seen a tag with a big SFO on Mason's luggage that night in the hotel room and made the incorrect assumption he lived on the West Coast. It'd barely registered at the time, but later, when she'd found out she was pregnant, it was a "lead" she'd tried to follow, to no avail.

"It turns out I was wrong," Eliza continued. "Your daddy lives here in Nashville." She swallowed hard and worked to keep her tone matter-of-fact. "Mr. Mason is your daddy."

Her normally boisterous son's eyes popped wide open as he stared at her in shocked silence, as if waiting to make sure it was true. He darted his gaze to Mason, who had an expectant but possibly nerve-filled half smile on his handsome face.

Mason nodded once. "It's true, Calvin. I'm your dad."

An exuberant, nervous laugh burst out of Calvin, and Blitz sat up at attention. Calvin popped up and did another donkey kick, then sent a quick look to Eliza for confirmation. Smile pasted on her face, she nodded, and then Calvin walked up to Mason, nearly at eye level with him, grinning from ear to ear but obviously unsure what to do next.

"Come here," Mason said, arms out, and that's all it took. Calvin threw himself into his dad's arms, giggling like a banshee.

Eliza took in the scene as Mason closed his eyes, holding his son to him, breathing him in, Calvin's little arms wrapping around his neck, and damn if her eyes didn't fill with tears. Her heart felt like it would burst out of her chest. A ribbon of insecurity was there too, wrapping itself around her gut, but she ignored it for now, doing what a mom did—soaking in her son's undiluted joy.

And Mason's.

She couldn't deny that witnessing his gratitude and love for their son in this moment *got* to her. It made her wish for things that might not be possible—the whole package. Not the marriage but the love, the true family, the two-way devotion.

A foolish part of her wished she and Calvin could grow to be the most important parts of Mason's life.

A more sensible part told her not to get her hopes up.

When Mason finally opened his eyes, they were glassy and full of emotion as he shot a smile her way. It was like another punch to the gut to see this strong, confident, over-capable man leveled by a little boy.

Calvin stood there, his face lit up with joy, staring at his dad, speechless for the first time in his life. Mason planted a kiss on his forehead, which made the boy laugh.

"I'm so happy to be your dad, C," Mason said, and then he put his large, protective hand on Calvin's little shoulder. "The way I see it, we've got a lot of time to make up for."

"Will you come to my preschool when I'm Star of the Week?"

That was the last thing Eliza had expected to come out of her son's mouth, and she fought to keep a neutral expression pasted on her face even as her heart cracked a little. Averting her eyes, she gave herself a silent talking-to, reminding herself to focus on the joy of the moment, not her own feelings.

"I'd love to," Mason said.

For all these years, Calvin had longed to have a daddy just like the other kids, and she'd longed for it for him. And now he had it.

No longer being Calvin's everything was a positive thing. It was just going to take some getting used to.

Mason must have read her thoughts, because he pulled Calvin in close and half whispered, "I bet your mom could use a hug too," in his ear.

Without hesitation, Calvin leaped toward her and threw his arms around her, laughing again. "I can't believe I have a daddy, Mama!"

His elation was contagious, and Eliza gladly let her self-doubts fall away so she could share this life-changing moment with her son. After a deep hug, she kissed his nose and smiled as she looked into his sparkling eyes. "I'm so happy that you're so happy, sweet boy."

Looking between his parents, Calvin said, with a crinkle of confusion on his forehead, "Do I still hafta call him Mr. Mason?"

Eliza met Mason's gaze. They hadn't thought to discuss this.

"What do you want to call me?" Mason asked.

This time, Calvin didn't even glance at his mom. "Daddy."

The emotion, the deep love that washed over Mason's face made it hard for Eliza to swallow, impossible to speak for a moment.

Apparently affected similarly, Mason nodded, then managed to say, "I'd love it if you call me Daddy."

Calvin laughed and said, "'Kay, Daddy."

Mason stood and lifted his son up over his head, eliciting a squeal from the boy, and then he hugged him close again, their arms around each other, Mason's eyes closing as he savored the moment. The image would be locked in Eliza's memory forever —the gorgeous man clinging to his little boy. *Their* little boy.

After the embrace, Mason shifted Calvin to one hip, smiling as broadly as she'd ever seen him, his eyes crinkling at the corners with the depth of it. "What should we do next, C?"

"Can we go to the dog park now?"

As if Blitz understood, he got to his feet and shook, then looked at his humans expectantly. He wore his leash, but it wasn't attached to anything at the moment, as he'd been content to nap until now. Eliza grabbed the end of it just in case.

"You think Blitz is ready to run free?" Mason asked.

"Yes!" Calvin squirmed to get down and then jumped up and down, which excited the dog more.

"Let's clean up our mess and then we'll go over there."

"Why don't you three go ahead?" Eliza said. "I'll clean up and give you some time together." And time for herself to process the past few minutes.

"What do you say, C? Are you up for our first daddy-son adventure?"

"And doggy!"

"And doggy." Mason winked at Eliza, looking, she would

swear to God, twice as hot with so much joy emanating from him. "We'll be back in a bit."

"Bye, Mama!" Calvin said as she handed Mason the end of the leash.

"Bye, sweet boy. Be good for Mr. Ma— for your daddy."

The dog park was on the far side of the private park, with a multitude of shrubs and a black metal fence around it, including a lower section where the vertical pickets were only a couple of inches apart, to keep the smallest dogs from escaping.

Eliza hugged her knees to her chest as she watched her heart walk toward it, with his daddy at his side, holding his hand, Blitz on Mason's other side. Though she couldn't make out what was said, she could tell Calvin was talking nonstop, and Mason was paying rapt attention to him, answering, discussing, fully engaging.

She slid her phone out of her pocket and captured the image of the three from behind, her eyes watering with affection.

Once they let themselves through the gate, Eliza collapsed to her back on the blanket, feeling one-hundred-percent wrung out. She stared up at the sky, which was clear and blue, though the sun was low in the sky and they'd need to head home soon.

Home. Back to Mason's, she meant. It was not their home, and she needed to remember that.

After lying there for several minutes, she sat up and repacked their leftover food and gathered their trash. By the time the three males made their way back to her, Calvin riding on Mason's shoulders, looking ever so pleased with himself, everything was cleaned, and she stood and folded the blanket, as it was starting to get dark.

Calvin was as exuberant as ever, and it crossed her mind that it would either be extra difficult to get him settled down tonight or he would crash in record time. Fingers crossed for crashing in record time, because it was all she could do to muster the energy to walk back through the park to the private entrance, across the street, and up to the top floor.

"How'd it go?" she asked when they reached her.

"Good!" Calvin answered. "Blitz ran super fast and so did I."

"They raced," Mason said, shooting her a look that told her Calvin crashing in record time was a good possibility. "Multiple times."

"I won the time that Blitz saw a rabbit and went the wrong way," Calvin said as Mason squatted down to let him climb off.

"Life lessons," Eliza said with a laugh. "Sometimes it's not about who's fastest but who stays on the path."

"Words of wisdom."

"Mama, did you know I have another gramma?" Calvin said. "And a whole bunch of uncles and some aunts!"

"I did know that." And yet she hadn't given them a ton of thought, so caught up on the Mason element of the North family. "Mason has a big family."

"And they're all dying to meet you," Mason said. "Both of you. I've been ordered to invite you to our weekly family dinner on Sunday."

"This Sunday?" Her mouth went dry at the thought.

"Can we please, Mama?"

The dry-mouth reaction, she realized, was on her own behalf. She was more worried about meeting Mason's whole family herself than she was where Calvin was concerned. For him, it meant that many more people to love him, support him, be in his life. For her, it was daunting, but…

She nodded. "We could do that. If you're sure—"

"I don't know how much longer I can hold my mother off from meeting her first grandson," he said, his voice teeming with affection.

His mom was the scariest one of all for Eliza to meet. What would she think of a girl who had a one-night stand with her son and didn't even try to get his contact info? It didn't paint Eliza in a great light.

"Sunday," she said, faking her courage, and Calvin cheered.

"Are you ready to go?" Mason said to Eliza.

She picked up the bag of trash and held it out to Calvin, having saved it for him to take to the nearest trash can, which was a hundred yards away. "Think you can take this over to the trash and throw it away?"

"By myself?" Calvin asked, his eyes big with the possibility of an important responsibility.

"Do you want me to go with you?" she asked.

"Nope!"

"We'll watch you the whole way," Mason said, still holding on to Blitz's leash.

Calvin took the bag and headed away from them in a careful, important walk.

Eliza and Mason stood side by side, watching him in silence for a few seconds, and then she felt Mason's hand on her back. He slid it to her other side, rested it at her waist, pulled her into his side for a moment. Her defenses were down, and his touch warmed her to a melting point inside. She managed to resist the urge to rest her head on his shoulder.

Calvin was about halfway to the trash can when Mason turned his head and said in a low, private voice, "Thank you, Eliza."

His tone, his intent, the whisper of air over her ear… The intimacy of the moment, of his sentiment made her shiver.

Her resistance crumbled further.

She had to clear her throat to get her voice to work. "You're welcome." She hesitated. "Thank you. For loving him. For making him happy."

He met her gaze then, and an almost tangible current of tension buzzed between them. As she peered into his arresting blue eyes, he stole her breath with his intensity…and, okay, his damn good looks.

This so wasn't a fair fight.

"Mama! Daddy! I did it!" Calvin's voice reached them from across the park, jolting them out of their moment. Mason dropped his hand from her side, and they turned their heads to watch their son race back at a sprint.

"He's going to pass out as soon as his head hits the pillow," Eliza said.

"Good going, C!" Mason called out to him, grinning. "You take the dog and I'll carry the kid," he said quietly to Eliza. He handed the leash to her, and she picked up the picnic bag.

As Calvin approached, Mason held his arms out, and their son leaped into them. When Calvin wrapped his arms around him in another hug, Mason shared a private look with Eliza, and then the four of them headed off toward the main gate.

Not a fair fight at all, she thought.

CHAPTER SIXTEEN

Mason had no proof, but he could swear Eliza had been avoiding him since the picnic three days ago.

He could admit to being insanely busy with work for those three days, as he'd been doing everything within his power to get the opening of the westside Nashville store moved up, so there was a chance Eliza's avoidance was in his head. But he didn't think so.

As much as it would help the bottom line to open the new store early, it didn't look like it was going to happen. Instead, they'd have to pin all their hope on the Colorado opening and the chain-wide promotions they'd added to the calendar to chip away at their financial goals.

But back to Eliza.

He'd barely seen her Friday, what with both of them working, her until after midnight. Saturday, after she'd gone to pick up Calvin at Lettie's, she, Grace, and Calvin had spent the day out of the condo, shopping, going to lunch, and running errands, she'd told him later.

Saturday evening, he and Eliza watched the Cardinals game with Calvin—complete with fan attire for all of them. Though their son had entertained himself with his train, Poopy the otter looking on, he'd peppered them with baseball questions and been glued to the screen for the "exciting parts," making Mason beam with pride. He couldn't wait to take him to his first in-person game.

Once they'd put their son to bed on the twin-sized mattress Mason had bought, he'd been hoping to spend time with Eliza alone. His cousin Logan, the IT director for NBS, had called to discuss an IT issue that couldn't wait till Monday, and though the call had been short, when he'd returned to the main floor, he'd found Eliza had closed herself in her room for the night with the lights out.

Hiding from him?

He couldn't help but think so.

It was confusing as fuck, because the one thing he didn't question was the chemistry between them. It'd been in their faces four-plus years ago, and it was still there now, every time they were in a room together.

If you went by the heat level of his dreams, it was there even when they weren't in a room together.

He'd never wanted a woman the way he wanted Eliza. He'd never met a woman who'd resisted him the way she did. He'd never felt so utterly powerless, and as someone who preferred to be in control of just about everything, he wasn't a fan of the situation.

She couldn't avoid him for the next few hours though. They were on their way to his mom's house, where everyone would meet his son. He was driving her car, back from the shop and starting fine, since his was a two-seater.

Eliza had been extra quiet since they'd gotten into the car, leaving Mason to respond to Calvin's excited chatter from the backseat.

When they pulled up to a stoplight at a corner with a fire station, every ounce of Calvin's attention was on the trucks in the bay, and he counted out how many there were, trucks and ambulances, then spotted a firefighter and enthusiastically searched for more. All of it made Mason smile.

He glanced toward Eliza to share a look, except she didn't seem to be paying attention, to him or their son. Her gaze was locked on the dash in front of her, and she was biting her lip, as if she was nervous.

After a glance in the rearview to ensure Calvin was still distracted by the station, Mason reached over and took her hand, which was resting on her lap. Her nails were painted a deep garnet, and she wore a single ring on her middle finger, a silver knot that formed a heart and a musical treble clef. Not for the first time, he was awed by the thought of how much talent rested in her long, slender fingers, and he caressed them with his thumb.

Eliza swung her head toward him, eyes questioning.

You okay? he mouthed to her.

She forced a smile and nodded.

"They're going to love you both," he said in a low voice.

Another smile and nod, but he could tell she didn't feel it.

He wasn't sure how else to convince her other than to let her find out for herself when she was welcomed into the family. She would be. He didn't have a single concern about it. Only about getting *her* to let *him* in, to accept *him*.

Minutes later, they pulled up to his mom's house. The driveway and curb in front were full with Gabe's Tesla, Drake's Jeep, Sierra's truck, Connor's Bimmer, and Aunt Liz's Lexus.

"Looks like the whole gang is here," he said as he pulled up in front of the Wilkensons' house next door. "If they beat me here, they must be excited." Especially Drake, although Mackenzie had made a big improvement on his punctuality record.

"Is this a party?" Calvin asked as Mason killed the engine.

"Kind of like a party," Mason said, again noting Eliza's silence.

Mason and Eliza got out, and by the time Mason came around the car, she had Calvin's door open. Calvin unbuckled himself and slid to the ground, then picked up his Thomas the Tank Engine backpack, where Eliza had packed his cars, books, and an engine with freight cars in case he needed something to entertain himself, being the only kid in the family. Mason had assured her he wouldn't need them, but it seemed both Calvin and Eliza felt better bringing it.

"Ready to meet your new grandma, uncles, and aunts?" Mason asked Calvin, who bounced as he nodded with exaggeration. To Eliza, Mason sent a questioning look that asked the same without words.

Eliza inhaled, making her chest rise and fall, and then she flashed him a smile that looked less fake, more courageous. Between her determination to face what she considered a tough moment and her gorgeous brown eyes and the kiss she bent down and pressed to the top of Calvin's head, Mason had a hard time keeping his hands off her, showing her how she made him feel.

He swallowed down all of that in order to focus on another giant moment in Calvin's life—and in Faye North's.

"Let's do this," Eliza said.

Calvin took each of their hands, and they walked down the sidewalk to the North home.

Before they reached the front door, it opened, and there stood his mom, bursting with joy, her eyes glued to Calvin.

"Hello, hello," Faye said as she eased the screen door open.

As the three of them went up the single step, Mason said, "Mom, meet your grandson. This is Calvin. Calvin, this is your grandma North."

Faye stepped onto the stoop. "Look at you, sweet boy." She crouched down and held her arms out and said, "Can I hug you?"

Calvin let go of Mason's and Eliza's hands and gave another exaggerated nod, his grin so big it could split his face. The only sign of nerves or shyness was that he didn't do his usual launch but walked into her arms at low speed. He wound his arms around her as Faye engulfed him in a hug.

Watching his mom as she squeezed her eyes shut, her love and acceptance so blatant, Mason felt his own emotions jam up in his throat. He'd anticipated this moment, but the reality of it was so much more powerful than he could've imagined.

Still watching his mom, who continued to hold on to Calvin,

he felt Eliza's fingers wrap around his, and he squeezed her hand as she sidled closer. When he looked down at her, he saw everything he was feeling reflected at him on her face.

Faye finally loosened the hug and held Calvin back enough to look him over again. "Look at you. I am overjoyed to meet you, Calvin."

"Hi, Gramma North."

As Faye stood, she swept Calvin up with her and Mason watched for any sign of too much strain. "What do you think about calling me Mimi?"

"Mimi!" Calvin said. He laughed and nodded and then pressed a kiss to her cheek, and there wasn't a doubt in Mason's head that his son had stolen his mom's heart in that very moment.

After another tight hug, Faye slid the boy down to the floor. "I have a bunch of other people who can't wait to meet you, but there's someone else I need to meet first. Do you want to introduce me to your mom?"

Calvin nodded importantly and pulled Faye toward Eliza and Mason. "This is my mama."

Eliza released Mason's hand as she became the center of attention. She smiled warmly, but Mason could see the nerves beneath the beautiful smile. Calvin stepped over to Mason and grabbed his hand. Mason did one better and hoisted him up.

"Eliza," Faye said, her voice full of emotion. "I'm so happy to meet you. Don't mind me. I'm a hugger." She wrapped Eliza in a motherly, love-filled hug, and Mason heard her whisper, "Thank you. He's a beautiful child."

As they parted, Eliza said, "It's wonderful to meet you, Mrs. North."

"Please call me Faye. Welcome to our family, my dear."

"Thank you…Faye. Thanks for having us."

"You're welcome here anytime. We do dinner every Sunday evening, and you and Calvin can come whether this one makes it or not." She squeezed Mason's arm.

Though Eliza remained somewhat stiff, Mason noted the moisture in the corners of her eyes.

It occurred to him he didn't know a lot about her family. She rarely talked about her parents, and he wanted to know more. He'd guess they weren't close, not like the Norths, so she wasn't sure how to take his affectionate, accepting mother.

"When was the last time I missed?" Mason said and then leaned forward and kissed his mom.

"Only when you're out of town," she acknowledged. She turned her attention to Calvin. "Are you ready to meet the rest of your family?"

Calvin nodded, and beside them, Mason noticed Eliza taking another fortifying breath.

With his son in his left arm, he reached out to Eliza with his right and wrapped it around her waist—to boost her confidence, sure, but even more, he was having a hell of time keeping his hands off her. Not only did he burn to touch her but, if he was honest, he needed to stake his claim and broadcast that she was his...or she would be.

AN HOUR AND A HALF LATER, Eliza sat with Cole's fiancée, Sierra, Drake's fiancée, Mackenzie, and Lexie and Gabe on the patio. She was surprisingly at ease, comfortable, and enjoying the evening.

Calvin, on the other hand, was having the absolute best time of his life.

The North family, as Mason had promised, had welcomed him, well, both of them with open arms, and she couldn't help liking every single one of them.

Mason's brothers were loud and lovable, and Eliza's respect for Faye had skyrocketed upon meeting them. Even without their fifth—Zane was on deployment with the navy—it was clear they must've been a handful to raise, even with a husband for many of those years.

The guys had taken Calvin under their collective wing and had kept him entertained, welcoming him as if he were one of them—albeit a shorter, younger one of them.

Currently, Mason, Drake, their cousin Connor, and their aunt

Liz had Calvin enmeshed in a noisy game of bocce ball out on the expansive back lawn.

The rest of the group—Faye, Cole, cousin Miranda, and Geraldine, who was BFFs with Faye and Liz, were inside prepping dessert and after-dinner drinks.

Eliza had taken an instant liking to the women who were marrying into the family. She and Sierra had bonded over Sugar Babies Sweet Shop on Hale Street, of which, she'd learned, Sierra's sister was one of the owners. Eliza sometimes played in the Hale Street Recording Studio and knew the bakery—as well as the other businesses on the street—well. It turned out Sierra had lived on Hale until a few months ago, when she and Cole had purchased a hundred-year-old farmhouse and moved in together.

Eliza had a lot in common with Lexie, who'd recently gone into business for herself as a mural artist. They'd discussed the challenges and advantages of owning a creative-based business and planned to get together for lunch soon.

Mackenzie was also easy to like and had wild stories from her job as a high-end honeymoon planner. She was finishing up a tale of a couple who'd requested an outdoor space at their Caribbean resort so they could do daily yoga—naked—when Eliza noticed Mason stepping away from the bocce crowd to answer his phone.

"Gabe, take over for me with Calvin. I have to take this," he said as he beelined for the house and some quiet. "It's Logan. POS system update from hell."

Gabe jogged out to Calvin and picked him up. "What color's ours?" he asked the boy, who informed him they were the yellow team.

Eliza's gaze trailed after Mason as he went inside, and she couldn't help wondering when he ever got a full day off. *If* he ever got a full day off.

When she returned her attention to the women on the patio with her, Sierra was watching her and smiled knowingly, as if she'd busted Eliza pining for Mason.

To clarify, Eliza said, "He works seven days a week, huh?"

"For as long as I've known him," Sierra said. "Which admittedly isn't all that long, but he's one dedicated man."

"Maybe you'll be the one who changes that, gets him to focus on something besides work," Mackenzie said, raising her brows suggestively.

"I'm not sure anyone or anything could get him to do that," Eliza said.

"Eliza, you had his baby," Mackenzie said. "I'd say you're on your way."

"If anyone can, it's you," Sierra said.

Eliza knew from experience it wasn't that simple. "Does anyone else worry it's not good for him?"

"I've known Mason since he was a kid," Lexie said, "and honestly, he thrives on it."

"On work?" Eliza asked, and she couldn't help comparing him for the hundredth time to her dad.

Leaning forward in her Adirondack chair, Lexie said, "It's not work for work's sake. It's Mason's role in the family. He runs the family business. He's ultra-conscious that it's his dad's and uncle's legacy and that they created it to provide for all the Norths."

Sierra nodded. "I think taking care of the business is how he takes care of his family, and he feels that responsibility deeply, being the oldest and with a father who died young."

"They're a tight-knit group," Eliza said, filing away everything to pick apart later.

She could see it now that they said it—Mason was a typical first-born overachiever—she had some of that herself as an only child—but maybe what drove him was different from her dad. If what these women said was true, North Brothers Sports was a labor of love, and maybe a bit of an obligation he'd never asked for. Not an addiction or an escape.

"The Norths are super close," Mackenzie said. "Being welcomed into this family is kind of incredible, to be honest."

"Which you are," Sierra said. "Welcomed."

"Speaking of which, you need to come to our wedding!" Mackenzie said, her eyes sparkling with excitement.

"Oh," Eliza said, surprised, then reeling her excitement in. "I don't want to mess up your guest counts at this late date."

There'd been wedding talk since she'd arrived, what with Gabe and Lexie married for a month and two other engaged couples—Sierra and Cole, who were planning a January wedding, and Lexie and Gabe, whose nuptials were in just a couple of weeks.

Lexie laughed. "Family's first with the Norths, and an extra guest doesn't make them blink financially."

"That's the truth," Sierra said, then took a sip of her wine. "You definitely don't want to miss this one."

"It's really soon, though, right?" Eliza asked.

"Two and a half weeks," Mackenzie said, then laughed. "Not that I'm counting or anything."

Eliza's mind went to her calendar as it always did, sifting through what needed to be juggled. "I'll have to see if my roommate can stay with Calvin."

"You can bring him," Mackenzie said. "It's going to be pretty laid-back."

Mason came back out the door onto the patio, looking sidetracked as he slid his phone into the pocket of his khakis.

"Hey, Mace, we got you a date," Lexie said, grinning up at him.

"Huh?"

"A plus-one for my wedding," Mackenzie said, the sparkle in her eyes turning a little teasing.

Eliza's gut tensed with nerves as they put their brother-in-law on the spot. She watched for him to stiffen or frown as what they were telling him sank in.

But he didn't. When he caught on, he looked down at Eliza, and a smile eased across his face, replacing the worry from his phone call. "You're going with me?"

"I might if you ask me," she said, hearing the flirtation in her own voice.

He pulled up another chair and sat next to her, and she caught a hint of his masculine scent, found herself breathing in deeper, hoping for another hit.

"Go with me to Drake and Mackenzie's wedding," he said.

Sierra laughed. "She said ask, not tell."

"I don't know about this sister thing," Mason muttered lightly. Making a show of it now, he took Eliza's hand between both of his. "Eliza, would you do me the honor of accompanying me to Drake and Mackenzie's wedding?"

Laughing, she said, "I will. They said Calvin could come?"

"Hell yeah," Mason said. "We're not leaving him home while we fly off to Malta."

She snapped the smile off her face. "Wait. What?"

As her heart raced with…nerves? Shock? Concern?…Mason eyed the three other women, his brow raised as if he suspected wicked intentions.

"You didn't tell her the details?" he asked them.

"We hadn't gotten there yet," Mackenzie said. "We're having a destination wedding in Malta," she said to Eliza. "Followed by a three-day Mediterranean tour on a private yacht for everyone."

"Malta," Eliza repeated, reeling. "I'm embarrassed to say I'm not even sure where Malta is, but it sounds far away and expensive and like too much trouble to put you to—"

"Really, it's not." Mackenzie had gone serious. "We'd love to have you there."

"It's not," Mason confirmed. "It's south of Italy in the Mediterranean."

"Wow." Eliza couldn't fathom how one paid for a wedding here in the States, never mind something so exotic and far away. "I'm not sure how that would be for Calvin…"

Mason squeezed her hand gently and explained, "We're taking the company jet. There's a bedroom if he needs one and plenty of room for him to be up and around. Not like a commercial flight where he'd be strapped in a seat for hours."

"We don't have passports—"

"I'll get you both expedited ones," Mason said.

The back door opened again, and Cole and Miranda emerged, carrying various drinks to pass around, followed by Faye, who had a large tray, and Geraldine, toting paper plates and napkins.

"We'll all help you keep an eye on him once there," Sierra said, "and he'll love the ship!"

"Can I think it over?" Eliza asked. That her son would lose his mind over a private yacht was unquestionable but...a private yacht?

"Of course," Mackenzie said. "However long it takes you to get to yes."

"What's this?" Geraldine asked as drinks were delivered and the bocce group headed toward the patio for a break.

"We invited Eliza to our wedding," Mackenzie said. "She's worried about Calvin."

Among other things, Eliza thought. *So many other things.*

"Oh, heavens yes," Faye said. "Bring my boy. Please," she hurriedly added. "Between all of us, he'll never be bored."

"What's that, Mimi?" Calvin asked as he came up between Eliza's and Mason's chairs. He said it as if he'd been calling this kind, loving woman Mimi since he'd learned to talk. No hesitation whatsoever.

"This is a very special treat," Faye told him. "Baked just for you and your mama."

Mason dragged an end table in the middle of all the chairs.

Calvin's eyes were huge as she set the tray on the little table. He climbed up on Eliza's lap. "What's it say, Mama?"

Once Calvin settled on one leg, Eliza could see the tray full of two dozen cupcakes. Each one had a single blue handwritten letter on top of thick white frosting. "Welcome, Calvin and Eliza," she read, then pressed her lips together.

She did feel welcome. Like they considered her a part of the family, even though she technically wasn't.

Calvin hopped down, because what three-year-old could sit still when there were cupcakes?

Eliza had to work hard to keep her eyes from tearing up too much.

When Mason had told her today would be okay, she'd figured it was lip service. She'd been wrong.

His family, it turned out, was kind of incredible, the men protectors who, she sensed, would do anything to keep her son safe and happy, the women beautiful souls who could become true friends.

And maybe they would, but she was getting way ahead of herself. Because while this was technically Calvin's family, it wasn't hers. Wouldn't be hers unless some miracle worked out between her and Mason someday. And as much as she was attracted to him, she still had reservations. They were still becoming acquainted, and to plan for more would be setting herself up for a big fall.

"Thank you for welcoming us, Faye. All of you," she said, glancing around at the whole group, who'd gathered around them. "It means the world to us, right, Calvin?"

"Right! Let's eat cupcakes!"

Everyone laughed and voiced their agreement, as Eliza put Malta and the wedding out of her mind.

Later, she'd have to weigh the pros and cons of a trip to the Mediterranean with a man she could very easily fall for. A man who might never fully be able to put a wife and family first, before his incredibly demanding job.

Even understanding more about what drove him, she wasn't sure she could put her son or herself in that position and feel okay about it.

CHAPTER SEVENTEEN

It was getting harder and harder for Mason to keep his hands off Eliza.

Not surprising, considering she was a beautiful woman and living under his roof.

What did surprise him, though, was this ongoing desire to spend time with her, talk to her, get to know her better. Even when he should be working.

Like now.

After they'd come home from his mom's and put Calvin to bed—who'd fallen asleep, with Blitz at the foot of his mattress, before they'd finished reading a story—Mason had come up to his second-story office to check in with Logan, his cousin and the IT director, one last time. After two days of fighting with the point-of-sale system, they had a plan to fix the problem overnight, hopefully before the East Coast stores opened tomorrow. Mason had some unpleasant email follow-up to do with the hardware company.

However, his office door was open, and he could hear Eliza in the kitchen. And they had unfinished business regarding a trip halfway around the world.

He could tell by the clink of a mug and the beep of the microwave that she was making tea, and he would bet she was digging into her stash of chocolate cream-filled cupcakes, which she kept hidden from Calvin. Knowing her habit of carrying her phone everywhere, he pulled his out and typed a message to her.

Got any tea to help a guy sleep?

Tea and sleep were only a small part of what he really wanted, needed, but they were a starting point.

I do, she messaged back. *Do you know a guy who wants to sleep?*

A sorry-ass sleep-deprived sucker up here in the office.

I can bring the sorry-ass sleep-deprived sucker some chamomile.

Thank you, gracious sleep fairy, he replied, then laughed to himself at the misnomer.

If anything, thoughts of her kept him up half the night, pun intended.

Mason stood and wandered to the window. He leaned against the wall to the side of it and gazed out, not really seeing anything because his body was on full alert, waiting for Eliza. The grandfather clock along the wall—the one item he'd taken from his dad's home office after his death—chimed the bottom-of-the-hour melody, then went back to its soothing ticking.

He felt anything but soothed though.

When she appeared a few minutes later in the doorway of his office, he looked her way and took a moment to collect his wits.

She wore a hoodie, unzipped, over a tank and sleep shorts, feet bare, hair in a single braid, and her legs stretching out for miles from those tiny shorts. He was pretty sure she wasn't wearing a bra but fought not to peer at her chest to confirm that.

"Hi," he said, then cleared his throat because the gravel that came out was not his usual voice.

"Hi." With a shy smile, she held up a mug with a tea bag hanging over the side as she entered the room.

Pushing away from the wall, he met her at his desk and moved the empty coaster where she could easily set the mug down.

"Thank you. So that's guaranteed to work?" he asked her lightly.

Eliza laughed quietly. "You would have to stop working for that. Do you ever stop working?"

Grinning, he averted his gaze to his feet, suspecting the question was rhetorical. "I'm beginning to think it's in part a bad habit." That topic wasn't going to get them anywhere, so he changed the subject. "Did you have fun tonight?"

"I did. Your family is"—she stepped to the window and took in the nighttime view—"very different from mine."

From where he stood, he could see her frown for a second and then pull her thoughts away from whatever caused it.

"I really like them. Every single one of them," she said. "Your mom is incredible. She was so awesome with Calvin. You heard him going on and on about Mimi practically until his eyes closed."

Mason sidled up next to her, gazing out the window but his other senses tuned in fully to her. "My mom is special. The kind of person who rules the roost with an iron fist but couches it in so much love that you don't really notice."

"She seems like a strong woman."

"She had to be when my dad died and she became a single mom of three teenage boys at home, plus Gabe and me."

"I can't even imagine."

Mason studied her profile in the warm, dim light of his desk lamp. Her lashes were long, her nose delicate, her lips tempting. Multiple strands of her dark hair had come out of her braid and fell over her cheek.

Unable to help himself, he reached out and brushed her hair back with one gentle finger, craving so much more than that barely there touch.

"It didn't escape my notice that you never gave a definitive answer about Drake's wedding," he said.

Eliza turned toward him, her arresting brown eyes meeting his. She inhaled deeply, and again, he had to fight not to watch her chest rise with the breath. "I don't know. There's a lot to consider, first and foremost, Calvin. That's a long trip. I'd have to take him out of school…"

"Think how much he'll see and learn visiting Malta. A few days off from the ABCs would be worth it, wouldn't it?"

"I'm not sure how I can make it work with my schedule

either. I committed to work on Steele Hearts' next album in October, but I don't know the dates yet."

"We'll be gone for a week," Mason said, trying not to think too hard about that, reassuring himself he would be able to check in with NBS from anywhere—even the ship. He'd checked.

"I'll ask the producer." She bit her lip in thought. "I don't want to back out. I've spent all these years building up a rep for reliability, and the Steele Hearts guys are a dream to work with. Plus, money…"

"You won't have to pay for anything."

She stiffened.

"Eliza, I admire your independence. We've already gone over that. But you can't believe I would invite you on a trip out of the country as my date and let you pay for anything."

"Did you invite me as your date?" she asked, and her expression was genuinely insecure. "Because technically Mackenzie was the one who asked me."

Mason took both her hands in his. "I'm asking you as my date. Not as the mother of my son but as the woman I want to spend more time with. I want you and Calvin by my side on that beach, watching my brother exchange vows with the love of his life. And any other objections you come up with, I'll do whatever it takes to get rid of them. Work, school, passports, money, time, fear of foreign countries—"

She laughed. "What? I don't have that."

"Then say yes."

Without waiting for her to say anything else, he tugged her closer, his blood pounding through him, and kissed her. Reining himself way in, he kept it gentle, light, and brief, because he did want her to give him an answer. The answer he wanted. He peered down at her, waiting.

"What?" she whispered.

"Waiting for a yes." Her heavy-lidded eyes were full of desire at this moment and killing him. "Please?"

"Yes."

He let out a breath of relief that he wouldn't have to mount a days-long campaign to convince her, then pulled her fully into him, kissed her again.

Not gentle this time.

Not rough but definitely fervent, overeager, the result of spending hours with her this evening and not being able to touch her as he wanted, to hold her, to kiss her if he was so moved, which he had been repeatedly. Not on guard with his family's eyes on them. Not worried about whether Calvin would see and misinterpret, although at this point, Mason suspected it wouldn't really be a misinterpretation.

Her hands went to his chest, then eased around his neck. As the kiss deepened, she pulled his head to hers, as if she didn't want it to end quickly this time.

He had no plans to end it quickly.

Easing his hands beneath her tank, he reveled at the contact with the soft, warm skin of her sides, her slender back. He caressed his fingers over her hip, where he remembered she had a sexy tattoo that was like a twisting, tantalizing, teasing trail from her hip bone toward her center. One day soon he swore he'd lay eyes on it again, have her stretched out, naked, on his bed like a feast for all his senses.

He'd been right about no bra, and he caressed up and down her back, trying to get his fill of touching her as he devoured her mouth the way he wanted to devour the rest of her.

He trailed his hands lower, slipped them beneath the waistband of her shorts, and cupped her ass in his hands. It was rounded and soft and fucking perfect, and he couldn't get enough of it. Pulling her hips into him, he pressed his rock-hard dick into her softness, relishing the little moan that escaped her, determined to draw more from her.

He couldn't get close enough to her, couldn't get enough of her flesh, her kiss, her body. Turning them slightly so her back was against the window, he burrowed his body into hers from their thighs up to their mouths.

With her hips wedged between him and the window, he continued his exploration of her gorgeous body, trailing his hands up her sides and to her lush, sumptuous tits, a little more than a handful. He longed to see them again, remembered the brownish-rose tint of the tips as if it was yesterday. They were hard pebbles for him to play with, fondle, pinch, caress, and she responded to all of it with her hands on his ass now.

When her fingers found their way under his khakis and boxer briefs, he paused for a moment to gather his control and keep from stripping her down and plunging into her here and now, standing up, against the window. His instincts said he needed to slow the hell down.

As he continued to ravage her mouth, he plucked at one nipple with one hand and dropped the other to her belly, lower, dipping under her shorts. He found the wet, silky heart of her and slipped his finger inside, groaning at the heavenly feel of her tight, welcoming sheath.

Eliza arched her body into him as she threw her head back against the glass, breaking the kiss and letting out a sexy, needful gasp.

He pumped one finger in and out of her, then two, his thumb playing with her hard little nub. He pulled his head back enough to watch her beautiful face, her eyes closed, her mouth open as she came apart.

Afterwards, she didn't move beyond the rising and falling of her chest for several heartbeats, then she grasped his upper arms as if she couldn't support her own weight, and then, slowly, she opened her eyes, met his.

For a full second, they gazed into each other's eyes, and time stopped, as if the connection went beyond the physical, and then Eliza lowered hers, as if it was too much, too intimate. He actually felt the connection sever as she mentally retreated.

As much as he didn't want to, he released her body, put a couple of inches between them, because he sensed that was what she needed.

She proved him right when she said, "I'm sorry. I shouldn't have let that go so far—"

"No need to apologize." His voice came out a low, needy growl.

"It's just... Calvin's downstairs. I can't... I don't want to mislead you."

"Eliza." He found one of her hands and pulled her close again, pressed a kiss to her forehead, then wrapped his arms around her, trying to reassure her. "It's okay if you're not ready for more."

It took a couple of seconds, but finally he felt her hands on his back as she returned the hug.

"I don't know how most of your dates work," she said into his chest, "but Calvin and I will need our own room."

Mason chuckled quietly. "I haven't been on a date for so long that I don't know how most them work either. But you and C will have your own room."

And he would hold out hope that she'd choose to come to his.

CHAPTER EIGHTEEN

Friday night, Eliza left the bar within ten minutes of her gig ending—record time for her, but then that's what a mom sometimes had to do—and rushed home. Well, to Mason's.

Mason had again offered to stay with Calvin tonight, which had surprised her, because all week, he'd reverted to working late, missing dinner with his son, and barely managing to Face-Time at Calvin's bedtime in order to tell him good night. But he *had* made a point of checking in every single night. So this time, Eliza had agreed. She knew Mason had his hands full and wasn't used to having a three-year-old at home. She believed he wanted to spend more time with their son, and the knowledge that Faye was at home tonight, available with a quick phone call if Mason had any problems, had sealed the deal.

Still, she'd worried all evening, playing her fiddle with her mind half on the music and half on Calvin and Mason.

The elevator in the condo building seemed to take forever to get to the top floor. Finally, it let her out, and she hurried down the hall to Mason's door. When she let herself in, she froze for a moment and took in the scene.

The kitchen was a disaster, with dirty dishes stacked next to the sink, an empty microwave-popcorn bag sitting on the counter with unpopped kernels scattered around it, a smear of goop near the stove, and a dirty pan crusted with the remains of what looked to be mac and cheese still on the burners.

Two of the stools at the island were askew instead of their usual neatly lined up and tucked underneath, and the counter needed a good scrubbing.

A glance toward the living room showed the train set had been picked up and stashed in the toy box Mason had bought, but there were cars out on top of it, and the kids' books they normally stacked neatly on top were strewn everywhere.

When she stepped closer, she noticed Mason lying on the couch, sound asleep. From here, she could see his hair was sticking up, and an orange stain was smeared on the sleeve of his T-shirt. The biceps that bulged out below that sleeve didn't escape her notice either—a result of his crack-of-dawn visits to the fitness center on the third floor, she'd learned.

Eliza covered her mouth with her hand to hide her astonishment at the full scene. Astonishment and amusement. It appeared maybe there was something that wasn't quite so easy for Mason after all.

Attempting to be silent, she hurried over to her closed bedroom door to check on Calvin and Blitz. She eased the closet door open to her son's "room" and could see, by the night-light, he was sound asleep, with Blitz in his usual place at the boy's feet. The dog raised his head to acknowledge Eliza but then put it down and went back to sleep.

All was well with her son, and she backed out of the room, closed the door again, and breathed out fully for the first time since she'd left him.

In her dark bedroom, she took off her boots, then went back out to see if Mason had woken up.

He hadn't stirred, and she stared down at him, thinking he was handsome and sexy on a good day, but mess up his hair and show this imperfect side of him and he was downright irresistible.

The lamp on the end table was on, so she stepped to it and clicked it off, leaving just the pendant lights over the kitchen island to illuminate the space. As soon as the lamp went off,

Mason's eyes popped open, and he raised his head slightly until he saw her standing there near his head.

"Hey, sleepyhead," she said in a hushed voice, grinning. "Calvin must've worn you out."

Mason reached out and took her hand and tugged her down to the couch. She didn't fight it, because had she mentioned irresistible?

Her butt landed next to his hips, and he kept a light hold on her hand.

"What time is it?" Mason asked.

"Quarter till eleven."

"I meant to clean everything up before you got home." Embarrassment reflected from his face.

This was new. This hint of vulnerability from Mason North, CEO, family leader, and general bossy-pants... It was sort of adorable.

After another glance at the mac and cheese stain on his sleeve, she leaned down and kissed him. A sexy growl rumbled out of his throat, and she felt his fingers burrow into her hair, which she'd worn down tonight. Within seconds, their tongues were tangling, breaths mingling, heat ramping up.

As much as she wanted to climb on top of him and ride him, she was hyperaware of the bedroom door, where their son slept, not twenty feet away.

Reluctantly, she ended the kiss, pulled her head back a few inches so she could gaze into his sleepy but lust-filled eyes, and smiled at him. "Thank you for taking care of Calvin."

"Did you check on him?"

"He's sound asleep. So is Blitz. They appear to have fared a lot better than the condo."

She noticed his laptop, open but the screen black, on the floor near his head, along with a yellow legal pad where he'd scribbled some notes.

Mason's gaze followed hers. "I guess he did wear me out," he said with a sheepish grin.

"Sounds about right. I'm glad to know you're human after all." She stood to put distance between them, because her blood was pounding through her, and a painful throb had started deep at the core of her, just from that kiss.

Feeling shaky, she picked up the Hot Wheels cars from the floor and took them to the toy box, then straightened the stack of books. She heard Mason sit up behind her and felt his eyes on her body as she tidied up the room.

"I'm going to have some tea. Can I make you some?" she offered.

Since Sunday, it'd become a bit of a ritual, at least on the nights when he came home from work before she went to bed. The chamomile, he claimed, had made him sleep hard, so she offered each time she made herself some.

"Please," Mason said, standing. "I'm going to take this stuff up to my office, and then I'll clean the kitchen."

With his laptop and notebook in hand, he climbed the stairs as Eliza filled two mugs with water and stuck one in the microwave. She filled the dirty pan with water to soak, threw away the popcorn bag, then scrubbed the counter clean and righted the stools, all before the first mug was done. By the time the second one dinged, she'd loaded the dishes in the dishwasher and the kitchen was clean, but Mason hadn't returned yet. He'd probably gotten pulled back into his work.

She shook her head, thinking yet again how she wished he could work less, for his sake, and wondered if a little distraction would do the job.

All week, he'd been affectionate and caring but careful not to start anything beyond a lingering kiss, as if respecting her wishes after the scene in his office on Sunday, when he'd made her come so hard she could barely walk back down to her room.

She appreciated that respect, and at the same time, she was dying for another taste of him. At night, she literally ached for him, alone in her bed, able to hear his footsteps on the floor above, picturing him as he moved about in his bedroom, wondering if he might sleep naked.

Maybe tonight offered the opportunity for a little payback of the best kind.

With one more glance toward her bedroom door, she made

her way up the stairs, his tea in hand and a plan taking shape in her mind.

Sure enough, she found him in his office, sitting in his big leather desk chair, his phone pressed to his ear, apparently listening to a voicemail. He looked rumpled and still a little sleepy and not so clean-cut, his five-o'clock shadow more like a midnight shadow. She longed to feel that scruff against her skin. Her fingers itched with the need to mess his hair up even more. She closed the door behind her and walked over to him.

As he continued to listen to a male voice on his phone, Eliza set his mug on his desk, then leaned over him, cupped the back of his head, and kissed him unrelentingly.

Mason's phone fell to the floor as one of his hands burrowed into her hair and the other found its way beneath her shirt to the bare skin at her waist. The voice on the other end continued to ramble on, and she had the vague thought that it was lucky his office was carpeted. And then she had the less vague thought that this kiss would be worth losing a phone over as he came alive and plunged his tongue into her mouth and pulled her body closer.

Eliza climbed onto him in a straddle, her short skirt inching up her thighs. She slid her hands beneath the hem of his tee, trailed them up to his chest, loving the firmness of his abs, the definition of his pecs, the heat of his flesh. With a sweep of her shaking hands, she lifted his shirt, sat up momentarily to remove it from him, tossed it to the floor next to his phone, which had gone silent.

His chest… God, she loved his chest. She took a moment to drink in the perfection of it with her eyes, then lavished it with attention, caressing it with her fingers, trailing kisses over it, teasing one of his nipples with her tongue.

Mason let out a slow, needful moan and settled farther back into his chair, shifting to give her full access to him, and she couldn't think of a greater gift.

For the next several minutes, she continued teasing him with her tongue and fingers, inching downward, gently removing his hands when he tried to take her shirt off, telling him it was his turn tonight.

When she eased her hand under the waistband of his athletic pants, he said, "Let me take you to my bedroom, Eliza, and make you feel amazing."

Following the trail of hair from his bellybutton down with her mouth, she groaned, because a part of her wanted nothing more than to spend the night in his arms, in his bed, in wild abandon. But there would be no *abandon* with a three-year-old downstairs, at least not for her, not all the way. And Mason deserved, they *both* deserved for it to be one hundred percent when and if they got that far again.

"As much as that tempts me," she said, her voice lower than normal, heavy with desire, "I can't. But I want to make you feel amazing the way you did to me a few nights ago."

There was a little bit of payback involved, for sure, because every night since then, she'd regretted not giving him the same pleasure he'd given her, but even more, this was one part *thank you for staying with our son* and two parts *I burn with the need to touch you, make you lose it.*

When he stared down at her without arguing, she pulled his cock out of his pants and ran her tongue over the tip. Mason dropped his head backward and gave up the campaign for the bedroom with another deep, gravelly groan.

She took him into her mouth, breathing in the musk of him, tasting the saltiness of his masculinity. It didn't take long to get him worked up, and she smiled to herself, feeling her power in this moment as this take-charge, in-control man handed everything over to her and let himself go.

As she worked her mouth over him, she felt his grip on her hair tightening, heard his breathing go shallow, quicken. She took him in deeper, worked her hand in concert with her lips, driving him higher and higher, until finally, he stiffened, arched into her, and ground out a raw, earthy "Fuuuck."

Several seconds passed as he caught his breath and she continued to press kisses to his abdomen, swirling her tongue over his navel, slowly making her way to his chest.

Eventually, Mason raised her so their lips met and kissed her, slowly, sensually, thoroughly. She felt his fingers between her legs, under her skirt, pushing beneath her underwear until he found the spot that pounded for him. He teased it way too briefly, then dipped his finger into her, discovering how ready for him her body was.

Eliza gasped and squirmed as he strummed her body like a maestro, and in a blink, she felt herself climbing toward release, begging him, grinding against his fingers until ecstasy finally overtook her, and she bit his shoulder to keep from screaming loudly enough to wake her son…and the rest of the building.

As she came down from the best orgasm of her life, she sank into his body, boneless, spent, sated to her very soul.

Mason shifted, cradling her onto his lap, making her feel safe, protected, and beyond content.

As the room filled with the ticking of the grandfather clock, her breathing slowed to match it, and she searched herself for any kernel of regret, but she didn't find any.

Maybe this, getting physical again, was a mistake, but she was beginning to believe it was an inevitable mistake and something that was going to happen whether she fought it or not.

CHAPTER NINETEEN

The setting of Drake and Mackenzie's wedding was stunning.

Eliza took it in as she and the others on the short guest list took their seats on the beach.

A simple arch served as the altar on the sand, only a few feet from the calm waters of the Mediterranean. The arch was a thing of beauty, woven of long, graceful pieces of driftwood. A delicate white gauzy material draped and flowed from it, and the focal point was the large arrangement at the top left corner made of white and light blue flowers, a beautiful assortment of greenery that ranged from sage-green to deep forest, and three elegant white starfishes as accents.

The sky behind it was an explosion of oranges, pinks, and lavenders as the sun was minutes from dropping below the horizon. The timing of the wedding had been intentional, centering around sunset, but the sensational display Mother Nature was putting on was pure luck. It was as if the universe was sending Mackenzie and Drake its blessings for a long and happy marriage. After spending time with both of them the past three days, Eliza believed they deserved it.

To light the area once the sun went down, simple driftwood tiki torches were planted in the sand, spreading out from both sides of the arch, and matching ones bordered the white-carpeted aisle that Mackenzie would walk down soon.

There were fourteen chairs set up for the gathering, and Eliza was in the second row, which consisted of Hayden Henry, who was a close friend of both the bride and Sierra, on her right, and Calvin and Mason on her left. There was an empty chair on the aisle in front of Hayden, and then Lexie sat with Gabe. The two rows on the other side of the aisle held the matronly trio—Faye, Liz, and Geraldine—as well as Cole and cousins Miranda, Logan, and Connor.

"Is there gonna be dolphins at this wedding?" Calvin asked. He was standing on his chair for now, his gaze locked on the sea, with Mason holding on to him.

"We'll have to watch and see," Mason said. "You never know when you'll see dolphins."

"Like on the boat ride." Calvin nodded knowingly, as if he was now a dolphin-sighting expert.

They'd gone on a boat cruise and visited multiple beaches and seen incredible rock formations and arches, taken in the aquarium, toured several historical sites, and Eliza had to admit, the things her son was being exposed to were so much better than a few extra days of the ABCs at preschool, as Mason had said.

Just the private jet alone had been an eye-opening experience, for Eliza as much as Calvin. She'd had no idea such capsules of luxury existed in the sky. She'd pinched herself several times, wondering how the heck it'd come about that she was in a private jet, flying to Malta, with one of the most down-to-earth, loving families she'd ever met.

Calvin had been a trooper and had loved the plane ride and the places they'd visited. Mason had bought him a cheap digital camera so he could capture it all to look at later. His photography skills left a lot to be desired, but his enthusiasm was priceless. Neither he nor Eliza would forget this trip anytime soon.

"Is that our boat, Daddy? Calvin asked of a small fishing boat some distance offshore.

Mason grinned and shook his head. "Ours is bigger. Much bigger. You won't believe how big it is."

Calvin kicked his legs in excitement.

"He is so adorable," Hayden said quietly, not for the first time this week, as she watched Calvin on dolphin alert with a grin. "He almost makes me want one of my own…if not for that pesky man part of the equation."

"There's always a downside," Eliza said, laughing.

She'd only met Hayden three days ago, when they'd arrived on the island, but it was impossible not to like her. She was Sierra's best friend of many years, and through Sierra, Hayden had become close to Mackenzie and Lexie as well.

Those three women, plus Mason's cousin Miranda, had embraced Eliza with a warmth she hadn't expected. They seemed to accept Calvin as one of their own, spending time with him and catering to his needs as the only child in the bunch.

Eliza had always gotten along well with most people on the surface, and back before Calvin, she'd had dozens, maybe hundreds, of contacts and acquaintances as she and Grace worked the Nashville music scene. But since Calvin had been born, Eliza had pulled back out of necessity. Part of that was due to the luck and opportunity of getting into studio work, so she didn't have to work the live music scene as she once had. Part of it was due to being a single mother with no time for a social life.

She hadn't made any true, lasting female friendships besides Grace in the years she'd lived in Nashville. But these women she'd met through Mason's family… She was quickly developing deeper ties.

Sierra was the practical one of them, the one who made sure things got done, probably in part because of her position as the maid of honor and Mackenzie's only attendant.

Mackenzie always, always had a smile on her face. Part of that could be because she was marrying the man of her dreams, coincidentally her brother Ezra's best friend, in minutes. But she seemed to love life anyway, and it was impossible not to like a person like that.

Lexie was the quiet one of the bunch, but there was a solid

confidence and a strength behind her quietness that Eliza admired. And her bond with her new husband, Gabe, was undeniable. Apparently they'd been friends since kindergarten, and she'd grown up with these rowdy North boys. Only recently had she and Gabe let their relationship go deeper, and they'd married in the mountains just over a month ago.

Miranda had flown in a couple of days later than Eliza and Mason, so she didn't know her as well, but she was funny and friendly and could obviously hold her own with her two brothers and five male cousins.

Hayden, Eliza knew, was both a businessperson and a creative person, something she had in common with both Eliza and Lexie. She was the owner of Henry Interiors, a home decor and interior decorating store on Hale Street that Eliza had admired from the window but never gone inside, knowing it was over her budget. Most of Eliza's furnishings were secondhand or discount-store sale items.

She couldn't help but like Hayden though. She had a wide independent streak and reminded Sierra and the others she didn't want or need a man—every time they pointed one out to her. It seemed to be a game, as Sierra, especially, but also Lexie tried to convince her there were upsides to romance. Eliza suspected Hayden had been hurt badly in the past.

The officiant walked past them down the aisle, seeming to come out of nowhere. It was an older gentleman who greeted their small party with smiles and nods and hellos.

"Who's that, Mama?"

"He's the man in charge of marrying Mackenzie and Drake," Eliza told him.

"Where's Mackenzie and Drake?"

Mason glanced at his watch and said, "They'll be here soon. It's almost time for the wedding to start. How about we see if we can read one of your books before they get here?"

Bless that man, Eliza thought as he dug through the bag of kid supplies they'd brought.

"The boat book!" Calvin said, climbing up onto his daddy's lap.

They were halfway through the board book when the string quartet set up to the left of the arch started playing. Not two minutes later, a golf cart from the resort pulled up carrying Drake and a man in a US Navy dress uniform—Drake's fraternal twin, Zane, Eliza realized. She hadn't met him yet, as he'd been scheduled to arrive today, on a short leave, in time to stand up as Drake's only attendant. The bride and groom had elected to go traditional and were making a point of not seeing each other today until the wedding, with the women in the party spending the day at the spa and the men golfing.

"Hell-oo, Mr. Military Guy," Hayden said under her breath at the same time she gripped Eliza's forearm.

Drake and Zane walked across the sand to stand next to the officiant, who Drake greeted and then introduced Zane to. Drake looked super handsome in a suit and bare feet, and Zane… In that uniform, he would turn heads in a crowd of thousands.

"Thank you, Jesus, for inventing dress uniforms," Hayden said so softly only Eliza could hear. And Lexie, apparently, whose shoulders shook with laughter as she turned and eyed Hayden.

Holding in her own laugh, Eliza leaned close to Hayden's ear and whispered, "I thought you didn't want a man."

Still watching the two at the altar, or more specifically, the one, Hayden leaned in and replied, "Not long-term. Short-term is up for debate." Then she frowned. "But not really, not with this small of a group. Awkward."

Eliza nodded and made eye contact with Mason, who she was pretty sure understood her exchange with Hayden, whether he'd heard their actual words or not. His grin was knowing, and he shook his head, then read the last page to Calvin.

Calvin hopped down to return the book to the bag just as another vehicle drove up and stopped with the passenger door perfectly centered at the end of the white-carpet aisle. It was a white Jeep with dark windows, so it was hard to see who was inside. On the door was painted *Bridal Brigade*, and Eliza knew it must be Mackenzie and Sierra.

"Is the wedding now, Daddy?" Calvin asked.

"Just about," Mason told him and patted his chair to get the boy to sit.

For nearly a minute, the Jeep sat there with no one getting out. Eliza could make out the driver, who looked to be a man from the resort, and she was pretty sure Sierra was riding shotgun, but the back seats were impossible to see.

Finally, the driver hopped out and came around to the front passenger door and opened it. Out stepped Sierra, looking gorgeous in a periwinkle gown that reached to the sand, the design simple and flowy and elegant. Her gaze went to her fiancé, Cole, first, and then she smiled at the group as a whole and started down the aisle at a measured pace and took her place to the side of the officiant.

In the next few seconds, the music changed to the processional, the guests were invited to stand, and the driver disappeared to the other side of the Jeep once again as everyone looked on. Mason lifted Calvin to his shoulders, his eyes big and expectant, and Eliza met Mason's gaze as he moved closer to her. He wore a charcoal suit that was made for him, literally, and Eliza had to force her eyes from him to the Jeep.

After two Jeep doors shut, the driver was back in the driver's seat. He eased the vehicle forward without shooting sand anywhere, and once it was out of the way, there stood Mackenzie and her brother, Ezra, who was giving her away.

Mackenzie's exquisite gown fluttered in the light breeze, looking iridescent in the dusky light. On her head was a floral crown, and on her face, a smile that could light up the entire beach resort behind them.

Eliza whipped her head around for the best part of the show —to see the look on Drake's face as he laid eyes on his bride for the first time.

Drake, the fun-loving, lighthearted, rarely serious brother, interrupted his wide smile to suck in a deep breath. His eyes went wide, and he blinked a few times, as if he was fighting off tears as he watched the beautiful woman approach him. As Mackenzie neared, Drake blew out his breath, and his handsome face broke back out into a shaky smile. He shook his head at his bride, as if to say, *You slay me*, and Eliza swallowed around a giant lump of emotion.

She hadn't realized it until this very moment, but *that* was exactly what she wanted. She wanted a man to look at her with his love and respect and adoration for her overflowing.

Discreetly wiping the corners of her eyes, she risked a glance at Mason, who peered down at her. She couldn't help but wonder if this man had it in him to give her what she needed.

———

THERE WAS no denying the love between Drake and Mackenzie, Mason thought. It was tangible. Pulsing between them as they turned to face each other to exchange vows. Maybe it was even filtering into the air and dispersing to everyone witnessing the moment, like some kind of magic elixir in the breeze. He felt it that strongly—something he couldn't quite describe, something he couldn't reason through. Something in the vicinity of his heart, and it had everything to do with the woman sitting next to him.

When they'd sat back down after the processional, Calvin had climbed on his lap, and Mason had shifted to the seat right next to Eliza and laced his fingers with hers, their hands resting on her thigh. Eliza's scent teased him, drifting to him on the breeze.

As Drake repeated his vows after the officiant, the words rang out for everyone in their intimate group to hear.

Though Mason wouldn't admit it if anyone asked him, for the second time in as many months, watching one of his brothers bind his life to the woman he loved had a profound effect on him.

He'd never been a sap at weddings, but with his brothers, his younger brothers, it was different. Drake was not only joining *his* life with Mackenzie's but was expanding their tight-knit family, giving the rest of them a sister, just as Gabe had. Someday, there would be kids added to the mix. Calvin would have cousins.

It drove home like never before that it was their generation's time to flourish, to love, to carry on the family name. Six months ago, Mason would've said let his siblings do that. Today...

He slid his gaze to Eliza as Mackenzie started her vows, softer yet still audible. Eliza's attention was glued to the bride and groom, allowing him to admire her unnoticed.

Her coral dress was simple but breathtaking, or rather, she was breathtaking in it. It had spaghetti straps and dipped low between her breasts, and he couldn't resist taking in her cleavage —again. The flowy fabric wrapped at her waist, and the two sides tapered down at an angle, revealing a whole lot of leg in the front, especially as she sat with her legs crossed. Like most of the other female guests, Eliza wore flip-flops—blinged-out ones—in deference to the sand. He wasn't normally one to think about a woman's feet, but an image came to him of massaging hers, rubbing her arches until she moaned, then working his way up her fantasy-inspiring long legs...

As Calvin shifted on Mason's lap, he dragged his thoughts back to a more PG level.

Mackenzie finished her vows, and there were several seconds of silence as they attained the rings from Zane. Eliza lifted her gaze to his for a moment, and he noticed the dampness in her eyes. Without thought, he lifted their entwined hands and pressed his lips to her knuckle.

"Did you kiss my mama?" Calvin said in his outdoor voice, and every last person—musicians and officiant included —laughed.

Mason rubbed Calvin's head with affection and leaned to his ear and whispered, "Shhh. But she looks pretty tonight, doesn't she?" He winked at the boy, who looked at his mama and nodded. "Our little secret?"

"Okay." Calvin's voice was closer to a whisper but still a fail, and their family laughed again but turned their attention back to the bride and groom.

Mason waited for Eliza to pull her hand away from his, but she didn't. Instead, she leaned her head on Mason's shoulder. His heart thundered as the significance of that, of the fact that he'd basically outed them in public and, worse, in front of Calvin and she'd gone with it instead of fought it, washed over him. Either the wedding had weakened Eliza or he was gaining ground.

For him, the wedding had clarified everything.

What he wanted from Eliza wasn't a marriage of convenience. He wanted the real thing, like Drake had found with Mackenzie, Gabe with Lexie, Cole with Sierra. He wanted a partner, a lover, a wife, a mother for his son, and a mother of more babies if she was open to it. He wanted a family to come home to, not just for the next couple of weeks but forever.

Mason tuned back in once the rings were exchanged and the officiant suggested they seal their vows with a kiss. Drake, in typical Drake style, kissed his bride wholeheartedly and then dipped her, eliciting a happy squeal from Mackenzie as he deepened the kiss and drew laughter and cheers of approval from the family.

When the bride and groom straightened, they were declared husband and wife. The family stood and cheered, then watched the couple walk down the short aisle, the collective joy palpable.

Calvin was in Mason's left arm, getting squirmy, so Mason let him slide down to the sand and took his hand instead. At the same time, still holding Eliza's hand with his right, he tugged her to him and their eyes met, hers full of the same happiness running through him—and then the connection between them went deeper for an instant, and the truth hit Mason.

He loved Eliza Bancroft. And he suspected she loved him too.

CHAPTER TWENTY

With her hand in Mason's and the blackness of the vast Mediterranean Sea at night out the windows of the luxury yacht, Eliza couldn't help wondering if this was really her life right now.

The elegance of the beach wedding and the luxury of the posh resort they'd stayed at for their first three nights in Malta were a drop in the bucket compared to the giant yacht they'd chartered. Her mind was blown, and that was an understatement.

The wedding reception was in the main *salon*—she was certain she'd never used that word before today except to mean where she got her hair done—where all the plush sectionals had been pushed to the outer walls to make room for mingling and dancing. Yes, pushed. There was plenty of room to move furniture around, and a gorgeous white baby grand piano sat at one end of the room.

Their party of seventeen—everyone who'd been at the wedding except for Zane, who couldn't take the full three days of the private yacht cruise and had to return to his base tomorrow—had come directly from the wedding to the ship, their luggage being handled by hotel personnel and placed in their cabins.

Though they were a small group as weddings went, the party was in typical North style—loud and celebratory and full of love. There was dancing and dinner and drinks, and although Eliza had been to several weddings in her time, she'd never been part of such a close, welcoming group. *Family*, she amended.

Calvin was on top of the world. His eyes when the hotel van had driven them up to the docking area had been as big as silver dollars, and his excited chatter had been nonstop. And then the "party"… He'd danced, he'd eaten half his weight in dinner and wedding cake, and he'd been about to collapse an hour ago when Faye, bless that dear woman, had insisted on taking Calvin to stay overnight in her cabin.

Eliza had put up a fight, not wanting to burden anyone with childcare, but Mason had sided with his mother and pointed out that Mimi was salivating to have her first grandkid sleepover—and on a ship, no less. So Eliza had relented and could admit, if only to herself, that her heart raced at the thought of spending more time with Mason. Grown-up time. Maybe, if she was lucky, some private grown-up time. Because being next to him today, even more than staying at his condo back home, made her craving for this man almost unbearable.

She and Mason joined everyone else lined up near the door that would take Drake and Mackenzie to the honeymoon suite. They all had mini bottles of bubbles, and they showered the newlyweds in suds as they made their exit, laughing and so beautifully, undeniably in love.

Once the bride and groom were gone, half the group gravitated to the bar in one corner, tended by one of the twenty-five crew members, and Gabe whisked a laughing Lexie to the makeshift dance floor and pulled her close even though it was a fast-tempo song that the DJ—another crew member—started.

"Surrounded by newlyweds," Mason muttered as he watched them, trying to act like it was offensive, but his smile overtook his face as he gazed down at Eliza. "Come with me."

She followed him blindly to the door at the other end, which led out to one of the decks and fresh air and relative quiet.

With his hand at the small of her back, he directed her to the railing at the bow. Grasping her hand, he tugged her to face him, instead of the sea, and before she could say a word, his lips were on hers, kissing her greedily as his hands trailed up the sides of her dress, the heat of them penetrating through the thin fabric.

"Hello there," she managed with a laugh when they came up for air.

Mason's reply was a growl low in his throat. "I've been dying to do that for hours."

"Yeah?"

The wind ruffled his hair onto his forehead, and she couldn't resist running her fingers through it as she went in for another taste of his lips. As he pressed his body into her, the ache deep inside of her intensified.

"So," he said between kisses, "it seems like, with Calvin in my mom's cabin, we have our choice of private rooms tonight. *If* we were to want a little more priv—"

"Yes," she said before he could finish. She might not have reconciled how to handle Calvin in the long-term equation, but she'd wrangle with that later. Right now, she needed this man all to herself, naked and all over her.

Without wasting a second, he grabbed her hand and led her to the middle of the ship and inside, toward the elevator, avoiding his family, she noticed and thanked God for, because she didn't want any more delay. They'd waited long enough.

Instead of waiting for the elevator, they took the stairs down a level to where most of the cabins were.

"Yours or mine?" Mason asked.

"Mine has two twins."

He led her to his door, let them in, and held her to his side as she took in the luxurious room. It was roomier than hers, with plenty of space on three sides of the queen-sized bed. The bedding looked thick and high-end, like a cloud you could sink into, with a pile of throw pillows. There was light wood paneling, plush carpet, and a small bathroom attached, with marble counters. A single lamp at the side of the bed was illuminated, casting a low, warm glow over the space.

And then Mason had her in his arms, and they could've been on an empty deck in a rainstorm and she wouldn't have cared.

He ran his hands hungrily up her sides, then around to the

zipper in the back. "Your dress…" he said between kisses, "you in this dress…beautiful. But it has to go." He pulled the zipper down and pushed the thin straps off her shoulders, and that's all it took for the whole thing to fall to the floor around the nude-colored heels she'd changed into once they'd boarded the ship.

Mason took a half step back and devoured her with his eyes. Her dress hadn't allowed for a bra, so she stood there in lace-trimmed cream-colored bikini-cut underwear and shoes and nothing else, her body on fire as he looked at her.

"Jesus, you're gorgeous, Eliza. Even better than I remembered," he said, pulling her into him, "and believe me, I spent more time than I want to admit remembering."

She had too, but she kept that to herself as she shoved his suit jacket off his shoulders impatiently, then began unbuttoning his shirt.

Their lips met again in a hot, lust-filled frenzy. As she finished with his shirt buttons, he dipped his hands into her underwear and palmed her butt, eliciting a moan from her, lighting her on fire in two seconds flat. It'd been that way the night Calvin was conceived, and it was that way now, all these years later, even though her body was different. He didn't seem to notice and made her not worry about it.

He peeled her underwear down her legs, and she stepped out of them, completely naked and aching.

As she undid his belt with shaking hands, then the button and zipper, he slid his fingers between her legs, and she gasped.

"So wet for me," he growled, and then he dipped a finger inside of her, and she clutched to his upper arms, still covered by his unbuttoned shirt.

He pumped his finger into her a few times, and Eliza let her head fall back, gave herself over to him, but then he stopped, and she nearly wept at the loss. Before she could protest, he whipped his shirt off and dropped it on the floor. His mouth returned to hers as he backed her toward the bed.

"Need to taste you," he said into her mouth as he eased her onto the mattress.

Before she could say *yes, please*, he went to his knees on the floor, between her legs, easing her a few inches back on the bed, running his hands all over her body. She arched into his touch as she reclined.

When she felt his hot breath at the core of her, she bit her lip with anticipation. Then he put his mouth to her, and she moaned low and long as she lost herself to him, to the bliss this man brought about with his tongue, his lips, his tenderness, his devotion to driving her over the edge.

She came apart in record time, contracting and trembling and clinging to him as the orgasm went on and she forgot how to breathe.

As if he knew exactly when the sensations became too much, he turned his head slightly and nipped her inner thigh, kissed it, then trailed nibbles and kisses up her body, over her abdomen, between her breasts, to her collarbone as she lay there with her heart pounding and her breath returning and her thoughts stuck on how talented his tongue was.

Before long, his full focus was on her breasts as he sucked one nipple into his mouth and fingered the other until...good God, she felt her body responding again, the tightness deep inside of her turning into a needy throb.

He kissed his way back down her belly, swirled his tongue around her core, nibbled a path down one of her thighs, her calf, to her feet, which she only now realized were still in her heels. As he worked to unfasten the tiny buckle at her ankle, his continued to lavish her with kisses, and then the shoe dropped to the floor and he moved to the other one, which momentarily followed.

Mason stood and took his pants and boxer briefs, shoes and socks off, then bent over her, pressed a kiss to her lips, and said, "Be right back."

He walked the three feet to the closet, and Eliza rose to her elbows and admired his strong, muscled body, her eyes getting caught up on his beautiful butt. A butt like that could inspire an entire symphony.

When he faced her again, he'd sheathed himself with a condom. She scooted farther up the bed, never taking her eyes from him, her body feeling hollow and achy and in need of him filling her.

As he climbed over her, he pressed a kiss to the inside of her knee. Just when she thought he might actually kill her with more slow attentiveness, he propped himself over her body, lining himself up with her opening, guiding his tip to it as he penetrated her with a gaze so intense she shivered.

His lips met hers at the moment when he pushed inside of her, filling her so perfectly she could weep. Her breath caught as he seated himself to the hilt and paused, as if letting her adjust to the beautiful invasion. As he gazed down at her, his pleasure and torture both shining in his eyes, she'd never felt so vulnerable, so connected to another human.

"Mason," she whispered.

He kissed her, slowly, thoroughly, making love to her mouth as he began to slide gently in and out of her. With each stroke, she felt herself climbing again, reaching. She locked her legs around him, deepening his thrusts, and gripped his butt cheeks in both her hands as if she could force him deeper.

Before long, his thrusts turned less gentle, more desperate, growing faster, harder, pushing her into the nest of pillows they hadn't bothered to move. Eliza clung to him as if her life depended on it, and quite honestly, it sort of did, because she needed the release that was thundering down on her more than she needed food or air.

"Eliza," he breathed into her ear. "All I've wanted… All I've needed…"

His words plunged her right over the edge she'd been dangling from, and he swore and stiffened into her at the same instant she cried out.

"Jesus," he said after a few seconds, after their bodies had gone limp, breathing heavily. "Incredible."

She nodded and smiled, still catching her breath. The same thing had happened the night they'd met, the mutual fulfillment, the orgasm at the same moment. She'd never experienced it with another man, couldn't imagine it would be possible with anyone but him because they were so physically in tune with each other.

His weight sank into hers, and she held him to her, loving the feel of so much man bearing down on her, still inside of her, surrounding her. Within seconds, he shifted to the side just enough that she could get a full breath, her heart still racing.

Slowly, she came back into her senses, noting the sheen of sweat that covered them both, the scent of Mason and sex in the air, the vibration of his growl as he leaned in to kiss her neck.

A couple of minutes ticked by, and then he said, "You good?" as he traced his fingers along her curves, up and down, as if he still couldn't keep his hands off her.

It took two tries to get her voice to work, and then she managed, "So good. You?"

His handsome face eased into a grin, and he laughed as he stared into her eyes. "Good doesn't do that justice."

She simply nodded, her brain not firing on all cylinders.

Mason propped himself on one elbow and kissed her, the urgency gone but the passion still evident in the slow, thorough sweep of his tongue. When he ended the kiss, he peered into her eyes, cradling her cheek in his palm. "I love you, Eliza."

Eliza felt lighter than air at the exact same time a hard knot tightened in her gut.

"I…" She swallowed. "I love you, Mason…"

He studied her for several seconds, not smiling, and his eyes narrowed. "It sounds like there's a but."

"There isn't…" She closed her eyes, trying to calm her fear. "Not exactly."

"You're scared."

She let out an unnatural laugh. "Scared. Yes." She'd been curled into him, but now she rolled flat to her back, gaining a little space to try to think straight. "I've been trying not to let my heart get involved."

"Why? I'm not going to hurt you, Eliza."

"I believe you won't mean to hurt me," she said in a voice barely over a whisper. She worked up her nerve to level with him. "But you're so devoted to your job, and I get why, and on the one hand, I admire that."

"And on the other hand?" he prompted.

"I need to go to the bathroom." While that was true, what she needed even more was a chance to think straight, to figure out how to explain without sounding like a selfish brat.

Mason looked less blissful, more concerned, but he said, "I'll be here."

Eliza closed herself into the small en suite and relieved herself quickly, too quickly, because she still didn't know how to explain her hesitancy to Mason. After washing up and wiping a smudge of mascara from the corner of her eye, she opened the door.

Mason had gotten rid of the condom and was stretched out on his back, still on top of the blankets, in all his glory, and the man had considerable glory. How could she not love him? For so many reasons, far beyond what he looked like.

She did love him. She'd admitted it to herself before, but only in the dead of night, when she was stuck alone with her thoughts…usually centering around him.

He watched her every step as she returned, still naked, to the bed, and she couldn't help feeling exposed.

"Can we get under the covers?" she asked.

He rose and peeled the blankets back, slid his large body under them, held them up for her to join him. She did so and automatically curled into his hard body again, craving contact in spite of her nerves.

"So you don't like how much I work," he stated rather than questioned.

"That's not it exactly."

"Why don't you tell me what it is exactly," he said, his voice a sexy, middle-of-the-night growl that had her pressing her body into him even more.

"It's just…my experience growing up with a dad who worked all the time…"

"You said he was a workaholic."

She nodded.

"And he died young?"

Another nod. "Forty-four. Heart attack. He worked seven days a week. Long hours every day. He spent more time at his office than at home, even when you counted sleeping hours."

"So you didn't see him much," Mason said, running his fingers gently through her hair, as if he knew how soothing it was.

"He missed things," Eliza said quietly. "Important days, once-in-a-lifetime moments. He missed my first high school concert when I was first chair violin. His missed most of my concerts, actually. He missed my graduation and more birthday parties than I can count. It…hurt. That's not what I want for Calvin."

Or myself.

Mason wove their fingers together and appeared to be thinking over what she said. "I'm sorry he hurt you. You deserved more from him." He kissed her forehead. "My dad…" He seemed to swallow down sadness as he shook his head. "Even as busy as he was, he was involved in all of our lives. That's the kind of dad I want to be. The kind of man I aspire to be. For you and Calvin."

She didn't meet his eyes, thinking about how late he'd worked almost every night in the weeks since she and Calvin had moved in.

Maybe this was different. They weren't married. He hadn't fully committed to them. In fact, the one time he'd brought up marrying her, she'd shut that idea down right away, giving him no reason to even pretend he was a family man.

"I haven't lived up to that at all, have I?" he said, rolling away from her, onto his back. He was pensive for a while, and Eliza kept quiet, because she didn't want to seem like the kind of woman who resented her partner's career. She didn't resent it. She respected the hell out of it…and him. It was just her baggage getting in the way, and if she could figure out how to get rid of it, she would.

She traced circles on his chest, admiring the muscles, the strength. "I…do love you." There was no debating it, and she didn't want him to doubt that, for whatever it was worth. "Just… that's why I'm scared. Which has nothing to do with tonight or this gorgeous ship we're on or this night we've been given as a gift." Even if it made her blush that Faye must know exactly how they were spending it.

As her fingers trailed down to his abdomen and lower, he snapped out of his thoughts and rolled toward her. "We shouldn't waste a second of it, should we?"

"We definitely shouldn't," she said as her physical need for him became an ache again. "Let's forget about jobs, put our son out of our mind, and—"

He pressed his lips to hers, cutting her off in the very best way, and pulled her on top of him, gliding the part of her that needed him most over his erection, the friction eliciting a purring sound from her like she'd never made before in her life. He reached to the little table, where he'd placed a pile of condoms when she'd been in the bathroom, and grabbed one, opened it, rolled it on. She sat up, straddling him, grabbed his cock, and slid it inside of her.

Mason let out a low rumble from his throat and then said, "When we get back, I'm going to prove to you I can put our family first. And tonight, I'm going to prove I can make you moan my name at least a dozen more times."

"Promises, promises," she said and then caught her breath as he thrust up into her.

Only time would tell on the first promise, she thought, but the one for tonight? She planned to hold him to every word of it.

CHAPTER TWENTY-ONE

wo weeks after the trip to Malta, Eliza hurried across Hale Street toward Clayborne's on the Corner during her lunch break for something she never would've believed could happen—a lunch date with Mason. *Initiated* by Mason.

Since they'd returned to Nashville, he'd stepped it up, become like a different man in some ways, some important ways. He'd made a point of being home by dinnertime each night to eat with her and Calvin and Grace when she was around. Most nights, he spent a couple of hours with them and helped her put Calvin to bed, then he submerged himself in his home office to work until midnight or sometimes after.

Eliza had spent hours in Mason's bed, but never the whole night. She was still adamant about keeping their developing relationship from Calvin, still afraid of getting their son's hopes up for a traditional family situation, still wary of letting him down or breaking his heart. Because she still didn't know if she and Mason would work long-term.

Being loved by that man was incredible and magical, but she wasn't sure it was enough to get them through to forever if he loved his job more. A part of her said she was asking too much and she should embrace the parts of him she could have, and she knew that was a valid point. She just wasn't sure if she had it in her.

The situation would change soon, one way or another. Her duplex would be fully repaired by the end of the month.

This week, Eliza was recording at the Hale Street Studio, a small but busy two-story space that producers and labels rented out frequently.

She was working on the new Steele Hearts album, which was proving to be challenging and rewarding at once. She'd worked with the band a year ago on their previous album and found them to be a great group of guys—lead singer Tucker Steele, drummer Micah Sloan, guitarist Zach Oberlin, and bass player Brandon Knox. In addition, they were bringing in a host of other musicians for this album—her fiddle, a string bass, keyboards, a trumpet, a trombone, and an extra percussionist.

As she entered the bar and grill, she scanned for Mason and saw him right away, sitting at a high-top table next to the window. It was impossible to miss him, her gaze drawn to his handsome face like a bee to a flower.

When she got to the table, he stood and kissed her, and she felt it down to her toes.

"Hey, good-looking," she said as she took her jacket off and hung it over the back of her chair.

"How's my favorite fiddle player?"

She laughed. "You know a lot of fiddle players?"

"Dozens," he said, his eyes sparkling.

"I'm good. Things finally clicked on one of the songs we've been working on for a few days, so everyone's in a good mood. How was your morning?"

"Exceptional."

He paused while a server came by for their drink orders, which gave Eliza the chance to really look at Mason. Somehow, he seemed lighter, like a weight had been lifted off his shoulders.

Once the tall, dark-haired server hurried off, she said, "Tell me about your exceptional morning."

Mason inhaled deeply, visibly, his chest under his suit jacket rising with it. "I think we might pull this off."

"*This* being the big annual goal to secure the big needed financing?"

"Exactly. This morning, three more of our vendors agreed to unprecedented cooperative deals to coincide with the Colorado store's grand opening, and they'll be at all our stores, nationwide, not just the new one. Marketing and Merchandising have worked their asses off to make this a big deal that should boost the bottom line throughout the chain. Between that and the ground we gained in September with the extra promotions, I'm optimistic."

"That's fantastic news," Eliza said. She grabbed his hand across the table. "Congratulations."

"It's early for congrats, but the news couldn't be more promising."

He'd explained how he was pinning all his hopes on making the Colorado grand opening big enough to pull them to their goal, since moving up the opening of the new Nashville store had turned out to be a no-go.

The server delivered their drinks and took their orders, both of them flipping the menus open and choosing something quickly since they hadn't taken time to read over the options. Frankly, she was more into talking to Mason than worrying about what food she ate.

Commotion at the bar caught Eliza's attention.

"There's the Steele Hearts guys," she said, smiling.

The bartender, a guy named Pierce, greeted the guys loudly, making it clear they frequented this place, and then a dark-haired woman came out from the back and planted a kiss on Micah, the drummer. Eliza had met Sloan, Micah's fiancée, a few days ago and knew she was the entertainment manager here at Clay-borne's.

"This place is crawling with country stars," Mason said. "Joey Bloom picked up food from the bar before you got here."

"She was in the studio this morning, recording vocals for one of the guys' songs in the other sound booth. She popped into our control room and listened for a while."

"You must meet a lot of interesting people at work."

"Every day," she said.

As she took a drink of her soda, Tucker spotted her, waved, and headed toward her in his usual high-energy way.

"Eliza!" Tucker said with an enthusiastic smile. "Best fiddler in the universe."

She laughed and shook her head at the flattery as he gave her a quick side hug.

"Hello," Tucker said to Mason, extending his hand. "Tucker Steele."

"Mason North. Good to meet you." The two shook hands.

"You too," Tucker said, then addressed Eliza. "That improvisation of yours today…" He nodded. "We're keeping it. That's exactly what that bit after the bridge needed."

"That's great news," she said humbly. "Some days the right thing comes out at the right time."

Tucker's brows went up his forehead. "You won't convince me you have any off days. Micah and I caught a couple hours of your gig last Friday night. Your stage presence is something else."

"Thank you," Eliza said.

"I gotta let the cat out of the bag. You'll be hearing from our manager, Rand Kippling, in the next couple of days about our tour. Spoiler alert—we'd love to have you tour with us."

"Oh," she said, stunned, her hand flying to her chest. "Wow. I'm honored."

"We'll be honored if you say yes. It'll be a bus tour. Mostly gone Thursdays through Sundays. Three months, kicking off in January. Rand will of course give you all the details."

Her heart raced as she stumbled over what to say. "I'll look forward to hearing from him, for sure."

"Really hope you can make it work. You'd be a stellar addition to our live show with your energy and your performance chops. The way you and Sanchez feed off each other…that's along the lines of what we're thinking between you and me on the big stage."

"That would be a blast," she said, meaning it.

"There's Gin," Tucker said, eyeing the side door as his wife entered. "I better go grab her before some other guy does."

Gin was the assistant producer for the Steele Hearts album, so Eliza was getting to know her. She was a musical wizard and a really sweet person on top of it.

"You definitely should," Eliza said, laughing. "Tucker, thank you. I'm sort of blown away."

"Thank *you*," Tucker said. "We'll see you after lunch. Nice to meet you, Mason." He nodded as he hurried off toward Gin, who'd joined his band at the bar.

Before she or Mason could say anything, their server arrived with their food and set their burgers in front of them.

"What else can I get you?" the guy asked.

Mason looked to her for confirmation as he said, "I think we're good, thanks," and Eliza nodded distractedly, astounded by the past five minutes.

As the server strode off to another table, Eliza stared at her plate, added ketchup to her burger, salted her fries without tasting them first, all on autopilot.

"Eliza," Mason said, his excitement for her dripping from his voice. "That's a big deal, right?"

She met his gaze. "It's a dream opportunity."

It would almost certainly be a lot more money than she made in the studio, it would be an incredible experience to play all over the country, and for her personally, the chance to perform live night after night... Her heart raced at the thought of it.

"Congratulations, best fiddler in the universe. We need to celebrate."

She swallowed and laid out the truth. "There's no way I can do it, unfortunately."

"What?"

She raised a brow at him, waiting for him to catch up with reality. "There's no way I can be gone four days a week every week, Mason. I can't even do that for one week. The touring life isn't a possibility right now."

"Because of Calvin," he said, frowning slightly as her situation sank in.

"He's why studio work is ideal for me," she said. "So I'm

really lucky to have that. Hundreds of people would kill for the regular studio calls."

"And I'm guessing thousands would kill to have Tucker Steele of Steele Hearts invite them on tour."

Eliza forced a shaky smile as she nodded. "Truth."

Mason dipped a fry in ketchup, then shoved it in his mouth, and Eliza made herself take a bite of her burger, her appetite gone.

"If we were married," Mason said once he'd swallowed his food, "maybe we could make it work."

"That's not a reason to get married," she said quickly.

Ever since he'd suggested they get hitched, it had been in the back of her mind. The possibility of it, of being Mason North's wife. There were a lot of parts of it she liked, but they so weren't there yet. Not if they were going to marry for the right reasons. Yes, he'd said he loved her, but he hadn't breathed another word about marriage until now. That it was a casual suggestion to solve a problem… It made it easier not to give it serious consideration.

"Besides, there's no way you could manage him for four days a week, even if Grace was around to help out, and I'm not comfortable asking her to do that."

He didn't disagree. There was no way he *could* disagree. Two hours a day of spending time with his son was a start, but the reality was that Mason's job required more than forty hours a week, even if he were to cut back to the bare minimum. And they both knew it.

"At least get the details from the guy," Mason said. "See what he has to say. Maybe we can come up with a solution in time."

"Yeah," she said, feeling zero optimism. "Of course I will."

———

MASON HAD BOTCHED YET another attempt at the marriage topic. How he could run a billion-dollar enterprise competently and yet repeatedly screw up the most basic of things with Eliza was beyond him.

He agreed that it was preferable to get married for reasons other than co-parenting, and he'd be marrying her for so many other reasons, the most important one being that he loved Eliza and Calvin, but he needed to step up his game and figure out how to propose right.

"Did you decide on what you're getting Calvin for his birthday yet?" Eliza asked between bites of burger.

Mason stuck another fried mozzarella stick in his mouth, wiped his hands off, and pulled his phone out. "As a matter of fact, I need your input." He tapped on the screen as he said, "I thought I'd get him some LEGOs. Every kid needs LEGOs, right?"

Eliza grinned and shook her head. "I'm not sure about *need*… Honestly, I've put off buying him any, one, because they're not cheap, and two, because of their reputation for being stepped on by innocent parents."

"You're afraid of a little building block?" he teased.

"An army of a thousand building blocks, yes." She dipped another fry in her ketchup. "Calvin would love LEGOs. It's a great idea."

"The bike from you for outside days, and the LEGOs from me for inside days. Or we could give them both to him from both of us."

Her eyes narrowed slightly, barely enough for him to notice, and he'd already fumbled into one clumsy push toward a traditional family.

"Don't want to mislead him," he answered himself before she could, and then he nodded. "I'm okay with that. For now." He bobbed his brows upward and smiled, lightening what wasn't truly light in his mind. Because he did very much want to be a traditional family.

"Anyway," he continued, "the first question is which theme. There's space, Minions, superheroes, City, Minecraft—"

"I don't even know what Minecraft is. Is there one with trains and fire trucks?"

"That'd be the city one. Kind of what I was thinking, but I'd rather not get him the train since he has the wooden set."

"Good point. So which one?"

"That's what I wanted you to weigh in on." He held his phone out with the options on the screen. "I can't decide which one's the best."

"Look at you," she said, smiling as she took it from him. "Only planning to get him one?"

"I might be picking up some tips from this woman I know. Parenting tips. Like, don't spoil your own kid."

"She sounds super smart," she said, her eyes sparkling with flirtation, luring him in like no one ever had. "You Norths are turning out to be good at showering him with affection and not spoiling him materially. I admit I was a little worried."

"After the bedtime meltdown on Friday while you were working, I got a reality check of what spoiling might do," Mason said.

Calvin had been overtired, over-sugared, and overemotional about letting go of the day, half of which Mason had only figured out after the fact, when Eliza got home and he'd told her about the tantrum. It'd caught him off guard because their son was usually so easygoing and happy-go-lucky.

"Trust me when I say it's very important not to spoil our kid." He grinned sheepishly as he pushed his empty plate away.

"You made it through just fine. Sorry to say, I'm glad you saw the...challenging side of kids, we'll call it. With him, it doesn't surface often, but when it does..."

"Gird your loins," Mason said, and they laughed together.

She went back to swiping through the LEGO options on his phone. "The fire station," she said confidently, then handed it back to him.

"That's what I was thinking. Thanks." He took out his wallet and handed the server a credit card as the guy delivered the bill.

"I can get mine," Eliza said as the server walked off to cash them out.

"This," Mason said, leaning forward on the table, peering into her brown eyes, "is a date. And it's not over yet if you can spare five minutes on our way back to the studio."

"You're walking me back?"

"I am. And I'm buying you dessert on the way." He gestured out the window at Sugar Babies Sweet Shop, the bakery across the street, the one Sierra's sister was part owner of.

The server returned his card and he signed off, then he helped Eliza into her jacket. As they went out the door into the sunny October day, Mason put his arm around her, pulled her close, feeling anything but casual. While they weren't open about their relationship, they didn't necessarily hide it in public, and he kissed the top of her head, breathed in her feminine scent, savored the rightness of the moment. Of her. Of them.

As they crossed the street to the bakery, Mason acknowledged the need to step up his game and make Eliza his for good, in every way.

He held the door open for her, and they were enveloped by the aroma of chocolate and sugar and cinnamon.

"FYI," Eliza said to him as they approached the line at the counter, "*this* might be the way to a girl's heart."

Though she was kidding, Mason took that to heart. Because this girl's heart was exactly what he wanted.

He needed a grand gesture, something to show her he was serious about spending their lives together, not just looking for convenience.

A chocolate cupcake might not be a grand gesture, but it was a start, and if it helped him win her over, he'd buy her a lifetime supply.

CHAPTER TWENTY-TWO

*E*liza woke up slowly three days later, contentment and satisfaction, bone-deep satisfaction, rolling through her even before she could form a full thought.

She inhaled deeply, her eyes still closed, and the scent of Mason and their lovemaking filtered in. Her arm was around his naked abdomen as he slept on his back, she on her side curled in next to him.

Slowly, in a haze of bliss, she opened her eyes to a dark room, as Mason had closed the curtains on the city view at some point last night, but she sensed dawn was near.

As she let the details of their night together seep into her mind, her body warmed, tightened.

Faye had invited Calvin—and Blitz, bless that woman's kind heart—to stay at her house last night, as an extra birthday treat, she'd said, allowing Mason to go to Eliza's final scheduled Friday night gig downtown. Eliza had savored the live-performance high, knowing that the Steele Hearts opportunity, as awesome as the terms were, was not feasible. She'd told Mr. Kippling that a few days ago. Last night's crowd would have to hold her for now, and they'd made the night memorable, showering her and the other musicians with enthusiastic applause and generous donations to the tip jar.

After the handful of Friday night gigs, Eliza could pay for

Calvin's birthday—presents, party, supplies—in full by herself, but she'd agreed to let Mason split the cost with her. She was stashing the extra away for Christmas.

Once they'd made their rounds in the bar, touching base with friends and fans, Mason had whisked her off to a quaint, romantic restaurant for a cocktail and a piece of out-of-this-world triple-chocolate cake.

That was reason enough to love him forever, but then he'd taken her back to the condo to spend their first full, glorious night together in his bed, without worrying about Calvin. They'd made up for numerous times when she'd had to sneak back down to her bedroom in the dead of night in case Calvin woke up early.

Today was Calvin's birthday party, so it would be hectic and loud for hours. Tonight, though, Mason had something up his sleeve just for the two of them. He'd been secretive and only told her Lettie was coming over to stay with Calvin for a few hours once the party and the special birthday dinner at Faye's house were over.

Her body tingled with excitement and hope...and desire for this rock-solid man.

As Eliza started tracing a loving finger over Mason's chest, his phone rang from the nightstand, blaring into her contentment and jolting Mason awake.

He rolled over, grabbed it, and answered. "Yeah?"

Curious and concerned, Eliza stretched the opposite way to pick up her own phone and check the time. It was 5:42 a.m. This couldn't be good news.

Mason bolted upright. "Fuck." He listened to the caller, a male, Eliza could tell although she couldn't make out the words. "Is everyone okay?" he asked, which set her adrenaline to pumping as it hit her that Calvin wasn't safe in his bed downstairs.

With wide eyes, she watched Mason, her heart thundering. When he glanced at her, she mouthed, *Calvin?*

Mason shook his head, and she breathed a little easier and scooted in to sit close to him, against the headboard, pulling the blankets up over their naked bodies. His body was stiff, and not in a good way.

"Yep," he said. He swung his legs away from her, to the floor as he prepared to get up. "I need to call Roberson. I'll touch base with you in a few."

He ended the call and sprang into action. "That was Cole. The Colorado store's on fire."

"What? North Brothers?" It was a stupid question as she tried to catch her brain up.

"They've got the fire under control. No one hurt, thank fuck. I need to make some calls, get more info." Naked, he went to the walk-in.

Eliza climbed out of bed, picked up her underwear from the floor where it'd landed last night, slipped it on, and went to his closet as well. She opened a drawer and helped herself to one of his T-shirts.

With his own clean underwear and undershirt in one hand, he cradled her neck with the other and pressed a kiss to her lips. "I'm sorry. This wasn't how I planned this morning to go."

With a squeeze of his hand, she shook her head. "No worries. Make your calls. Do what you need to do. I'll go start coffee."

He kissed her one more time, then headed to the bathroom.

Eliza pulled the shirt over her head. It was just long enough to keep her covered, not that it mattered terribly. Grace was likely home but in bed after working her bartending job until closing. She and Reed had broken up for good a couple of weeks ago, so she was home a lot more.

She and Grace had made plans to run some last-minute errands before Calvin's one-p.m. party, picking up the cake and the helium-filled balloons and taking them to the Party Palace, an indoor play place that specialized in birthdays. Faye would meet them there with Calvin. The four of them—Eliza, Grace, Faye, and Mason—would chaperone along with the staff, and the nineteen kids they'd invited, his whole preschool class, would have parents present as well.

As the coffeemaker started to brew, Eliza checked the refrigerator for breakfast possibilities and pulled out the carton of eggs and a box of frozen sausage links. She set both on the counter, waiting to see if Mason would have time for a sit-down breakfast or if he would need to rush out the door to his office.

She wandered to the floor-to-ceiling windows and looked out at the city, where the sky was starting to lighten for the day, enough that she could see the buildings as dark outlines. The view was one she'd never get tired of, and yet she still didn't think this was where she'd choose to live if she had all the money in the world. The condo was beautiful and stunning, but it wasn't a family home.

When she heard Mason coming down the stairs, she turned from the window and walked toward the kitchen to meet him. He wore dress pants and a dress shirt, no tie, and his hair was still damp at the edges. She noticed he hadn't shaved, which was not like him at all, and then she found out why.

"I'm flying to Colorado," he said when he reached the island, his work bag and a duffel over his shoulder and a jacket over his arm.

"Oh," she said, taken aback, even though maybe she shouldn't have been. Her next thought was their son, and a pang hit her in the chest. "Calvin will miss you."

"Yeah. Damn. I'll miss his party," he said, as if just realizing it. "I'll make it up to him somehow. You'll take loads of pictures?"

Swallowing down on the ache, she nodded.

"I'm sorry, Eliza." He set his bags on the floor and took her into his arms. "I don't have a choice. Our opening will likely have to be pushed back, if we can open at all. This is going to affect…everything."

She nodded again, working hard to be the support he needed even as her heart was breaking for their son. "I get it, Mason. You have to go."

She honest-to-God did get it. She grasped how crucial this was, how much of the future of North Brothers Sports was on the line, depending on whether the Colorado store could open and when.

The stakes were sky-high, for Mason more than anyone else. She knew he'd do anything in his power to ensure the company's future, regardless of the setbacks, but at the same time, she was grasping the price of that. Not for the first time in her life. Not by a long shot.

Standing on her toes, she pressed a kiss to his lips, then said, "I'll make your coffee to go. Do you have time for me to make some toast or…?"

He shook his head as he picked his bags back up. "I'm meeting Cole and Connor at the airport. The jet is being prepped and we hope to be wheels up within the hour."

With a shaky inhale, Eliza took down one of the travel cups and filled it with steaming hot coffee, put the lid on, and held it out to Mason. She forced a half smile to show she was okay, whether to herself or Mason, she wasn't sure.

"Have a safe trip and let me know what's going on as soon as you can," she said, feeling helpless in her need to somehow make the situation better for him.

"I will." He took the travel cup, kissing her as he did. "Thank you. Tell Calvin happy birthday for me. I'll FaceTime him as soon as I can." Grasping her shoulder, he peered down at her, pausing for long enough to say, "I love you, Eliza."

She swallowed hard, willing her eyes not to dampen, and said, "Love you too. Safe trip."

Seconds later, he was gone, the door closing quietly behind him.

Eliza's eyes filled with tears. Her chest constricted with heartache for their boy, who'd been so over-the-top excited to have his daddy at his first birthday party.

She couldn't fault Mason for needing to tend to a horrible emergency. But she wasn't sure she was cut out for a life with him, where business could come first and her little boy's heart could be crushed the way hers had so many times.

Sliding her back down the cabinet, she sank to the floor, her heart torn.

CHAPTER TWENTY-THREE

*E*liza wasn't sure how much time had passed when she heard Grace's bedroom door open on the other side of the living room. Footsteps sounded across the floor, heading toward the kitchen.

"Eliza, what's wrong, sugar?" Grace rushed over to where she still sat on the kitchen floor and crouched down in front of her, taking her hands.

Sucking in a shaky breath, Eliza swiped at the remaining moisture in her eyes. "Mason's new store in Colorado is on fire," she began, and then she filled her friend in on the few details she knew and their brief morning before he'd hurried out.

Grace slid down to sit next to her, putting her arm around her and pulling her in for a side hug.

"Shouldn't you be sleeping for a few more hours?" Eliza asked her night owl friend.

"I saw the light on out here. Wanted to make sure things were okay."

"Things are okay."

"But you're not."

Eliza shook her head, her eyes watering again. "He's going to miss Calvin's party. It's flashing me back, Grace."

Grace nodded. They'd discussed Eliza's family more than

once since Mason had come into their lives, comparing his dedication to his work with Eliza's dad's workaholism.

"It's natural for this to trigger your memory, but remember Mason is not the same person as your dad," Grace said.

Eliza nodded. "Not at all."

"Mason is a warm, loving man once you get past his hard-ass CEO exterior. From what you've told me about your dad, he wasn't like that."

Eliza let out a scoff. "No. My dad wasn't like that. He definitely wasn't warm. I think..." Eliza pressed her lips together as she inhaled deeply, gathering her courage as some hard truths settled in, clearer than ever before. "I don't think my parents loved each other. Like, ever. There wasn't any affection between them. They got married because my mom got pregnant."

A soothing, sympathetic hum came from Grace. "It's possible your dad felt trapped. Or both of them."

Eliza nodded. That realization should have been disturbing, but instead, it was the first time her family started to make sense to her. "I know they loved me on some level, but my dad wasn't outwardly loving, like you said. My mom... Who knows what it would do to a person to live in a loveless marriage for years."

Grace squeezed her again. "That's no way for a child to grow up. And that's *not* how Calvin is growing up, love."

"Calvin knows he's loved to the stars and beyond."

"Even before Mason came along. Calvin knows he's first in your life, Lize, and he has me and Lettie too. You add in Mason, who is obviously wild about him, and Calvin is up to his eyeballs with love. Even if his daddy needs to tend to his company sometimes."

"That's true. And Mason's family too..."

"His mimi is over the moon," Grace said, grinning. She'd met Faye yesterday when she and Eliza had dropped Calvin and Blitz off for the night. "She's fantastic."

Eliza's own grandparents had not been a big factor in her life. She didn't remember three of them because they'd died before she was born or when she was a baby, and her paternal grandmother was nothing like Faye North. She'd been a detached woman, overly practical, and very seldom affectionate.

"I can't fault Mason for needing to go today," Eliza said. "It just hurts my heart."

"I know." Grace hugged her again. "But I believe he *will* make it up to Calvin. Mason is the most dedicated man I've ever met. Dedication and devotion are positive traits. If Reed could've had a tenth of that dedication, to *anything*, maybe we'd still be together."

"He wasn't the right guy for you."

"No," Grace agreed. "I want a guy more like Mason. As dedicated as he is to his company, he's just as dedicated to you and Calvin."

Eliza let that sink in, and she was surprised to realize she couldn't argue. "Part of what I love about him is how devoted he is to the things that matter to him," she admitted. "He cares hard."

"Yessss," Grace emphasized. "The question is, can you learn to handle it when he has to put work first? Or is it too much? Is there too much baggage there that makes him the wrong guy for you?"

Eliza sat up straighter, everything inside of her rejecting the thought of not having Mason in her life in any way except as Calvin's father. This had nothing to do with custody or parenthood and everything to do with her heart. She shook her head. "No. There's not too much baggage. You're right that he adores Calvin, and I believe he really does love me—"

"Hell yes, he loves you."

Eliza pulled herself up off the floor, gripping the counter, determination sweeping through her. Determination and a sense of harmony and contentment...and love like she'd never felt before. Deep love. Lasting love.

"He's the one for me, Grace. Pure, plain, and simple. You and Faye and I've got this party today. Calvin will be sad for thirty seconds, and then he'll run off with his friends. And he'll be excited all over again when Mason FaceTimes him. And I know

Mason will make it up to him when he gets home." She did. With her whole heart.

"I agree," Grace said as she stood, "with all of that. If you walk away now, I might have to kick your bodacious little tush."

Eliza laughed, and she didn't have to fake it. "No need to pull out the tough-girl act." She hugged her best friend. "Thanks for talking me down. Hours before your alarm's supposed to go off, at that."

"That's what I'm here for, sugar. Day or night."

"Works both ways," Eliza said.

When they ended the hug, Grace took Eliza's hands in hers and looked her in the eyes. "I am so damn happy you've found your man. You deserve it, Lize."

"Thank you." She was tearing up again, but this time in a good way.

"And now we have the best four-year-old in the universe's birthday party to prep for, so we better get our tushes busy."

"You get in the shower. I'm making us breakfast," Eliza said. "We're going to need the energy."

———

THE CORPORATE JET was cruising at forty-one thousand feet, and the flight was on track, turbulence-free, uneventful. The complete opposite of Mason's head.

He, his cousin Connor, who was VP of Operations, and his brother Cole, who was special projects manager and oversaw company construction projects, sat around a table in the main cabin, laptops out, monitoring the info coming from the Colorado site and organizing an action plan for pushing the opening back.

Based on the photos they'd received less than two minutes ago, now that daylight showed the extent of the damage, there was no choice but to push it back. They'd be damn lucky if they could manage to open the doors before the new year.

Which meant there were no more options to hit the objectives set by their investors. Their financing was dead in the water.

NBS's expansion plans had been destroyed just as the new store had been.

"Fuck," Mason said into the silence as they all three stared at the photos on their screens.

"Double fuck," Cole said, then shook his head.

"We'll rebuild," Connor said. "It's not a total loss."

It depended on what you considered a total loss.

The building that housed the store was not a total loss. In fact, only the front corner, which housed Footwear and Team Sports, had sustained damage that was visible from the exterior. There weren't interior photos yet, as Roberson, the contractor, couldn't get in to survey it, probably not for another twenty-four to forty-eight hours.

As far as all the plans they'd made, though, the goals they'd hoped to achieve...those were dead.

Connor was right though. They would rebuild.

The thought of it wore Mason the fuck out.

His mind wandered to Eliza, to having her in his arms, to listening to her soothing, sexy voice in his ear, telling him it would be okay and he'd figure it out. To losing himself in her for a few hours...or a few days.

"Thank God we only had about half the merchandise in there," Connor said. "We'll see what we can salvage, if anything. Need to contact all our vendors ASAP and stop whatever shipments we can."

"Yo, Mason. Where are you at?" Cole asked, snapping his fingers.

"Right here," Mason lied.

As Cole and Connor continued to lay out the thousand tasks that needed to be handled, Mason sat back in his seat and rubbed his fingers over his temples, trying to snap into action on the goat fuck that was recovery and moving forward. He hadn't gotten a lot of sleep, had spent much of the night making love to Eliza, talking, acting like someone who didn't have so much riding on his shoulders.

The crazy thing was, he couldn't make himself regret a single second of it. Because, damn, was it good between them. The things that woman could do with her mouth—

"What the fuck is wrong with you?" Cole demanded, jolting Mason back to the shitty present moment.

"I'm missing Calvin's birthday party today," Mason said, surprising himself. It was on his mind, of course. That look in Eliza's eyes when he'd said he was leaving… It gutted him even now. There was so much hurt there. Disappointment.

"Aw, man," Connor said. "He's turning four?"

Mason nodded, all too aware that this was probably the first birthday his son would remember when he was older, and Mason was missing it.

"What the hell are you doing flying to Colorado when it's the first birthday you could spend with your son?" Cole asked.

"I was planning to propose to Eliza tonight as well." He'd been working on the details all week, getting all his ducks in a row for the future he hoped to have with her. It would have to wait.

Cole's reaction was to lean back in his chair and scoff, as if Mason was the dumbest man alive.

"Seriously, man," Connor piled on. "You don't need to be here."

"Why wouldn't I need to be here?" Mason asked rhetorically, on autopilot, as he scrubbed his hands over his face. There hadn't been any question in his mind that he would fly out with Cole and Connor. There was a crisis, his company's jet was going, and he'd be on it.

"There's nothing you can do that we can't," Cole said. "I'm the point guy on construction. This is what you hired me for."

"You can't do everything alone," Mason said.

"That's what I'm here for," Connor said.

"Why should the VP of Operations have to deal with the crisis instead of the CEO?" Mason had always prided himself on being a leader who stepped up in challenging situations. He didn't shy away from the hard stuff. He charged through the hard stuff, doing what was best for the company and his people.

"Because I don't have anything better to do on a Saturday,

dumb ass," Connor said. "No gorgeous woman, no adorable birthday boy, no home life to speak of."

"Kind of sounding pathetic now," Cole said to Connor.

Connor flipped off Cole as he said, "Cole and I could've handled this, Mason."

An email notification sounded on Cole's laptop, and he turned his attention to that. Connor opened his travel bag and took out a package of chips, then pushed the button to call Cher, their flight attendant. She approached from the crew area before any of them could blink, and Connor let her know they were ready for food.

Mason shook his head when she asked if he wanted anything besides more coffee, then tuned all of them out. He rose and strode toward the back of the aircraft, into the lounge area with a couch and video screen, then into the bedroom, where he stood, lost in his thoughts.

I fucked up.

He sank down to the edge of the mattress and covered his face with his hands as that truth soaked in.

God dammit, he'd made the wrong damn decision. Whether it was out of habit or an inflated ego or having his head up his ass, it didn't matter. He'd screwed the pooch.

He'd hurt Eliza deeply, even though she hadn't said a word. She didn't need to. He might be slow, but he comprehended now. She wasn't the kind of woman who would rant and holler and beg him to put his family first. She understood the demands of his career, and she respected them, even when she wished things were different.

Eliza was a goddamn gift from the heavens.

It was up to him to *make things different*.

He could line his future ducks up all he wanted, but when it came to emergencies like this one—because there would always be emergencies of some type when it came to running a large company—he needed to step up and handle it like a family man. There was always the chance that he'd have to choose work over family temporarily, but fucking hell. This was not one of those times.

He glanced at his watch, ran some calculations in his head. They were thirty-five minutes from ETA in Colorado.

Mason stood and looked down the length of the aircraft, currently an open line to the cockpit, where he could see the door was ajar. Decision made—the right one—he headed toward it, without a glance at Cole and Connor as he walked past. Cher was in the food prep area as he continued right by.

At the doorway between the cockpit and the rest of the plane, he stopped. Both pilots—Adriana and Brett, their regulars—greeted him warmly.

"How fast can you get me back in the air to Nashville after we land?" he asked.

CHAPTER TWENTY-FOUR

*E*liza heard Calvin's exuberant voice entering the Party Palace with his mimi before she could see him. She and Grace, in the private party room closest to the main doors, shared a look of affection for the boy and laughed at his excitement, tangible from here.

"God, I love that kid," Grace said as she continued to set out the favor bags on a side table.

"Faye said he took a long time to get to sleep last night." Eliza had texted with Mason's mom earlier this morning to firm up their plans for the day, especially now that Mason was gone. The family birthday dinner at Faye's was still on for this evening.

"Mama!"

She turned in time to catch her boy as he leaped into her arms, making her laugh.

"Happy birthday, sweet boy!" Eliza squeezed him tight and closed her eyes as she inhaled his clean-kid scent. "I missed you like crazy."

"Missed you too," he said nonchalantly as he squirmed to get down and ran to Grace, who greeted him as enthusiastically.

"Faye." Eliza went to the woman who was slower to enter but looked just as happy as her grandson. They hugged. "Everything went okay?"

"He was an angel," Faye said, beaming.

"Maybe you could give us some lessons to get that angel effect at home," Eliza said with a laugh. "Thank you again. He obviously had a fantastic time."

"Me and Blitz had a super-duper time," Calvin said as Grace kissed his forehead and released him. He zipped over to the table that was already set with train-themed plates, napkins, and cups for twenty kids. "Wow!"

"Before the chaos starts, I'm going to find the ladies' room," Faye said and then walked off.

Eliza sidled up next to her son, determined to get the bad part of the day over with. She might have made peace with Mason's work obligations, but that didn't mean she didn't dread breaking the news to Calvin that his daddy would miss his party.

"What do you think?" she asked him, bending down to his level. "Does the table look good?"

"Really good! Where's the place for my presents?"

With a laugh, Grace said, "Right over here, next to the favors, which are the presents for your friends."

"We all get presents!" Calvin did a little stomp-dance thing with his feet, and it was like soul medicine for Eliza to finally give him a birthday party with a long list of friends.

"It's going to be a great day," Eliza said. She pulled out one of the kid-sized chairs and sat it in, facing Calvin. "One thing I need to tell you. Your daddy had to fly out of town this morning for an emergency. There was a fire at one of his stores."

"More fire trucks?" Calvin said in a tone that said he was an expert on the subject.

"More fire trucks for sure."

"Ambulances?"

"Nobody was hurt," Eliza said, managing to keep a straight face at his earnestness.

Calvin nodded solemnly, his eyes wide.

"Daddy won't be able to make it to this party or your dinner at Mimi's tonight, but he's going to FaceTime you later to wish you happy birthday, and he promised he'd make it up to you when he gets home."

With a big grin, Calvin said, "Okay! If he FaceTimes while I'm playing, will you come get me?"

"Of course."

The ruckus of kids arriving sounded outside of the party room, and Calvin craned his neck past Eliza to look.

"It's Ryan!" Calvin yelled. "And Jacob! And Maddie! Mama, can I go play?"

"As soon as I get the waivers turned in, I'll take you."

"I can take him," Grace said.

Calvin raced to the door and hollered out his friends' names.

Grace paused next to Eliza. "It didn't even faze him. Because he knows he's loved. That's on you, Mama."

"And you," Eliza said, nodding. "And Lettie and Mason and his whole family."

"Sugar, you got knocked up by a good one."

Eliza swatted at her as Grace hurried off to catch up with the birthday boy, and then she went to her bag to dig out the waivers for each kid that she'd collected beforehand.

She set the stack on the table, then rechecked her cell phone battery, planning to send Mason a video of Calvin and his friends playing—plus a jillion photos. Satisfied to see it was still at seventy percent, she straightened just as she heard the door to the room close. She whipped around and nearly fell back into the kid-sized chair in surprise.

"Mason? What the…?"

He stood in front of the closed door, grinning, one hand in his pants pocket, looking so damn handsome in the dress clothes he'd been wearing when he'd rushed out of the condo this morning. His eyes were tired and the scruff on his jaw had thickened in the past few hours. Normally, he was clean-shaven until the evening, but this extra day of growth… Rugged Mason made her body hum like the engine of an old pickup truck in need of a tune-up.

"Hi," he said quietly, stepping away from the door, approaching her.

"Hi." She met him halfway, stunned to see him, trying to

figure out what had changed. "I thought you'd be in Colorado by now."

"I was."

She glanced at the big clock with the Party Palace's raccoon mascot, maybe to verify she wasn't caught in a time warp. It was four minutes till one o'clock.

"I'm missing something," she said as he took both her hands.

"*I* was missing something. I screwed up." He kissed the knuckles of one of her hands. "I had the pilot turn around and bring me back as soon as we landed."

"I don't understand. What about the fire?"

He sobered up. "It's out. The damage is bad but could've been a lot worse."

"Any chance of opening on time?"

He shook his head. "The grand opening's off."

"I'm so sorry, Mason."

"We'll figure out how to proceed later. Cole and Connor are handling everything on-site so I could come to my son's birthday party."

Eliza, finally daring to believe this was real, threw her arms around him. "He's going to be over the moon."

Mason slid his hands to her waist, pulled her into his body. "We'll get to that."

"The kids are arriving," Eliza said with a glance toward the closed door. "I should—"

"My mom's here, right?"

She nodded.

"Grace?"

"Yes, but—"

"Just five minutes. I need to say some things. Please."

"Okay," she said easily, knowing Grace and Faye and the staff could, indeed, handle the kids as they arrived.

Mason glanced toward the door, which had a window, and then he tugged her over to the wall, out of the line of sight for anyone on the other side of the door. He pressed her back against the wall. He cradled her chin, tilted it upward, and kissed her.

With a reluctant groan, he ended the kiss and wove their

fingers together, both hands, and pressed her hands to the wall next to her face. "I'm sorry, Eliza. Out of habit, I made the wrong choice this morning. I'm so used to handling everything and not having the love of my life lying next to me that I jumped to my usual ways and rushed out to handle the emergency."

Her insides warmed at his words, and if it was possible, her love grew. "It's okay, Mason."

"You were upset, and I get it."

"I was, but I figured some stuff out."

"Yeah?" He dropped one of her hands and ran his finger down her jaw, under her chin, over her lower lip, melting her heart with his gentle, loving touch. "Like what?"

"North Brothers Sports is who you are," she said. "And it's a big responsibility, and it's part of what I love about you. You take care of your family by taking care of the company. You give it everything you have and yet still give so much to Calvin and me. You pay tribute to your dad and your love for him with your work every single day. You're a warrior for your family—your whole family and Calvin and me—but instead of putting on armor and fighting a physical battle, you're protecting our futures by driving the company."

He averted his eyes to the floor and sadness weighed down his handsome features. "Until there's a setback like today."

"That's all it is, though," she said, "and you know it as well as I know it. You'll figure out how to proceed and how to do it successfully, and I love that about you. I wouldn't want you to be any other way. Even if it takes you away from us here and there when there's an emergency."

He looked back into her eyes, as if ascertaining whether she meant it, and then the corners of his lips twitched upward just before he kissed her again. He pressed his forehead to hers, his eyes still closed, and said, "You're the perfect woman for me, and I came back, one, to make it to Calvin's party, and two, because I want to spend the rest of my life being your partner. I've got a lot to learn, but I've worked some things out over the past few hours just for you."

"Me? Mason, what the… Your business is going through a crisis today. I'm fine—"

He pressed his finger to her lips. "You're more than fine. You're incredible. You could handle a birthday party for twenty screaming preschoolers in your sleep. Practically speaking, Calvin doesn't need me."

"He needs your love."

He nodded. "He's got it. But you know what I mean. You've been both parents to him and could continue to for as long as you needed to. But that's not what I want."

Her heart started racing as he stared into her eyes intently.

"I want to be a family man to you and Calvin. My mom always says I was never content to just be good at something. I always wanted to be the best. And I want to be the best damn family man ever."

She laughed, because she could totally imagine twelve-year-old Mason aiming to win the science fair and sixteen-year-old Mason striving for a perfect score on his driving test and twenty-two-year-old Mason graduating at the top of his college class. "I don't think there's a way to measure that," she said, feeling light and hopeful.

"Maybe not, but there are ways I can do better. I made a few calls, tried not to step on your toes, haven't committed you to anything yet, but the spot on Tucker's tour bus is yours if you want it."

"Oh. Mason, that's sweet but—"

"I know. You said it doesn't work for your life right now, but you're not alone anymore. I'm committing to it right now—I'll be with Calvin every weekend you need to be gone. On top of that, my mom is going to spend Thursdays and Fridays taking care of Calvin."

"No," Eliza said automatically. "She doesn't need to do that."

"Are you kidding? I know my mom well, and I never would've asked if I didn't think she'd be all over it. She jumped at the chance."

"Really?" She was torn by the idea. "I trust her implicitly, of course, and Calvin loves her so much, as if he's known her since the day he was born. I don't want her to feel locked in though. I don't want him to become a burden."

"He's the opposite of a burden. He's the biggest light of that woman's life, Eliza. I say that with zero hesitation. But something else I was thinking is that we can look for a nanny if you want one. You can continue to work in the studio the days you're home if you want, or you can spend the extra time with Calvin. Whatever you need."

"Oh." She tried to take in the implications, tried to pinpoint what she wanted, but really, what she wanted was standing an inch—if that—away from her. And the rest was running around, probably shrieking like a birthday boy, out in the main play area. "You and Calvin are all I need."

"You've got us. But you've put your career on hold for long enough, and I want you to think about what will make you happiest in that regard too."

"And you talked to Mr. Kippling?" she asked, her mind racing with possibilities.

"I spoke to Tucker himself. He and the band want you badly on that tour. He was talking a mile a minute, telling me they hadn't found the right person to fill your spot yet, that they were hoping you'd come around. I believe his exact words were, 'Shit, Mason, if you can get her to accept, we'll name our next album after you.'"

Eliza laughed, reeling, brimming over with optimism. "That'd be quite an honor."

"I don't give a damn about that," he said, peering down into her eyes, and she could see his love there, his determination, and it was wild to be the object of all that masculine desire.

"It's a lot to think about," she said, suddenly aware that it was a few minutes after one and the party had officially started.

"I have one more thing for you to think about," Mason said, going even more serious as he took half a step back. "I'm fucking up my grand gesture six ways to Sunday, but what the hell."

Before she could process what was happening, he dropped to one knee, clasping her hands in his, and her eyes popped wide open and her brain forgot about everything else.

"I never in a million years thought I'd be doing this before I was forty and sure as hell never pictured doing it in the middle of a kid party haven." With a self-conscious grin, he continued. "I have a ring for you, but it's at home. I'd planned to pop the question tonight, but screw it. The right time is right now. Eliza, will you marry me? Not out of convenience but because I love you and I love our son and I want to be a family in every sense of the word."

Tears sprang into her eyes, and if Mason wasn't holding her hands, she would've pressed them to her mouth. As it was, a happy sound burst out of her mouth, half laugh, half scream, and then a resounding, "Yes." She had no doubts left in her mind. "I'll marry you."

Mason got to his feet and pressed her into the wall, trapping her there with his solid body as he kissed her for all he was worth and turned her inside out.

"Tell me," she said when they came up for air, "what grand gesture did you screw up?"

He touched his forehead to hers. "I set up a tour of three houses tonight. Three family homes in the best school district in the city. Big yards, at least four bedrooms each, because if you're up for it, I want to fill those with siblings for Calvin, and they all have what would make an ideal music room for you. I'd planned to propose after you picked one—"

Eliza yanked him in for another kiss, overcome with joy, unable to figure out the right words, because this man... He was perfect for her and Calvin.

THE DOOR OPENED, the din from outside the room rushing in, and then Calvin said, "Mama!"

As Mason laughed and put a few inches between himself and Eliza, she looked over at their son. The little boy froze, his eyes big.

"Daddy!" He ran full speed into them, Mason catching him and swinging him into his arms. "You're here!"

"I'm here," Mason said as Calvin hugged him. "Happy Birthday, C! I couldn't stand to miss it, so I had the pilot turn the plane around and bring me back here just in time."

Calvin's answer was a happy laugh as he threw his head back. "Daddy's here, Mama!"

Eliza laughed. "I know, baby." Lord, did she know in the best way possible.

Mason met her eyes. "Should we tell him the news?"

Eliza nodded as she wiped her eyes.

"What is it, Daddy?" Calvin said.

Mason shifted Calvin into one arm and then took Eliza's hand with his empty one. "What would you say if your mama and I got married and we three became a real full-time forever family?"

The look her son shot Eliza, with the biggest, most hopeful eyes, completed the melting of her insides, and she nodded. "It's true. Mason asked me to marry him and I said yes."

Calvin squealed—there was no other word for it—and threw his head back again and closed his eyes, a vision of pure joy that echoed exactly what Eliza felt in her heart.

"Family hug," Mason said, pulling the two of them into a happy tangle of arms and kisses.

Eliza held on to both her guys. Never had anything felt so amazing, so right, so perfect.

When they ended the hug and Mason slid the wiggling boy down to his feet, Calvin did a little dance in a circle, let out another happy shriek, and then said, "This is the best birthday ever!"

EPILOGUE

"Never thought I'd see the day." Zane shook his head as he watched Cole, their formerly grumpy black sheep brother, dancing with his brand-new wife, gazing down at Sierra with the biggest, happiest grin on his face as the entire room full of wedding reception guests looked on.

"Wild, isn't it?" Drake said. "The Colester is whipped."

Mason smirked at Drake. "Like you have any room to talk."

"Like any of you fuckers do," Zane said, shaking his head.

Mason couldn't actually argue that.

"Guilty," Drake said with a shrug and a self-satisfied grin.

Mason and Eliza had tied the knot a month ago, and he'd never been happier. After a quick, no-nonsense courthouse marriage with his mom and Calvin present, he and Eliza had flown to Turks and Caicos for an unforgettable few private days of bliss. He wasn't sure he'd ever used that word for himself before in his life, but that's what it was—pure bliss. Not only had they made some scorching naked memories in their luxurious beachfront villa but they'd explored the islands, snorkeling, shopping, and lounging on the postcard-perfect beaches, and they'd bonded deeply through everything they'd shared.

Calvin had spent the long honeymoon weekend with Mason's mom and had a fantastic time, as had Faye, who insisted her grandson made her feel young and purposeful again. Mason fully realized there would be more grandchildren soon—who knew which of the three other newlywed couples would win that race—but he was selfishly grateful for this time his boy had to be the only grand, the center of Faye's attention. It was allowing them to make up for the years they'd missed.

The night Mason had proposed, he'd taken Eliza on the home tour he'd planned, and she'd fallen in love with the house that was also his favorite.

Calvin had the "best bedroom in the universe," outfitted in a train theme, naturally. Eliza had the bonus room above the three-car garage as her music room. And Mason? He had everything he ever could've dreamed of—a gorgeous wife who was caring and kind and sexy as all get out, a little boy with a zest for life that made Mason slow down and appreciate the little things, like beetles, for instance, and a home filled with the noise and music and harmony of a family.

Thanks to his wife's connections and a good dose of luck, he also had new investors for North Brothers Sports. A power couple in country music who knew both Mackenzie and Eliza had been looking for a local opportunity to invest in and had decided NBS was it.

As Cole and Sierra's first dance as husband and wife continued, Mason searched the room for Eliza, knowing the bridal party was slated for the next song. He spotted Mackenzie and a very pregnant Kennedy standing near the bridal party table in their silver bridesmaid gowns, but there was no sign of Eliza. Finally, he saw her sitting at a table, with Lexie standing next to her, along the edge of the room in the historical inn Sierra and Cole had chosen for their reception.

He narrowed his eyes, looking closer as Eliza wiped her forehead, as if she wasn't well. Concern was beginning to pulse through him as the last notes of the song wound down.

"We're up next. Guess you better find Hayden," Drake said to Zane.

Zane let out a frustrated groan that no one but his two brothers could likely hear.

"You don't like Hayden?" Mason said, surprised. She was one of those women who was hard not to like.

Zane shook his head. "Opposite of that." He swore and headed off around the dance floor before Mason or Drake could reply.

Drake let out a howl of laughter while Mason's amusement was slightly more contained—but definitely present.

"Predicting it right now. That sucker's going down." Drake laughed again and then headed off toward Mackenzie.

Mason went in the other direction toward the woman of his dreams, frowning as he wondered again if she was okay.

The clinking of forks on glasses sounded, a few at first and then becoming a roar, demanding for the bride and groom to kiss.

Mason didn't pause to watch them, his sights on his wife, who was still sitting, in spite of them being due on the dance floor.

"Hey, gorgeous," he said as he walked up to her, smiling as he continued to gauge her. "You doing okay?"

Eliza flashed him a wide smile that almost rang true. Mason squatted down in front of her and took her hand in his.

"What's going on, sweetheart?"

Eliza brushed her fingers over his jawline and then stood. "Come on. We've gotta dance."

The music had switched to the bridal party's song, and Eliza tugged at his hand, leading him toward the dance floor. He followed her, confused and curious.

Her smile was almost normal as she wound her arms around his neck and he pulled her in close, feeling the rightness as he always did whenever he touched her.

"Talk to me," Mason said. "I saw you during Cole and Sierra's dance, and you looked like you didn't feel well."

"Just exhausted," she said. "Someone kept me awake late last night." She shot him that private grin that turned him inside out every time.

"You shouldn't have been so irresistible," he said with a suggestive raise of his brows as they swayed to the music.

"Back atcha, husband."

He kissed her, because he needed to, even though he still sensed she was off somehow. Pale. Missing her usual spark.

When he ended the kiss, he said, "Do you feel okay?"

She was silent for several beats, and he wondered if she hadn't heard him.

"I will be," she finally answered and then looked up to meet his gaze. As she searched his eyes, she smiled and said, "If I told you a secret, could you keep it to yourself?"

"Of course." He didn't take his gaze from hers, even as she hesitated. "Eliza," he said sternly. "Out with it."

She peered up at him for another eternal three seconds, then went up on her toes, her lips brushing his earlobe as she whispered, "I'm pregnant."

He clasped her to his body as the words resonated through him and worked their way into his brain. A sound of joy came out of him in the form of a laugh, and he clung to her, probably too tightly, but fuck, he never wanted to let her go. She was the light of his world, and she'd just given him the happiest news ever.

Even if it was earlier than planned.

He sobered for a moment and looked down at her. "Is this going to affect the tour?"

Steele Hearts was slated to start its weekly traveling in less than two weeks.

With a smile that told him she was as ecstatic as he was, she shook her head. "I mean, I can throw up on a bus just as easily as anywhere."

He frowned. "You threw up?"

With a nod, she explained, "This afternoon, after the first round of photos. Lexie came into the bathroom and heard me and swore I was pregnant. We sent Miranda out to get a test— Lexie insisted. She bought two and both were positive. Nobody knows but those two."

"Okay," he said, studying her, trying to ascertain her feelings. "This is earlier than we wanted. Are you…okay?"

She made a face and then laughed. "Does it matter? We might not be ready, but were we ready for Calvin? Not in the least. And look at us now."

"We're lucky."

"Blessed. Double blessed."

He nodded but furrowed his brow. "I just hate for your career to be put on hold again."

Eliza lifted one shoulder in a semi-shrug. "I'll go on the road with Steele Hearts and then see where we are. Pregnant women can still play the fiddle, you know."

"Of course you can. *If* you want to. I want you to be happy."

She pulled his head down to hers and kissed him emphatically. "I'm ecstatically happy!" She again moved her lips right next to his ear. "We're having a baby. Another baby."

"A sibling for Calvin," he said, his grin widening. "Grandson number two for my mom."

"Um, yes and no."

He tilted his head at her in question.

"Another secret, but I have permission to tell you if you can keep it to yourself. The reason Lexie was so fast on the pregnancy draw…she's pregnant too."

Mason shot a look to his brother Gabe, dancing across the way with Lexie, looking like a cat who ate a whole flock of canaries.

Mason could relate to that feeling.

"Did Lexie tell Gabe our news?"

Eliza shook her head. "You were first in line. She's keeping it quiet, but I told her she could share it, just with him, after tonight."

He nodded and touched her forehead with his. "I already love our baby." He swiped a finger discreetly over her abdomen where the baby would grow. "I love Calvin. And I love you. I'm the luckiest man alive."

"That makes two of us then, because I'm the luckiest girl."

"We make a good team," he said.

"A, um, fertile team, apparently. It's almost like we're meant to be."

"No *almost* about it, sweetheart."

~~~
~~~

NOTE FROM THE AUTHOR

Thanks for reading *True Harmony*! I hope you loved Mason and Eliza's story.

You can order Zane and Hayden's story now! Find out what happens when Zane is home for a wedding, not at all looking for love, and is matched up with Hayden.

If you missed Cole and Sierra's story, you can order or download it right away! Find out what happens when Mr. Socially Awkward spontaneously volunteers to be his beautiful boss's fake date.

You can also read Kennedy and Hunter's story right away. Find out what happens when bartender Kennedy's new boss, Hunter, has her shaken *and* stirred.

"I loved this story—from beginning to end, it had me!" —5-star reader review

———

If you liked *True Harmony*, I hope you'll consider leaving a review for it. Reviews help other readers find books and can be as short (or long) as you feel comfortable with. Just a couple sentences is all it takes. I appreciate all honest reviews.

———

True Harmony is part of the North Brothers series, which includes these stand-alone stories:

- True North
- True Colors
- True Blue
- True Harmony
- True Hero

North Brothers is a spin-off of the Hale Street series, which includes these stand-alone stories by me:

- Sweet Spot
- Sweet Dreams
- Soft Spot
- One and Only
- Last First Kiss
- Heartstrings

ACKNOWLEDGMENTS

Thank you to my early readers, Kay L., Rachel C., Edie L., Kathy P., Heather C., Lisa G., and Meshanna B. Your feedback helps me find the little things that can be so important and gives me confidence there's a story in what I've written. I appreciate each one of you so much!

To my lake sisters, Tasha, for your blurb wizardry and ongoing support, and Emily, for encouraging me with pretty words at the exact moments when I need them most. Malone better be ready for us because we have a lot to make up for this year!

Thank you to Melissa Chambers, my twin from another family and partner in the BBB Readers Group. I feel like I've known you for ages and don't know what I did before I met you! Thanks for being my sounding board, cheering squad, wise counsel, source for all things Nashville, and most importantly, dear friend. People don't realize how frightened they should be now that we've connected!

Thank you, once again, to my family. To my mom and dad, who've always supported and nurtured my love of books. To my boys, who've been my cheerleaders and author assistants and generally cool humans. And to my husband, who is my plotting partner, my parenting partner, my life partner through all the ups and downs, those that come from me doing this author thing and those that come from everything else. I couldn't do it without your love and support.

ALSO BY AMY KNUPP

<u>Henry Brothers Series</u>

Untold (prequel)

Unraveled

Unsung

Undone

<u>North Brothers Series</u>

True North

True Colors

True Blue

True Harmony

True Hero

North Brothers Box Sets:

North Brothers Books 1-3

North Brothers Books 4-5

North Brothers: The Complete Series

<u>Hale Street Series</u>:

Sweet Spot

Sweet Dreams

Soft Spot

One and Only

Last First Kiss

Heartstrings

<u>Hale Street Box Sets:</u>

Meet Me at Clayborne's

Clayborne's After Hours

It Happened on Hale Street

<u>Island Fire Series</u>:

Playing with Fire

Heat of the Night

Fully Involved

Firestorm

Afterburn

Up in Flames

Flash Point

Fire Within

Impulse

Slow Burn

Island Fire Box Sets:

Sparked (books 1-3)

Ignited (books 4-6)

Enflamed (books 7-10)

OR

Island Fire: The Complete Series

Themed Box Sets:

Friends to Forever (Friends to Lovers Romance)

Working It (Workplace Romance)

ABOUT THE AUTHOR

Amy Knupp is a *USA Today* Best-Selling Author of contemporary romance and a copy editor for Blue Otter Editing. She loves words and grammar and meaty, engrossing stories with complex characters.

Amy lives in Wisconsin with her husband and has two sons, four cats, and two box turtles. She graduated from the University of Kansas with degrees in French and journalism. In her spare time, she enjoys traveling, breaking up cat fights, watching college hoops, and annoying her family by correcting their grammar.

For more information:
www.amyknuppbooks.com

If you'd like to know when her next book is available, you can sign up for her newsletter and/or follow her on the social media below.